NINE MONTHS OF SUMMER

ISOBEL BLACKTHORN

PRAISE FOR ISOBEL BLACKTHORN

"Nine Months of Summer has all my favourite elements: politics, social justice and strong women characters. I applaud that Nine Months of Summer demands that its readers question the politics of asylum. Impeccably written in clear, succinct, yet sophisticated prose, Nine Months of Summer is a thoroughly enjoyable read."

JASMINA BRANKOVICH

"Nine Months of Summer gives us an English perspective on a subject matter that is so often associated with non-English speaking peoples."

JASMIN ATLEY

"I couldn't put it down! I judge by whether a book grips me or I can take it or leave it. Nine Months of Summer gripped tight!"

MARGO SHAW

"A was a pleasure to read. Within pages of starting the book I was drawn into the story of Yvette and her relationships with the permanent women and transient men in her life. Capturing the inconsistencies in policy and disgust many feel about current politics around who is welcomed to Australia, the story travels across Australia. I have never been to Perth or Fremantle but I felt myself transported."

KATHERINE WEBBER

"A highly readable novel, written in clear and direct prose. The story will win Isobel Blackthorn many friends, more so amongst women readers; the entire novel is fashioned from a distinctly female sensibility."

ROBERT HILLMAN

For my mother, Margaret Rodgers

ACKNOWLEDGMENTS

With special thanks to my daughter Liz Blackthorn for her astute and invaluable comments, and boundless enthusiasm for the work. My gratitude to visual artists Jude Walker and Rhonda Ayliffe for sharing with me their thoughts and experiences of art. My warmest thanks to Georgia Matthey for describing how she composed her artwork, *Not Saying No*. And many thanks to Vanessa Mercieca for her assistance with the Italian dialogue.

Until you make the unconscious conscious, it will direct your life and you will call it fate.

CARL GUSTAV JUNG

I
———
ONE

1.1

Dents in the loop-pile carpet marked the legs of once-present furniture. The walls, bare, rendered an insipid peach. There was a faint smell of acrylic paint. Shutting herself in, she closed the bedroom door behind her, the slap-back echoes jeering, a clamour of recriminating voices.

She would never be enamoured with shoulds.

It had been a shrine in here. A room for storing the past. A box of a room, smaller then with all the clutter. When Yvette was last here, a teak-veneer wardrobe and a white melamine chest of drawers took up one wall. A single bed occupied the full length of the other. Hanging above the bed was a whimsical print of a young girl in a shabby brown dress, standing in a cobbled street beneath an industrial-grey sky, walled in to either side by flat-faced Victorian terraced houses receding to a point behind her. That print hung in all of her childhood bedrooms. The chest of drawers was crowded with artefacts. The gaudy vase she bought for her mother's birthday one year. The pink jewellery box with the plastic ballerina that still twirled shakily to Fur Elise when she opened the lid. A content Snoopy lying atop his money-box kennel. The generous-faced alarm clock her mother gave her when she was ten which she had wound so tightly it never ticked again and had stayed stuck between eight and nine ever since. Yvette had been too ashamed to tell her.

A blade of sunlight sliced through the window's beige fabric bars and stung her eyes. She hefted herself out of bed and swished the blind aside.

The window faced northeast, protected from the intense sun of summer by the foliage of a silver birch. She was in no doubt her mother had lined up the angles to make sure. The crisp light of early morning shone through the branches, now wintry bare, making a filigree pattern on the frost-burnt grass. Two parrots, bright and keen, preened on one of the lower limbs. The birch was set in a neat garden of clipped lawn and rose beds. Dotted here and there were grevilleas and bottle brushes, all neat and trim. Her mother had a fondness for reds, stately reds, traditional and rich. There ought to be topiary. Box hedges and cascades of wisteria. And white picket fences. Instead the garden was hemmed by barbed wire strung between red-gum posts, electrified to keep out the cattle. Beyond, there was a backdrop of undulating paddocks peppered with majestic red gums. The entire valley embraced by an armchair of forested mountains. Bucolic paradise, worthy of the brushstrokes of Alfred Sisley.

The air was calm. Dew glistened on a spider web hanging under the veranda. A kookaburra's cackling crescendo burst into the silence.

Forcing herself into the day, she pulled a baggy red jumper over her head and slipped on the size-eight jeans she used to wear as a teenager. She could scarcely believe her mother had kept her old clothes. But she was grateful. She owned nothing but the handful of sarongs and summer dresses she'd squashed into her cobalt-blue travelling bag when she left Malta, rugged and dry, for the moist and fecund Bali. The same cobalt-blue travelling bag she used to move her things into Carlos's house. Her beloved Carlos. She couldn't bear to look at the bag. She'd shoved it behind some shoe boxes in the bottom of the wardrobe the moment she arrived.

Where was he now? Still in Bali? Heading back to Malta? No doubt coveting the backside of every stewardess on the flight.

She sat down on the edge of the bed without feeling the grip of her jeans against her belly. Weren't these the pair she used to zip up with the hook of a coat hanger? She was thin, a waif, sure to wander hither and yon, pulling her heart behind her like a clobbered plastic duck on squeaky wooden wheels.

Hearing a clatter of plates, she closed the door on her discontents and headed to the kitchen.

Her mother's presence permeated the whole of this open-plan Hardiplank kit-home. She was in the three-piece suite, the hearthrug and the pine dining table, so highly polished the reflection of the morning sun dazzled as Yvette walked by. She was in every framed print hanging on the walls, in every ornament and knick-knack, from the Spode plates, Wedgewood saucers and porcelain figurines right down to the glass rolling pin she kept in a kitchen drawer. Even the doormat had her footprint on it. In this house Yvette could only be her daughter, the prodigal returned after a ten-year absence.

Her mother, Leah, was bending down to reach into the cupboard under the sink. Her buttocks bulged like buns in the seat of the dull-blue track pants she wore around the house. Hearing Yvette enter the kitchen, she turned and raised herself up to her full height, much shorter than Yvette recalled, and smiled before her gaze slid away. Leah had aged. Short curly hair, ten years earlier a mop of nutty brown, now thin and white. The freckles on her face had joined together, giving her fair skin a sandy patina. Her hazel eyes were still vigilant, yet softer, more resigned. There was a slight downturn to the mouth. Her face had lines, wrinkles and creases where once there were none. Yvette found it hard to accustom herself to the changes. And there was a sluggishness in the way her mother moved. Yvette remembered her energy, always darting about, not exactly agile, but deft. She felt remote. And was

5

saddened by it. Too many years living intensely while her mother grew vegetables. Yvette was a stranger to her but she didn't seem to know it.

She grabbed a cereal bowl from the cupboard beside the cooker and opened the pantry door.

'Tea?'

Yvette turned to see her mother pouring boiling water into a second cup.

'We'll fill out the immigration forms after breakfast,' Leah said, heading out through the back door with an ice-cream container of vegetable scraps. Her mother was the most practical woman Yvette had ever known. She'd sent off for the permanent residency forms the moment Yvette told her she was coming.

She had to get out of Bali. She was too distressed to stay. So distressed that the travel agent in Kuta, a small and wizened man with a permanent and insanely broad grin, had driven her all over Denpasar on his scooter to help secure the holiday visa and the one-way ticket to Sydney.

Yvette went to the dining table with her breakfast, sitting with her back to the sun. She flicked through the form. She wanted to gain residency through the deadlocked back door. She thought she might be eligible under the family reunion category. She read through the instructions and found she wasn't. Her father was still in England. She hadn't seen him for years and had no intention of ever doing so, but he was a blood parent.

Her mother came back inside and joined her. Yvette passed her the form and watched her leaf through the pages, scrutinising the instructions, lips tightening.

'Perhaps there's a loophole,' she murmured.

A loophole that benefits a refugee? In the Department of Immigration and Border Protection's draconian rule system? Impossible. Besides, she could hardly claim that were she to return to Malta her life would be in danger. That when Carlos had reached across that restaurant table in Bali and pulled her hair, his fit of frustration constituted an act of persecution or torture. Yvette was seeking refuge from the wreckage of her life.

Leah leafed again through the pages. 'There might be compassionate grounds.'

'Mum, I don't...' She stopped speaking. They both knew there wasn't a skerrick of compassion in the Department of Immigration's institutional bones.

She drained her cup and took her breakfast things back to the kitchen then wandered across the living room and gazed out the window. A long lock of mist drifted in the valley, slipping through a stand of red gums.

Leah was watching her closely. 'You'll have to get married,' she said matter-of-factly, as if in the time it had taken Yvette to walk to the kitchen and back she'd conceived the solution.

'Married?'

'It's the only way.'

'I couldn't,' she said emphatically, shocked that her mother would even consider the thought. It wasn't the deception that bothered her. There was a part of her, the romantic and the fool, adamant that marriage had to be a contract founded on love, not convenience.

Without another word Yvette filled out the form and slid it into an envelope along with a vague hope of a miracle and the relevant photocopied pages of her British passport—the holiday visa, the page with the photo of her face with its wooden grin and harried brown eyes. She knew she was far prettier than that.

It would be months before she heard the outcome. Meanwhile she needed a job. For that, Leah told her she needed a tax file number. Even for the most menial of casual work.

'The post office will have the form,' she said. 'Shall I run you into town?'

'I'll walk.'

She stuffed the envelope in her pocket and went outside. The air was fresh, the morning bright. Taking up one of the plastic chairs beside the woodpile, she shuffled her feet into a pair of Leah's old volleys and tightly tied the laces to compensate for her size feet. Leah was a nine, Yvette an eight.

Her mother's cat, a plump tortoiseshell, rubbed against her calf. She ruffled her hand through its fur. The cat followed her to the fence then lost interest and trotted back to the house.

She closed the gate behind the garden and picked her way through the paddock, avoiding the spats of cow manure, and across the cattle grid. The farm straddled the lower reaches of gullied hills some two kilometres north of Cobargo. Heading for the highway, she walked up the dirt track that snaked through a neighbour's property. His paddocks were denuded. Dead trees, ghostly white, their contorted limbs stretching heavenward, stood like monuments to the forest pre-dating the squatters. The only surviving trees were the apple gums growing on batholithic hillcrests. Their roots smothered in middens of cow dung heaped by generations of paddock-clearing farmers.

Leaving the paddocks behind, she followed a dirt road that flanked a hillside of bush, and reached a T-junction. Directly across the highway, in a swathe of mown grass, the cemetery displayed the gravestones of the departed to every vehicle travelling up and down this remote stretch of road. Somewhere among the gathering of Catholic graves lay her stepfather.

She turned right and headed down to the village huddled at the bottom of the valley, a quaint gathering of gift shops and cafes housed in historic weatherboard and brick buildings. She crossed the road at the newsagency and passed the art gallery, formerly a petrol station. On the forecourt, in the shade of a deep awning, an elaborate sculpture spilling from an old iron wheel rim sat beside two defunct petrol bowsers. Ahead, on the other side of the creek, was the hotel, a brick and tile boozer no doubt frequented by she'll-be-right-mate beery blokes and their whisky-and-coke drinking sheilas. On a rise a short way up the road that wound west to the hinterland of dairy farms and wilderness were the primary school and the Catholic church. The Anglican church stared piously from its equally lofty location to the east. The village, with a history entrenched in milking cows, remained as self-sufficient as ever it was, supplying the needs of man and beast. There was a doctor's surgery, a vet clinic, a police station and even a swimming pool. The few back streets contained a smattering of vintage weatherboard cottages and contemporary brick and Hardiplank houses interspersed with vacant blocks. The village hadn't changed an iota since she was last here. The butcher, baker, supermarket and post office were exactly as she remembered them. The sweeping views that surrounded the village failed to inspire her. They might as well have been murals plastered to her mother's living-room walls.

The year Saddam Hussein was found guilty of crimes against humanity, her mother for the second time upped to a better life in this land of plenty, settling here in Cobargo with Yvette's stepfather and sister, Debbie, the moment they arrived in Australia, foregoing all the opportunities that Sydney might afford for a pastoral dream. Not a tree-change, they were too conventional for alternatives. They felled the remaining red gums on their hundred-acre block before Yvette followed, and six weeks later, left, before her stepfather, Joe, a robust gung-ho sort of man with a penchant for guzzling lager, lost his life to a chain saw. Leah and Joe hadn't been together long. A sudden and gruesome accident, the sort of tragedy that rips into all that is soft and vulnerable. But her mother was a tight-lipped woman; her letters never mentioned her grief. With Yvette back in England she turned to the only family she had here, Debbie.

When Yvette last saw Debbie she was a smug sixteen-year-old, proud to be engaged to a local boy. She had her own story; distinct from Yvette's as cotton wool and splinters, a cushiony narrative of stability and marital harmony. Now Yvette couldn't walk down the main street of the village without being identified as Debbie's sister. The moment she entered the post office a buxom woman, squeezing past on her way outside, looked her up and down and said, 'Are you Debbie's sister?'

'That's me,' she said with a forced smile, thinking, no actually, she's *my* sister since I was born first. Even as the words ran through her mind she felt contrite. Resentment wasn't becoming. Yet the people around here hadn't a clue who *she* was. And she wasn't about to tell them. Only she didn't want to be defined as her mother's daughter or her sister's sister, aligned with the secretary of the agricultural show society and the dairy farmer's wife.

Her mother was working on next year's show when she returned. Notepads, forms, old programs, raffle tickets and a cash box were spread across the dining table. Yvette sat in the chair furthest from Leah and read through the identification requirements on the tax-file-number form. Bank account, driver's licence and Medicare card, none could be acquired without showing her immigration status.

'It's no good, Mum,' she said, dropping the form on the table and leaning back in her seat. 'I can't get one.'

Her mother peered over the rim of her glasses. 'I thought not.' She put down her pen and folded her arms under her bosom. 'We should have become citizens before we went back to England.'

'You weren't to know.'

'At the time I never thought I'd come back. I'd had enough. I spent those last years here cleaning the corridors and classrooms of your old primary school.'

'And I caught the school bus.'

She'd started school the year Alanis Morissette vied with Celine Dion for first place in the charts. On that bus Yvette must have listened to *Ironic* and *Because You Loved Me* twice a day for months. Even then she preferred satire to sentimentality.

Those first years of school were fabulous. There were sleepovers at her best friend Heather McAllister's place. Fun in the park across the street. The orange tree beside the house, laden with the juiciest, sweetest fruit. She had the best year. Her mother had her worst.

It was her mother's decision to emigrate, both times. The first was in 1993. Leah wanted to leave the London of working-class council housing estates. Common-as-muck, she'd say. Leah had left school at sixteen to spend a few months skivvying as an office junior before moving on to work in a cinema kiosk and a shoe shop, then becoming a traffic warden—a career that appealed to her because she worked outdoors and alone, unmolested by bitchy co-workers, creepy patrons and dithering customers with smelly feet. Yvette's father, Jimmy, was a skilled factory worker. He was born a Cockney, his family relocated to South London during the post-war slum clearances. Leah wanted to better Jimmy. She thought Australia held the promise of a better life for her. That's what the brochures told her. So she filled out the forms and flew them to Australia.

Leah's best friend at primary school, Gloria, along with her family, had migrated to Perth twenty years before. They were ten-pound Poms. Gloria had written to Leah regularly ever since. One of a small store of Grimm-family vignettes was how fortunate they'd been to avoid the Nissen huts of Graylands. Poor Gloria—that was what her mother called her friend—had gone from a three-bedroom terraced house in London to bunk beds in a migrant hostel. Leah thought the conditions scandalous. The hut had unlined corrugated-iron walls and bare wooden floorboards. And Gloria's family had to share communal dining and communal ablutions with all the other migrants from Europe and the Middle East. Pentonville, Leah called it. Pentonville. For years Yvette thought her mother meant one of the pale-blue set in Monopoly. Leah was referring to the jail. You could stay there for months, a voluntary sentence, but a week had been enough for Gloria's mum.

It was Gloria who'd arranged the three-bedroom rental in Kwinana and suggested Jimmy apply for a position at the aluminium refinery. Leah went on to buy a brick and tile home in Perth's English-migrant capital, Rockingham.

Five years later, Leah was ready to move back to London. Australia didn't fulfil her expectations. She couldn't find satisfying work. She wasn't happy. She wasn't happy with Yvette's father.

Back in London, Leah returned to her preferred career of traffic warden, much to Yvette's teenage consternation. While Yvette chewed the ends of her Biros in class, her mother's life was unfolding apace. Leah Grimm became Leah Betts. With a new husband in tow, she emigrated a second time.

Yvette stayed behind, and stayed Grimm.

She couldn't fathom why, when she was just eighteen, her mother chose to emigrate for a country where she found so little happiness the first time around.

1.2

A red-gum log burned gently in the wood heater. Leah was watching *Days of Our Lives*, her weekdays cleaved by frothy melodrama. Yvette gazed out the window. She had no tolerance for her mother's habit. To her, the soaps were shallow, over-acted, lip-quivering drivel. She couldn't bring herself to admit she had enough going on inside her to fill an entire series.

Outside, a fierce southerly buffeted the grevilleas and bottlebrushes. Leah said she lost a shrub every year. Snaps off right at the base and rolls about like spinifex. Yvette watched the shrubs cower. She felt adrift, her own roots shallow, their grasp in the soil of a stable life tenuous. Her mother's soap addiction reinforcing feelings of tremendous isolation. Leah was an impossible anchor. She had an astonishing capacity to get on with the practical day-to-day that alienated Yvette at every turn. She'd rather her mother thrashed and flailed like a shrub decapitated by that uncompromising wind. At least now and then. If only she would let down her reserve.

In an effort to relieve her listless mood, Yvette flicked through the local paper that her mother had brought back from her bi-weekly run into the village. When she came to the last pages she scanned the small ads. The Cobargo hotel needed a cleaner. She felt a swirl of contempt; her life had come to this. Yet it was the only listing. In deference to her mother, she waited for the adverts then dialled the number, hoping the job would be cash-in-hand.

A woman answered.

'Hi,' she said. 'I'm Yvette Grimm. I'm calling about the cleaning job.'

'Are you new in town?'

Straight away she knew she was too well-spoken to be a local, and too well-spoken to be a cleaner, but she kept those thoughts to herself. 'I'm Debbie Smith's sister,' she said, knowing as she spoke that the claim was an appeal for acceptance.

'Ah.'

The woman warmed to her.

Maybe there was some advantage in being known as Debbie's sister.

She started work the following Thursday.

It was a cool and sunny day. Heading for the hotel, Yvette walked down to the village, glancing up the road at the Catholic church as she crossed the bridge over the creek. Debbie's farm was a short walk further on. Since her return, Debbie had been away visiting her sister-in-law. She'd returned yesterday. And she'd be at home now. Her boys at school. Alan in the paddocks with the cows. The sisterly thing would be to call in after the shift.

She pulled open the heavy wooden door of the hotel and went through to the bar, long and dark with too much tacky chrome. A sickly odour of yesterday's beer perfumed the air. She nodded at the old man seated on a stool over by the cigarette machine, who gave her a languid smile. Otherwise, the bar was empty.

Before long, a middle-aged woman appeared. She was in her thirties, dressed as if ready for the beach in T-shirt, shorts and thongs, her blonde hair pinned back in a ponytail. 'G'day,' she said. 'You must be Yvette. I'm Brenda.' She grinned as she gave Yvette a single appraising sweep of her eye. 'Come with me.'

She followed Brenda across the car park to the cleaner's storeroom, located in the centre of a row of motel rooms. Brenda talked her through the cleaning procedures, detailed and exacting, and handed her a bunch of keys. 'Cash all right?'

'That's fine.' Thank God, but already she was sinking at the prospect of the work ahead. The view of the rolling hills and the mountains did nothing to loosen the tightening knot of resistance in her guts.

She wheeled the cleaning trolley from one stuffy, pastel-coloured room to another. She stripped and re-made beds, emptied bins, polished, mopped and vacuumed. She did it all with no enthusiasm whatsoever. She earned ten dollars per room, slave wages, and only by cleaning three rooms per hour did she feel the work remotely close to worthwhile. She hated it. Her back hated it. Her self-esteem sloshed with the grime at the bottom of the mop bucket.

She walked back to her mother's house without glancing at the road to her sister's farm.

1.3

Yvette spent the solstice weeks in a numb haze. She helped in the garden, mowing lawns, pruning, weeding and harvesting, all performed under Leah's watchful eye, as if she were poised to kill or maim a darling member of the floral kingdom any moment. She soon decided her mother's passion for gardening was fanatical and unbearably tedious—who cared if this year's blooms won first prize in the show?

One afternoon, she could endure the watcher no more and downed tools, feigning exhaustion to sit in the warm sun with a sketchbook and pencil. She idly traced the lines of a dead tree in the neighbour's paddock, pathetic efforts, knowing what she was capable of. She missed the luxury of her studio space and ready access to materials at Goldsmiths and the Royal College of Art, luxuries she had taken for granted at the time.

Later, while her mother enjoyed her soaps, she lay on her single bed, isolated and apart. She felt tattered. A teddy bear come apart at the seams. All her stuffing gone. About now she'd have been plump about the belly, all flushed and expectant and busy knitting booties. She met the gaze of the forlorn girl in the print above her bed. Poor little girl. What tragedy wrecked her?

She knew she was wallowing in her gloom. Yet she had latched on to her loss with an unrelenting clasp. She had to let go, she would let go, she was poised to do just that, but not yet. Although even now her dogged sadness had begun to feel ridiculous.

When the living room went silent and she heard the fly screen bang shut, she traipsed to the living room and slumped on the sofa. Moments later the fly screen banged again. Yvette didn't move. Then she sensed her mother standing over her. 'Cheer up.'

'I'm all right,' she said. Leah had no inkling of Yvette's abortion and Yvette wasn't about to confide.

'You haven't seen Debbie since you arrived.'

'She knows where I am,' Yvette said sourly.

'She's waiting for an invitation.'

'It's hard. We don't get on.'

In her mind she was understating the emotional distance that had grown between them. They were estranged, Yvette had decided, having grown attached to the fact that only twice in their ten years apart had she received news directly from her sister and not via their mother, a card announcing the birth of each of her boys. She emitted a heavy sigh but her mother was steadfast, waving a finger in the direction of the telephone. Forcing down her own resistance, Yvette swung her legs to the floor. Satisfied, her mother went outside.

With no expectation of anything beneficial arising from this coerced reunion, Yvette lifted the receiver and stabbed the numbers on the keypad. A female voice answered.

'Hi. It's Yvette,' she said flatly.

'Yvette! How *are* you?'

'Good. And you?'

'Great to hear your voice. Welcome back!'

'Thanks.'

They chatted about the old times Yvette didn't care to remember, of their childhood days in Perth, teenage years in London. After what seemed an eon of small talk, she succumbed to an impulse to be convivial and invited Debbie over for coffee.

The following afternoon she watched an old Holden ute buck and bounce down the long dirt track, pulling up beside the machinery shed. A figure of average build, dressed in baggy pants and a sky-blue T-shirt, walked in strides towards the house with the easy-going gait of the Australian country woman. Yvette knew the woman was Debbie but strained to recognise in her the Debbie she'd grown up with—a cute, freckle-faced, impish girl with a self-conscious smile. She looked to Yvette now like every other twenty-something woman in the area, totally lacking in style. Her hair was long and brown and shapelessly cut. The T-shirt hung limply from her bust; the pants, on closer inspection, were pilling; and the fawn Crocs she sported to complete her outfit looked like foot boats. Yet her smile was warm, her brown eyes seemed genuine and Yvette softened in her company.

They sat in the garden on the north side of the house, sheltering from the cold southerly wind. Leah waved from the veranda and offered to make tea. She returned five minutes later with two mugs and a plate of Monte Carlos.

'Why don't you join us?' Yvette said, suddenly craving relief from the intimacy of just the two of them.

Leah mumbled something about needing to clean the house. Yvette knew it was an excuse. The house was immaculate.

Debbie took a few sips of her tea before blathering on about her two boys with that familiar need to prove her worth chiming with every comment. She glowed over their achievements at school—a merit award for this, a merit award for that, how good Peter was in the junior soccer team, the terrific progress Simon was making with the violin and how marvellous it was that they were both in the school choir performing at next year's folk festival held at the showground. Choir? At a folk festival? Forgetting she once loved to sing, Yvette couldn't imagine any pursuit more cringe-worthy. She couldn't countenance being part of anything amateur and looked down from an absurdly high height at anyone, young or old, who did.

She stared absently at the distant hills, doing her best to be polite while fending off jealousy over the doting interest Debbie took in her boys. Her sister hadn't the conversational grace to ask about the last decade of her life. But then again, it was probably better Debbie didn't know how far her sister had drifted from their mother's upright morality, campus adventures as she limped from one boyfriend to the next, and in Malta, where she'd taken unconventionality to a precipice with her flirtations in the iniquitous underworld of drugs and crime. It had been easy to do. Too easy. Easy to keep the truth from them too. Her letters contained the veneer of her studies at art school, then her sight-seeing escapades with her best friend Josie and their glorious life in the sun. And as for her mother and sister, neither visited her once in that whole ten years. Not once.

A pair of parrots, splendidly red and green, perched on the bird table, chortling to each other. Yvette raised a hand to slide her hair behind her ears and they flew away. She was wondering how to divert her sister's attention from her offspring when Debbie set her mug at her feet and said, 'I dreamt about you last night.' Her tone had an intimate ring. 'You were standing on my veranda in a long red dress, with a gorgeous young man beside you.'

'What happened?'

Debbie blushed. She seemed awkward. 'Nothing,' she said, averting her gaze. 'But I had a strong sense you were meant to be together.'

The wind gusted from the south, blowing a shaft of Yvette's hair in her face. She smoothed a hand across her cheek, feeling in her belly an echo of the childhood thrill of teasing her sister. She sat on the edge of her seat and lowered her voice to a whisper. 'That's weird.' She widened her eyes. 'Maybe it's a premonition.'

'Don't.'

'It's a coincidence at least.' Yvette relished in the game. Debbie had always been easily spooked. 'A psychic read my palm before I left

Malta. I was in a nightclub and an old woman with leathery skin and a mystical look in her eyes took hold of my hand. She said I would meet the father of my children before I was thirty.' And as she spoke, the words took on a potency they had lacked before that moment. As if in the telling she was imbuing the prophecy with all the significance of the cosmos.

'She was probably drunk,' Debbie said.

'She wasn't. She was emphatic. She grabbed my arm and told me he was definitely not the man I was with.'

'Carlos?'

'Carlos.'

'She got that part right.'

'What would you know?' Yvette said sharply.

'Sorry.'

Their mother's cat flopped down at their feet and arched her back.

'Maybe I was meant to come to Australia to find him.' Her voice had gone all misty.

'Who?'

'The father of my children.'

She knew it was ludicrous but the prediction had suddenly given her hope. Although she couldn't imagine encountering an Australian man she'd find desirable. None of the Aussie men she'd met had charisma, mystique or originality. They looked generic, they sounded generic and they were all into sport.

1.4

Yvette was sitting in the living room, teasing her cuticles to better show the half-moons. Leah was glued to *The Young and the Restless*. The phone rang. 'You answer it,' she said without moving her eyes from the screen.

She picked up the receiver expecting to hear her sister's voice. Debbie was the only person who dared call during the daily soap-opera marathon. Instead, Yvette heard a heavily accented male voice asking to speak to her. It was Carlos. Passion bolted through her. She slid down the wall until she was sitting on the floor with her knees drawn to her chest. She wasn't even sure she could speak. 'Ciao,' she managed.

'Ciao, il mio amore.'

She was silent. He called her 'his love', but she knew there was no substance to the words. He didn't love her. He didn't know how to love her. He didn't have it in him to love anyone but himself. But she couldn't stop her guts somersaulting.

'Sono qui,' he said, adding in slow accented English, 'The Gold Coast.'

He was here?

'Yvette. Viene con me.'

Go with him? 'No. Non posso.' She had to resist.

'Ho bisogno di te.'

He needed her?

'Mi dispiace,' she said. It was a vacuous reply. She wasn't sorry at all. She was torn.

There was a pause. Then he said, 'Per favore.'

Why was he persisting?

'Ti prego l'autobus,' he said.

'No. Non ho soldi, Carlos.' That was true. She was broke.

'Yvette. Ti amo.'

'Non ho soldi.' She tried to sound insistent. She felt limp. She wanted to run to him, badly, wanted to spend her whole life by his side, live in his house, birth a gaggle of his babies, be immersed forevermore in the culture she loved. Instead, she hung up the phone wishing she'd never given him her mother's number, and slouched on the sofa with a hard lump in her throat, knowing it was going to be hard to exorcise that man from her heart.

Debbie called as the credits rolled on the last soap of the day and invited Yvette to a friend's house for dinner. 'You'll like Tracy,' she said. 'She's an artist. She's your type.'

Yvette doubted it. She couldn't imagine any of Debbie's friends being her type. 'Thanks for thinking of me. But ...'

'I'll pick you up at five.'

'What about Alan and the boys?'

'Alan's taking them on a scout camp.'

She didn't feel like going, preferring the familiarity of her misery. Yet she couldn't think of a way to decline so she agreed and hung up the phone.

'Who was that?' Leah said, switching off the television.

'Debbie.' She went on to explain the invitation.

'It'll do you good,' Leah said.

She wasn't convinced.

She didn't bother to change out of the old jeans she wore as a teenager and the baggy red jumper that had become as symbolic to her as Linus' blanket. When she heard Debbie's ute, she left her mother half knitting, half watching a documentary, catching a glimpse of the wreckage of a boat washed up on a beach by a wild sea, the voice-over announcing at least twenty-two asylum seekers dead in the capsize. She paused then went outside, barely absorbing what she'd seen. In Malta, boat arrivals from Somalia were a frequent occurrence and never to a warm reception; the Maltese government claiming, with good foundation they thought, that the island was in the front line and if they didn't impose a deterrent the floodgates would open. Yvette had been as indifferent then as she was now, too busy with the travails of her own life to care that much about the lives of others.

Instead, as she opened the passenger door she wondered how her mother coped with her small and dreary life. How she would never, ever, end up living like that.

'Hi sis. So pleased to have you back,' Debbie said fondly. 'Truly I am.'

'Thanks.' She forced a smile.

'How are you finding it here? Bit of a change from your old life, eh?'

'It's strange.' She couldn't help sounding distant.

Debbie threw the gearstick into reverse and hit the accelerator, the ute lunging backwards towards their mother's rose bed. She braked, changed gear and hit the accelerator again, the ute charging through the paddock, juddering over the cattle grid and bumping over every rut and pothole in the track.

'You'll get used to it,' Debbie said. Was she referring to her driving or Australia? Right now it was hard to decide which was the more precarious.

Debbie slowed as they neared the highway, making a right turn and cruising down the smooth tarmac to the village. 'Maybe you'll settle down.'

Yvette didn't speak. They crawled through the village, Debbie accelerating hard up the hill on the other side. 'Do you think you'll stay here?'

'I doubt it.'

This time Debbie made no comment.

Yvette stared out the window at the scenery: the majesty of the mountain to the north that presided over the landscape like a benevolent mother, now silhouetted against a darkening sky; the red gums and apple gums casting long shadows over undulating farmland; the granite outcrops and the cute weatherboard farm houses; and the mountains to the west slumbering beneath a wide band of soft apricot.

About five kilometres on, after a sharp bend to the left, Debbie told her to look out for a flitch-clad shack perched on a hill.

'Nearly there,' she said brightly.

'So how do you know Tracy?'

'She's a voluntary scripture teacher at the primary school. She taught Buddhism to Peter and Simon.'

Debbie swung by the carcass of an old fridge and a rusty milk urn propped on its side on a trifurcated log, and hurtled up a long and liberally cratered driveway.

Tracy greeted them at the door. She was a stocky and weather-beaten woman with wild black hair. Dressed in a baggy, striped jumper hanging loosely beneath paint-spattered dungarees, either the sort of artist who liked to throw paint around or inept at her craft. She led them into a poorly-lit room that smelled strongly of Nag Champa. Once Yvette's eyes adjusted to the gloom, her senses were assailed. The room was filled with drab and grungy furniture. Two battered-looking sofas faced each other across a low-lying coffee table littered with magazines and ashtrays. Propped on an easel to the left was a large canvas streaked in black and grey acrylic, with a half-formed figure of a girl, open-mouthed and clutching her face in her hands. Tracy's interpretation of an Edvard Munch. It was ghastly. To the right was the kitchen, partitioned from the rest of the room by a red-gum bench strewn with dirty cups and plates. In the centre of the room a fire glowed in a wood heater.

'This is a charming house,' Yvette said with contrived enthusiasm, scanning the clutter of books, papers and junk piled on shelves, tables and chairs.

'It is,' a man's voice said. She peered into the room and made out the figure of a man coming through a far doorway. Tall, with dark hair, his lean torso defined in a tight T-shirt, eyes hidden behind a pair of black-framed sunglasses. Sensing she'd been set up, she was intrigued. She picked her way through Tracy's clutter and held out her hand.

'Hi. I'm Yvette.'

'I know.' He removed his sunglasses and looked at her intently, a smile lighting his face. She felt herself blushing.

'Yvette, this is Terry,' Tracy called from the kitchen. 'Terry Ford,' she added, as if his full name would mean something. It didn't, but the man before Yvette suddenly did. He had a broad, rugged face, with thin lips and deep-set brown eyes. Behind him, she noticed chinks of twilight filtering through gaps in the flitches. Immediately, he became the subject of a Gainsborough, a nobleman of the seventeen hundreds bedecked in rustic finery, a crosscut saw held proudly to his chest like a hunting pistol.

'Take a seat,' Tracy said, pointing at the sofa. 'Dinner won't be long.'

'I'll give you a hand,' said Debbie.

The sofa was little more than a fat man's armchair. Yvette perched on the edge of one cushion with her knees pressed together. Terry lounged on the other with his arms straddling the backrest. His knee brushed against her thigh.

'Tracy tells me you've just arrived in Australia.'

'I was living in Malta.'

'Named after the cross?'

They both laughed.

'It would be the other way round.'

'Err, Malta? My geography is failing me.'

She could hardly believe his ignorance.

'Malta is about a hundred kilometres off the coast of Sicily,' she said, wondering at once if he even knew the whereabouts of that island. Perhaps the mention of Italy might have been more helpful. She was instantly wistful, recalling the ancient cities, the honey-coloured stone, the turquoise of the sea. She pictured Carlos's house, the flat roof, the old stone walls and shuttered windows. And she yearned for Malta, the rugged landscape, the uninhibited freedom of her life there.

'What were you doing there?'

What to say? Artist? Too vague. Mafia mole? Too exotic.

'Market trader. I sold my hand-made jewellery.' Multi-coloured necklaces and earrings made from plaited thread. She thought of the pursuit, even at the time, as her hippy phase and no doubt her response conjured in Terry's mind an image of a barefooted nymphette with braided hair found in abundance in Kuta. Still, the handicraft sold well. And he seemed satisfied. 'And you?' she added, keen to steer the conversation away from her.

'I'm an artist. A leather sculptor.'

'Fascinating,' she said with enthusiasm, privately regretting she'd chosen to portray herself in such a commonplace if exotic fashion.

'You have to see his work, Yvette,' Tracy said, handing her a glass of red wine. 'He's a genius.'

A genius? Yvette stifled a smile. She couldn't imagine anyone living in this sleepy backwater as anything other than a hick.

Tracy passed round hunks of bread and plates of bean stew. Then she raised her glass with a 'cheers', and slugged her wine before sitting down with Debbie on the opposite sofa. The others reached for their glasses in reply.

Tracy and Debbie engaged in small talk as they nibbled through their food. Terry ate with gusto. Yvette forked from the edges of the mound on her plate, no longer hungry. Terry's presence was making her oddly nervous. He had an allure about him, yet she wasn't sure she found him all that attractive. He wasn't her type. Surely he couldn't be the fulfilment of the palm-reader's prophecy. Besides, she thought, glancing at her sister, you can't force fate.

Leaving Tracy and Debbie to the dishes, she followed Terry outside. The air was still and crisp. She gazed at the stars in the sharp, moonless vault of sky, struck by the luminosity and the depth of black, the void.

Terry was rolling a cigarette. 'Tracy tells me you came here on a holiday visa.'

'I did.'

'And you're planning to stay?'

'I'm going to try.'

'Good luck,' he said doubtfully.

'Yeah, thanks.'

'Lucky you came by plane.'

She frowned. 'What do you mean?'

He took a drag on his cigarette and inhaled deeply. 'If you'd come by boat you'd be in detention on some mosquito-infested island, sweating it out for months, if not years.'

An image of the capsized boat flashed into her mind. 'I'm not a refugee,' she said coolly.

'No. Of course not.'

They stood together in the silence, broken only by the forceful exhale of his smoke-infused breath. Then by a rustle coming from a pile of old timber stacked beside a shed. In the darkness she made out the shadowy figure of a cat slinking towards a copse of trees. She looked back at Terry, whose face was tilted heavenwards. Aware of her gaze, he smiled, and with the heel of his shoe he stubbed out his cigarette on a patch of bare earth.

'Would you like to see my studio?' he said casually.

'Sounds great.'

'I'll call you tomorrow.'

He didn't ask for her number.

1.6

One blustery morning in the following week, Yvette drove to the coast in her mother's station wagon. She was due at Terry's studio at eleven. It was a pleasant drive through a picturesque landscape, the mountain always to her left, wattle trees dotted here and there in full bloom, but she couldn't admire it. Running through her mind in a replay loop was the knowledge that Debbie and her mother had colluded and Tracy had been in on the whole thing. The situation was a sham and she could scarcely believe she was going through with it.

When she reached Bermagui she was a welter of emotion. Once an isolated fishing village sheltering in a deep bay guarded by the mountain to the north, the town had become a desirable tourist and early retirement destination, particularly for those wealthy enough to own a boat. She drove across a long bridge, glimpsing a pelican crouched on a post at the edge of the choppy waters of the lagoon. She passed the yachts nestling in the marina. She passed the sandwich boards stacked like dominoes near a polling station displaying the smiling faces of wannabe and soon-to-be has-been federal politicians vying for power with vacuous promises, and felt pleased she couldn't vote. And as she neared Terry's studio she passed a row of shops, squat on a low rise, housed in plain concrete buildings with garish façades that mocked the mountain, the shimmering ocean and the creamy sands of the bay. Main Street, pandering to the battery of holidaymakers, whale watchers, nature lovers and sports fishermen, who occupied the town through the summer. Across the road, beneath the shade of palms and sturdy Norfolk Pines, play equipment, benches, picnic tables and a toilet block were scattered along a tongue of lawn separated from the beach by a narrow strip of dunes. Now the park was empty. No children scampering about, whizzing back and forth on swings or hanging upside-down on monkey bars, no dogs sniffing and straining on leads, no parents pushing strollers, slathering their young in sunscreen or spreading out blankets in the shade. Even the seagulls, starved of unwanted chips, had flown back out to sea.

Terry's studio was in a café at the end of the parade of shops, situated between a motel and a hairdressing salon. The café was closed for the season. He'd told her to pull up at the far end of the park. She stuffed her sketchbook into her bag and opened the driver-side door. One foot on the tarmac and a squall buffeted the car, threatening to slam the door on her thigh. She leaned her shoulder against the door and battled it ajar as she stood. Wanting to regain her composure, she walked to the dunes and stared at the waves walloping the shore, grateful for the breadth of golden sand between her and that unbridled water.

Terry opened the café door before she knocked. He must have seen her arrive. He stood squarely in the doorway, blocking her entry. A heady mix of solvents and the rich smell of leather wafted outside. She was self-conscious and still filled with misgivings. A blast of wind pushed her forward and he took the opportunity to offer her a welcoming hug. 'Hi,' he said, and another part of her wanted to fall into his arms.

She followed him into a vestibule and through a set of glass doors. His studio took up about half the café's eating area, a cavernous space with an industrial-grey floor, whitewashed walls and floor-to-ceiling windows overlooking the ocean. Tables pushed against the walls were strewn end-to-end with leather in various shades of brown, from narrow strips to whole hides. Terry led her to his workbench, cluttered with scraps of leather and an array of hand tools.

'I'll just finish up,' he said without apology.

She watched him cut a swatch of leather. He had an industrious manner about him, focused and serious. Even so, she wondered if his apparent busyness were not contrived.

'How did you get into leather sculpting?'

'I used to be a saddle maker before I attended the Canberra School of Art.' He paused. 'There I became inspired by the work of Rex Lingwood.'

'Rex Lingwood?'

'*The* master leather sculptor.'

Without looking up from his bench, he described at length the processes of working with leather, the wetting, moulding and stretching, and the gluing, carving and polishing. Then he wiped his hands on a rag and passed her an arty magazine folded open at a leather-sculpting review.

She scanned the article then wandered around the room. A stack of large squares of plywood leaned against a wall. A few half-finished pieces that didn't draw her in. Then she noticed a finished piece leaning against the far wall. Mounted on a large rectangle of black-painted plywood was the three-dimensional form of a winged human torso. She was genuinely impressed. 'Wow!' she said loudly.

Terry looked up. 'It's for an exhibition in Sydney.'

'It's extraordinary.'

'It's Eros.'

'The god of sexual desire.'

'The god of passion.'

Terry's artistic mastery unexpectedly stabbed at her own creativity. Cast in his light, she had little ambition. The jewellery she made in Malta didn't qualify. And her incomplete sketches of the dead and limbless tree in the neighbour's paddock weren't even dabbling. She felt like a dilettante. She hadn't done more than dangle a pencil nib in artistic waters since she'd arrived in Australia. She wasn't sure she even wanted to. She'd lost her passion, her creativity shrivelled like a prune. She was a directionless fool. She wondered if in her, the light of Eros shone dimly. But that couldn't be true. Her passion for Carlos was intense.

Terry grabbed his leather satchel and car keys. 'Sorry about that. Now, I'm all yours.'

She was silent. She hadn't a clue what to say to him.

'Would you like to come back to my place?'

She hesitated. 'I'll have to let my mother know when I'll be back.'

'You are an adult, Yvette.'

'She'll worry.'

Terry and a male friend shared an A-frame cottage built on a steep slope on the outskirts of town. She walked up a wooden staircase to the front door. Terry followed close behind. The northern side of the house was elevated, with a veranda looking out at tall gum trees. Inside, an open-plan living area led on to the bedrooms.

1.7

On the days she wasn't cleaning motel rooms she drove to Terry's studio. After that first visit she left her sketchbook behind. Without it she was idle and listless. She watched Terry work. She sat on the end of a table and swung her legs. She flicked through his arty magazines until boredom drove her outside to wander about in the park and on the beach, kicking sand and collecting shells. Sometimes she stood at the waterline in awe of the heaving plain of sapphire, the crash and the quick suck of the waves. When she felt brave she dipped her toes in the spume.

At lunchtime she went down the street to the bakery for two meat pies. Terry loved meat pies. She didn't. She slipped into the supermarket for fruit.

She'd become attached to her waif-like figure. She found her size empowering. Terry liked her thin too, but for an altogether different reason. He said her shape was perfect. He would cup his hands over her breasts murmuring in her ear that more than a handful was a waste. He would squeeze her buttocks, smooth his palms across her flat tummy and circle her wrist with his thumb and forefinger. When he whispered he loved her, she was sure he only meant her body.

Which explained why with Terry she didn't enjoy sex. It couldn't have been because he smelled of meat pies. She wasn't that fickle. And there could be no other reason for her lack of desire for him. He had a great physique. He was bright, witty and chatty. And his love was a salve for her wounded heart. But she didn't connect with him. Her body was numb. Terry had no idea. She pretended to respond. She groaned over his caresses. She threw her head back and gasped to convince him that he satisfied her, every time.

And she lied when she told him that she loved him.

Terry owned a forty-acre bush block in the foothills of a nearby mountain. One warm spring day when the wind was still, he suggested Yvette might like to take a look. Ten minutes into the trip she'd lost confidence in Australian driving standards. Whoever had granted Terry a licence was either unimaginably lax or nuts. Terry spent more time looking at her than the road. He drove too fast. He held the steering wheel at six o'clock with his left hand, over-steering and veering towards the hard shoulder and bumping over cat's eyes to the wrong side of the highway. Seeing her grip her seat he patted her thigh and said, 'Trust me. I haven't trashed a car yet.'

Yet?

Leaving the highway, he headed up a dirt road that wound through the gullies and spurs of the mountain. Terry jerked his way round potholes, skidded over corrugations and charged along on the wrong side of the road. When he lurched into a bend and fishtailed out the other side, she gasped.

He laughed. 'You're safe.'

She didn't feel the slightest bit safe. She might be a risk taker but this was not the sort of risk she had in mind.

They pulled up in a small clearing beside a roofless mud-brick hut. Before she opened the passenger-side door she wiped the sweat from her palms. She felt like a marionette with its strings caught in a fan.

He took her hand and led her onto a rustic wooden deck. She poked her head through one of the window cavities. There were no interior walls. The floor was a crisscross of bearers and joists.

'What do you think?' he said, grinning.

She was dumbfounded. Mustering enthusiasm she said, 'Awesome,' privately hoping this wasn't leading where she thought.

She withdrew her head and looked around. The place was spooky. The forest of gum trees overshadowed the house, their writhen branches bearing down like witch's fingers.

'I dreamt about you last night,' he said. 'You were standing right here in a long red dress like a fairy-tale princess. I stood beside you holding your hand.'

She felt a ripple of alarm mingled with disbelief. Debbie's dream was almost identical. 'How romantic,' she said, masking her unease.

'I'll be your handsome prince.' He lifted her face to his. 'And marry you.'

She didn't answer. They'd only known each other a few weeks.

'You're vulnerable,' he went on. 'You need someone to protect you.'

What gave him that idea? He hadn't fallen in love with her. He was enamoured with a babe-in-the-woods fantasy. The knight on a steed set to rescue the distressed damsel. She'd be an extension of his ego. It was madness. But she felt herself yielding. He was a nice man, a good man, proud but sincere. He'd never hurt her in the way Carlos had. Could she force herself to love a man she had no feelings for?

Back at home she sat with her arms folded tightly across her chest, hands gripping flesh. She stared out the window at the mountains in the distance, furious that her mother and sister had colluded to influence her life. They had no right to interfere. The root of her reasoning was the loss of her unborn child. She wanted desperately to replace the baby she aborted, was urged to abort, by Carlos. And she would never risk having Terry's child. On their way back from his bush block he'd told her he dumped his last girlfriend because her post-childbirth stomach was not to his liking. She'd had a caesarean. He said he couldn't fancy a woman unless her stomach was pancake-flat. What sort of man thinks that? Surely not the fulfilment of the palm-reader's prophecy. She draped a protective arm across her tummy and resolved to bring the relationship, and the conniving, to an end.

1.8

Without Terry in her life she was restless again. She couldn't countenance a whole summer cleaning motel rooms. One afternoon, she was sitting on the floor trying not to engage with *Days of Our Lives* when her phone rang. It was Thomas, her friend from London who'd moved to Perth in July to be with his boyfriend. She'd met Thomas at a Noah and the Whale concert in Notting Hill six years earlier. It was her final year of her Masters. After the support band had left the stage and they were waiting for the main act, they struck up a conversation about David Hockney. Thomas had that day browsed the artist's works at the Tate. He seemed eccentric yet kind and they'd remained friends ever since.

After catching up on his new life down under, she was reticent and vague when he asked her where she was.

'Australia? I thought you were in Bali.'

'Long story. I finished with Carlos.' She went on to explain her circumstances as succinctly as she could and excluding the abortion.

'But you're an Aussie. Dual citizenship or something.'

'Afraid not.'

'But you can't overstay a holiday visa. You'll have one hell of a job gaining residency if you do.'

'I know.'

'You'll have to find someone to marry.'

'Not you as well. That's what my mother is saying.'

'She's right. It's common knowledge.' He paused. 'So where exactly are you, geographically speaking.'

'New South Wales.'

'Well, fancy that! We're neighbours.'

'Hardly,' she said, wondering if he even knew where New South Wales was.

'We could at least catch up.'

'I'd love to visit. The farm is, well ...' she glanced at her mother to make sure she wasn't listening. She wasn't. 'Intolerably dull.'

He told her he'd just purchased a one-bedroom unit in a suburb close to the city centre. 'Why don't you move here?'

'To Perth?'

'You can stay in my old flat until the lease runs out.'

After ten years apart, did she really want to sever her relationship with her mother again by putting the width of the continent between them? The only other comment the palm reader had made was that she would do better far from her family. She had dismissed the remark at the time, but after recent events she couldn't agree more.

'When shall I come?'

'As soon as you like.'

She waited for the credits to roll and Leah to disappear outside before she switched on Leah's computer and researched the cheapest route. She booked the bus to Melbourne and a one-way plane ticket to Perth. She'd leave in four days. A quick check of her inbox—there was nothing but junk—then she went outside and wandered around the garden, finding her mother picking broad beans.

'Mum.'

'Yes?' Her mother didn't look up.

'I'm moving to Perth.'

Leah shoed away a curious bee with a soft flick of her hand, then carried on picking beans. 'Perth?' she said. 'Why Perth?'

Yvette explained as the colander filled with bean pods.

'Are you sure?'

'I can't stay here, Mum.'

'You're not happy, that's obvious.'

'I'll miss you.'

'I'll miss you.'

'At least it's not halfway round the world this time.'

'Just a whole continent.'

'You can visit.'

'Well, good luck.'

She trailed her mother inside and helped shell the beans, wondering if she could ever face coming back to this sleepy, isolated backwater where her family, for a reason that remained inexplicable, had chosen to play out their miniscule lives.

II

TWO

2.1

She stood in the aisle beside her back-row seat. Behind her the other passengers jostled for a place in the tightly packed queue. After a ten-hour bus ride, another hour in transit to Tullamarine airport, and a tedious three-hour wait for a smooth four-hour flight across the desert guts of Australia, her skin felt dirty and sticky and she hankered for somewhere, anywhere, quiet, cool and still.

Instead, the steward opened the plane's rear door and Perth greeted her with a gust of hot, dry air. November, and it must have been a hundred degrees.

The heat was at once exotic and familiar, the heat she grew up with in Perth, the sort of heat she craved all those years in London, the heat that drew her to Malta. Heading for the shelter of the concrete and glass arrivals building she felt exhilarated, until memory stabbed its black through her head and, for a few seconds, she was light-headed. She slowed her pace and breathed deeply, and stared down at the tarmac. She was back at primary school. How she had loathed that school. More than anything she'd loathed morning assembly.

. . .

The morning sun was hot. Young as she was, to her English eyes the headmaster looked absurdly casual in a short-sleeved shirt and shorts and carefully measured socks. But Yvette took him seriously as he lectured the rows of kids with stern authority. Only she couldn't listen. She stood at the back of her class queue, eyes glued to the flagpole, willing the Australian flag to billow. It hung limply, and she went limp inside and staggered across the playground to the toilets.

She was six, a timid, scrawny Pom, an easy target for those rowdy Australian kids. She avoided them. At recesses and lunchtimes she would sit on a bench in the shade of the peppermint gum furthest from the tuckshop, and feed the hard lump in her belly with marmalade sandwiches. Her mother couldn't understand why she insisted on marmalade. She couldn't understand it either at the time. Now she knew. Marmalade was bitter. Even then she'd had a sense of the symbolic.

Weeks passed and she adjusted, to the heat, the buildings and the smell of gum leaves, but not to the Aussie kids. She made two friends, Melissa Kovac, a pretty, wide-eyed girl from Bosnia, and Heather McAllister, who immediately became Yvette's best friend. Heather was a plump girl with curly black hair and blue-green eyes, whose family arrived in Australia from Scotland about the same time as Yvette's. Heather was in the same class and they sat together in the shade of the peppermint gum to eat their lunch. Yvette's sandwich progressed from marmalade to lemon butter; still tart yet smooth and creamy.

Melissa's family moved to Melbourne about a year later and Yvette hadn't heard from her since. And when Yvette was about to turn nine her family left for England and she lost touch with Heather.

Young as she was, Yvette might have tried to keep in touch. Yet she'd preferred to keep Heather locked in her past. For a reason strange to her, she suffered an absurd resistance to maintaining old friendships. Friends frozen like photographs, with the same values, interests and beliefs they'd had when she'd known them, moss-gatherers while only she rolled through life like a bare pebble. Even Thomas. Last time they'd met he was recovering after being punched in the face by an angry young woman on the London Underground. His pride bruised more than his eye. And he was furious with Yvette for laughing so hard that rivulets of mascara ran down her cheeks. Now she was apprehensive. She had to force herself to embrace the possibility that Thomas was a little less paranoid and a little more trusting, and in the six months he'd lived in Perth, absorbed some of the laid-back Australian way of life.

The big acoustic chamber of the arrivals lounge housed a muted cacophony of bustling and chatter, thumps and squeaking trolley wheels, and a clear, high voice piercing above the rest with announcements. Yvette squeezed by a clutch of women with small children and noticed Thomas hovering beside a row of seats. He greeted her with a light kiss on her cheek. His round face, full lips and sharp blue eyes were exactly as she recalled. Short and sturdy, and dressed in a tight-fitting white T-shirt and jeans, shaven head framing his unshaven face, he'd taken on a sort of George Michael style, without the pizzazz.

'Good to see you,' he said.

She wasn't convinced he meant it. His eyes darted from her face to her feet and scanned nervously about the lounge. She was sporting a baggy purple T-shirt hanging over a pair of punky drainpipes, streaks of black and lurid-pink on a white background. When she found them in the Cobargo op shop she was ecstatic, the village instantly more appealing. Surrounded now by suntanned folk in shorts and thongs and others dressed uniformly in department-store chic, she suddenly felt ridiculous. She felt an overwhelming desire to merge, to belong to the ordinary. And an equally powerful urge to stand apart.

'Let's go.' She handed Thomas the canvas holdall her mother had given her, and grabbed a stray copy of the *West Australian* folded on a nearby seat. Then she adjusted the handles of her travelling bag that were pinching her shoulder and made for the exit doors.

It took Thomas five minutes to remove the heavy metal contraption he'd locked to the steering wheel of his Honda Civic. A vintage model painted a lurid pea-green, the car had the appearance of a jelly bean. At last he started the engine and crunched the gear stick into reverse.

She sat back in her seat in bemused silence as he manoeuvred the car out of the car park, his face riven with tense concentration. Heading towards the city, he drove slowly in the inside lane of a stretch of dual carriageway, cars sweeping past on the right. She didn't mind his caution. It afforded a leisurely chance to take in the streetscape. And she was shocked by the expansion of the American occupation that had occurred in her absence—a visual famine she hadn't taken in at the blinkered age of twelve—a sprawl of car showrooms, petrol stations, discount warehouses, furniture display rooms, fast food joints and drive-through bottle shops to wash down the cultural bilge. All manner of businesses advertising themselves with blatant disregard for any aesthetic. O'Keeffe would have packed up her easel in disgust.

'I can't believe what's happened to this place,' she said. 'And there's no cohesion, just a ribbon of businesses each with its own car park. Not even a connecting footpath. What were the town planners thinking?'

Without moving his head, Thomas sniggered in that distinctly Thomas way of his, at once familiar and comforting.

'American-style self-promotion,' he said.

'Gaudy and loud.'

'A poverty of style.'

'A mishmash lacking civic pride.'

They both laughed, but another part of her sank flat as the landscape, hoping with every passing set of traffic lights that the appearance of this metropolis would improve the closer they inched towards its centre.

An hour later, Thomas turned down a tree-lined street in Maylands, pulling up in the car park outside a block of high-rise flats.

She looked with dismay at the plain brick building fringed with rows of concrete balconies, the whole edifice totally devoid of charm.

There was no lift. She gave Thomas the holdall and, following behind him, heaved her travelling bag up six flights of concrete stairs, entering a carpeted corridor that smelled faintly acrid, stopping about halfway down on the left. She braced herself for what was to come.

Sure enough, the flat was vile. A rectangular room painted institutional cream, partitioned at the end by a kitchen bench. Beyond the kitchen was a sliding door leading to a balcony. Opposite the kitchen bench, a door led to a bedroom and through it, a windowless bathroom. She took in at a glance the plain grey sofa, small Formica dining table and three padded vinyl chairs, and in the bedroom, a battered melamine wardrobe and a double-bed mattress on the floor. The lack of bars on the windows and a key to open the front door were all that prevented her from screaming, 'Let me out of here!'

Hiding her displeasure, she turned to Thomas. 'Thanks so much for letting me stay.'

'I left the fridge on.'

As she went to open the fridge door he said, 'But it's empty.' He hesitated. 'There's a shop round the corner.' He glanced at his watch then caught her eye with an apologetic smile. 'Anthony's due at my place soon.'

She fought an urge to cry.

'I'll call you later.'

And he left.

2.2

She slid open the door to the balcony and stepped outside. The view was impressive in a modern kind of way, the jacarandas and the gum trees, the suburban rooftops and the Perth city skyline to the west. There was a satisfying depth of field, pleasing variations of height, but the light was too brash and the detail too bland to warrant the sharpening of a pencil.

She was about to lean over the concrete wall to survey the ground below when she noticed a black bin liner in the far corner of the balcony. Loosely knotted, the blowfly buzzing around was sure to find a point of entry. She picked up the bag by its knot and recoiled, the distinct smells of rancid food and rotten meat so strong she caught her breath. She went and propped open the front door, dashed back for the bag and hurried downstairs. Rows of green wheelie bins were lined up along a fence. She hurled the bag into one and followed a trail of fetid drips back to the flat.

Deciding to make the best of things, she used the skerrick of washing up liquid and the old rag that Thomas had left beside the sink, and cleaned the cupboards, inside and out, and the benches, cooker, fridge and floor. Then she walked to the shops. She didn't buy much. Partly because she was broke, and partly because whatever she did buy she had to lug up those stairs. She returned with two carrier bags of groceries.

Entering the flat again she recoiled. Was this a conspiracy of town planners and architects to depress the senses of the populace, render them dim-witted, numb and complacent, passive acceptors of the institutionalisation of everywhere? She had to summon all her resolve to endure it.

She divested the shopping bags of their contents, putting the milk, butter and eggs in the fridge along with a small selection of vegetables, and the tea and sugar, and a tin of tomatoes and a packet of pasta in one of the cupboards. Then she unpacked her things, setting free of her clothes a handful of cutlery, a bowl, two plates, two glasses and two mugs, and an old kettle and a toaster her mother had been keeping for a daughter-leaving-home eventuality. When done she filled the kettle and made a mug of tea, taking up one of the vinyl chairs and opening the newspaper she'd taken from the arrivals lounge, curious to see what passed for news in this state.

She waded through the usual bashings, drug hauls, rich and glitz scandals and political storms, stopping to read with mild interest a review of that documentary about asylum seekers her mother had been watching, the journalist explaining some of the humanitarian difficulties that had presented themselves over the years, citing one example in which there had been a stand-off between Australia and Indonesia over a boat of asylum seekers, neither country prepared to take the people to shore. What a ludicrous scenario. Someone needed to show some humanity, she thought. Otherwise, what were those folk to do? Bob about in the ocean forever?

The article was long, too long to hold her attention. She closed the paper in disgust and took a cool shower. Then she made the bed with the sheets her mother had given her and lay down, staring at the light globe hanging in the centre of the ceiling. What now? She thought of reading a book but she didn't have one. She couldn't listen to music. She'd left her CDs, along with her jewellery, laptop, photos, sketches, paints and brushes in Carlos's house. She didn't even have a radio. And the silence was claustrophobic. She reached for her shoulder bag leaning against the skirting board and rummaged about for a pencil and her sketchbook.

She leafed through ten sketches of dead trees, none of them worthy of her pencil's attention. Arriving at a blank page, she was unexpectedly crowded by memories, prisoners straining the highwire fence she'd long ago erected in her mind.

Perhaps returning to Perth wasn't such a good idea.

She drew a large oval and marked out where in the face the nose and eyes would go. His portrait. The one she painted in that first year here. She was so proud. She'd given him a shock of black hair, large ears, round eyes set close together, a long nose with flaring nostrils and a wide mouth full of dagger-like teeth. Looking back she viewed the work her one expressionist masterpiece. Her mother thought she'd captured him delightfully well. She supposed she had. Her father wasn't stupid, although her mother liked to call him gormless. He wasn't mad either, but when he smiled he had an air of mad stupidity, the sort of stupid, senseless madness that transfigured, along with his countenance, into something terrifying when his anger was triggered. Which was as often as sunrise. He wasn't a powerful man, lanky and barrel-chested, with sloping shoulders and a nervous blink. Her mother had other names for him. Sometimes she called him a silly old sod or face-ache. She must have hated him. Yvette had loved him. Which was why, when he saw her portrait of him and ripped it to pieces, she cried.

Yvette closed her sketchbook then her eyes.

Thomas phoned late that evening.

'How are you settling in?' he said.

'I've been cleaning up a bit,' she said brightly. 'I removed the bin liner you left out on the balcony.'

'Oh that? It wasn't mine. It was there when I moved in.'

Yvette's upper lip curled of its own accord. Thomas wasn't the most hygienic of men, the sheets on his bed in his functional London flat looked and smelt so grimy when he offered her the choice between his bed and the couch she always took the couch.

She accepted his invitation to dinner at his place the following evening, curious to see what sort of home he now had, and hung up her phone.

Deciding she'd had enough of the day, she turned to switch off the kitchen light. Something small and black scuttled across the floor. She thought best to ignore it. She brushed her teeth and changed into a T-shirt for bed. Back in the kitchen she opened a cupboard for a glass. Inside, scurrying to the back of the cupboard were three shiny, black insects. She opened the other cupboard doors. And there they were in all of them, crawling, scurrying, feeling their way about with long antennae.

Cockroaches.

She keeled with revulsion. Worse than ants, worse than flies, ranking joint-first with rats in her hierarchy of vile and dirty pests. And they were everywhere. One had even found its way into the fridge.

She slammed shut the cupboard doors and rinsed and filled her glass in the bathroom. Hoping the roaches had not found their way into the bedroom she rolled a towel and rammed it into the crack under the living-room door. She switched off the light and closed her eyes. She dared not open them for fear of glimpsing in the gloom a roach crawling up the wall beside the bed.

2.3

Thomas's unit was four streets closer to the city in the adjacent suburb of Mount Lawley. It was a warm evening. Yvette walked along the flat, suburban streets dodging the spray from the garden sprinklers watering the carefully mown lawns. She admired the canopy the jacarandas made, their floral display of purple trumpets, fallen blooms dusting the pavement like fat confetti. Had she been more like Séraphine Louis and less Georgia O'Keeffe in her artistic approach, more inclined to chaos than control, she would have been in creative paradise right here on these pavements.

Instead, she kept walking, determined to make the most of her new life in Perth, determined, therefore, to enjoy whatever social delights Thomas had to offer.

Accessed by an external walkway, Thomas's unit was on the second floor of a brick building fashioned in the style of government housing. The door to the unit was ajar so she pushed it open and entered straight into a steam-filled kitchen. Thomas was frantically snatching handfuls of spaghetti out of the sink and tossing them into a colander. On the cooker, on hard boil, a saucepan brimming with bolognaise sauce spluttered madly.

'Can I help?' she said.

Thomas emitted a small yelp before plonking a lid over the colander. Regaining his composure, he said, 'Are you early?'

'Bang on time. Smells terrific.'

She kissed his cheek before sitting down at a small wooden table. Beyond the kitchen, the living room was the same in size and appeal as her flat. A jumbled mess of books, papers, clothing and CDs occupied every seat and the whole of the floor, except for a small area occupied by a music stand and Thomas's violin.

Thomas handed her a glass of red wine.

'Where's Anthony?' she said.

'He didn't turn up.' A look of dejection appeared in his face. He seemed close to tears. 'It isn't working.'

'I'm sorry.'

He turned to fetch the colander.

She sipped the wine. It had a sharp, metallic twang.

'What's the problem?' she asked.

'He won't commit. He says he wants an open relationship.'

'I'm sorry,' she said again. Really, what could she say?

'Me too,' he said with his back to her.

He piled spaghetti onto plates, placed the saucepan on a board in the centre of the table and offered her a ladle.

'Help yourself to sauce.'

'Thanks.' Keen to reinforce her solidarity, she said, 'You didn't move halfway round the world to share him with other men.'

'He's always been a butterfly. But I thought he wanted me.' Thomas poured two ladles of sauce onto his spaghetti, thrust in his fork and twirled it round and round and round without a pause before shovelling a dribbling bulk into his mouth. She twisted a few spaghetti strands round on her fork without looking up at him. Poor guy.

'I don't know how you can stay with him,' she said, realising as she spoke she had been doing just that with Carlos until she fell pregnant.

'We might be splitting up.'

'What will you do? Go back to England?' She had to repress an unwarranted feeling of abandonment.

'I thought about it. But I've bought this place now.'

She couldn't see how anyone could bond with a unit like this. But she felt relieved.

'And then there's my job,' he continued, reaching behind him for the stained tea towel on the draining board to wipe his mouth.

'Computer programming? I thought you hated it.'

He avoided her gaze. 'It pays well and my colleagues are friendly. I seem to fit in.'

She let his justifications slip by without challenge.

They spent the rest of the evening laying diagonally on his unmade bed, discussing art, poetry and music, an elixir of conversation. They finished one bottle of the wine and opened another. Yvette felt drawn to him, not physically, but there was an intimacy between them, born of affection and shared history. They reminisced. Long walks on Hampstead Heath. Sunday mornings at Camden Market. The cinemas, pubs and cheap restaurants they'd frequented. Of the two weeks he'd spent with her in Malta. How they'd visited the old temples and strolled along the rocky beaches where the limestone cliffs met the ocean, their voices raised against the wind, dissecting the ravaged body of the island's culture with their scalpel-sharp minds. An island settled by stone-age farmers thousands of years before first the Greeks, the Phoenicians then the Romans came along. Embroiled in the Byzantine wars, colonised by Arab rulers from Sicily, then back to the West in the hands of the Normans, eventually ending up part of the British Empire. Poor beleaguered Malta, in sixty-four its people finally gained independence after many thousands of years, only now to be colonised by tourists, who at least, they had to agree, went home after their generally less harmful pillaging.

'I identified with the island so much,' she said. 'I refused to mix with the foreigners. Even the market traders. But the locals were a closed group.'

'So, you fell in with Carlos.'

'That's an interesting way of putting it.'

He propped himself up on a pillow. 'You're here now. Malta is the past.'

She turned away from him and buried her face in her hands. He had no idea how much his words stung. He couldn't fathom the depths of her attachment to that island. And she hadn't told him she'd fallen pregnant. She didn't want him to know Carlos had coerced her into having a termination. Now, with a hollow heart and a resistant mind, she faced the bland suburban landscape of Perth, with its suburban values, suburban aspirations, inane, urbane and nauseatingly bourgeois. She had no idea how she'd find her way. One part of her craved security. Another craved adventure. Both were drawn by the allure of the fortune-teller's prophecy. It was all she had to hold on to.

She left shortly after eleven. She could have stayed up all night but Thomas had to work tomorrow. And she had to *find* work. Casual work. Cash in hand. But she wouldn't clean motel rooms again.

2.4

With a mug of tea in hand, Yvette sat on the balcony floor, back against the wall, warming her legs in the morning sun, and squinting at the small ads in the local newspaper she'd bought in the supermarket yesterday. A Turkish café in Leederville was looking for waitresses. She pushed aside her misgivings, based on a rather superficial loyalty to the original inhabitants of her beloved island, Malta. She'd acquired a tendency to be wary of all things Turkish, largely from Carlos who held a number of bombastic prejudices, especially towards those descendants of the Ottoman Empire. She knew at the time her attitude was ludicrously inconsistent. Following that path, she ought to be wary of the French, the Lebanese and anyone from England. And she was hardly inclined to be wary of herself.

She went inside and looked up Leederville on her street map. It was just a few train stops away. She went back outside and dialled the number provided in the ad and arranged an interview for later in the day.

The newly opened café was in a newly opened shopping mall, pristine and smelling of fresh paint, with glass walls looking out on the car park and the main road. Muzak blended with all the chatter and bustle in the mall, culminating in a wall of loud but muffled echoes. A nominal attempt had been made by the interior designers to instil character into this intrinsically characterless box, towering philodendrons in large terracotta tubs book-ending park benches. But for Yvette, the singular attraction of the place was the air-conditioning.

Rows of circular tables filled the café's spacious interior. Three o'clock and there were no customers. The counter was long with an espresso machine at one end and a cash register at the other. Behind the salad bar a petite woman of about forty, with smooth black hair pinned back from her face, was piling baklava onto a large platter.

Yvette approached wearing a cheery smile and said, 'Hi, I've come about the job.'

The woman looked up, her eyes sliding down to Yvette's apparel, taking in the loose, thigh-length frock and leather sandals that Yvette had thought until that moment adequately smart.

The woman wiped her hands on her apron and Yvette followed her to a small table positioned against the back wall beneath a lively crewelwork wall hanging. The kitchen door swung open and a solid-looking man, also wearing an apron, carried a platter of sweetmeats to the counter. The woman smiled over at him before returning her gaze to Yvette.

'My name is Pinar,' she said in a strongly accented voice. 'My husband and I looking for nice waitress.'

She asked some questions. Yvette fabricated vignettes, holding Pinar's gaze, doing her best to exude charm. Pinar seemed doubtful. Yvette wondered what to say to clinch the interview. Glancing up at the wall hanging, she said with a measure of sincerity, 'What a beautiful tapestry.' She placed a hand on her chest. 'I wish I knew how to make something like that.'

Pinar's face lit with interest. 'My mother made it.'

'Really? I adore it.'

Pinar looked over at a woman with four children walking towards the counter. Then she leaned forward and said in a low voice, 'You work for cash?'

'Yes.' Yvette was at once relieved and bemused. Pinar must be taking an enormous risk in this regulation-bound nation. Still, she was not about to question her new employer's subterfuge any more than she questioned Brenda's at the Cobargo hotel.

'You start work tomorrow?'

'Yes.'

'You be here at nine.'

Pinar told Yvette to wear black with closed-in shoes. On her way home she went to Vinnies and bought a pair of black drainpipes and a loose-fitting black T-shirt.

It was a mistake.

When Yvette arrived at the café for her first shift, Pinar was neatly dressed in black tailored pants and a pressed cotton blouse. She looked at Yvette with mild disapproval before ushering her behind the counter. Humiliation pinged in Yvette's guts. Already she regretted insinuating her way into a job she knew she'd despise.

Yvette followed Pinar up and down the servery, watching attentively as Pinar taught her how to use the espresso machine and assemble and wrap kebabs. She served her first customers with Pinar watching her with equal intensity.

Yvette was keen to impress. She split the pitta bread with finesse. She rolled kebabs tightly. She was polite to customers. Pinar seemed satisfied and left her alone. Determined to convince Pinar of her worth, Yvette cleared tables without being prompted. She cleaned. She restocked. She did everything well. She even managed to make acceptable lattes and cappuccinos. But Pinar prided herself on perfect coffee, the milk topped with velvety foam, and decorated with a love-heart pattern. Yvette applied all her training and determination but whenever she passed by with a cup in her hand, Pinar looked disappointed.

2.5

The customers didn't seem to mind Yvette's distorted love hearts. One woman of about her age had come in every morning in that first week, ordered a latte and sat at a table by the window. She was a large woman with a kind face and she'd opened a book the moment she was seated. She seemed self-contained; Yvette hardly gave her a second glance. Their only interaction occurred when Yvette set down her latte and the woman made a brief comment about the haphazard brown shape floating on the froth.

On Friday, as Yvette set down her cup the woman chuckled and said, 'Different every time, eh?'

'I'm not good with love hearts,' Yvette said apologetically.

'I'm sure you are.'

The woman beamed good will. She was dressed today in a flowing burgundy frock. Long beaded necklaces rested on her full bosom. She closed her book and held Yvette's gaze. Framed by locks of curly black hair, she had a round face with a pert nose, cupid lips, and blue-green eyes. Yvette felt a vague pulse of recognition. 'Do you live near here?'

'I work in that building across the car park.' The woman pointed out the window at a white office block.

'What do you do?'

'Holistic counselling. I'm Heather.' She held out her hand.

'Yvette.'

'Yvette?' Heather paused and looked wistful. 'I went to school with an Yvette.'

'Rockingham Primary School?'

A look of amazement appeared in Heather's face. 'You're never Yvette Grimm?' She looked at Yvette closely and with genuine regard.

'That's me.'

'You do remember me?'

'Heather? Heather McAllister?' She repressed a cascade of feeling, at once cautious and intrigued. 'You are still McAllister?'

'Yeah. After a spell as someone else. And you're still Grimm?'

They both laughed.

Heather still exuded the same maternal vibe. She had been, even at six, motherly and protective, shielding Yvette from the playground bullies. Heather wasn't rough, but her bulk and the fiery look of her when roused were enough to arrest even the keenest thug. Heather had been Yvette's fortress. School life hadn't been easy back in London; she'd had little success on her own fending off the toughs.

'We must catch up,' Heather said eagerly. 'I'd love to hear what you've been up to all these years.'

'We must.' Yvette glanced back at the counter. Pinar was watching. 'I better get back to work.'

A lonely, wispy cloud meandered across the face of the afternoon sun. Her phone rang. It was her mother.

Yes, she was settling in. Yes, she was enjoying the job. No, she hadn't heard anything yet. Then Yvette mentioned Heather.

'I went to school with her. I used to go to her house for sleepovers.'

'That fat girl with the green eyes?'

'She was my best friend.'

'She was Scottish, wasn't she?'

'She was lovely and kind.'

'I'm sure she was. You had a nice time with her anyway.'

A far, far better time than I'd had at home. She didn't say it. She told her mother she was about to take a shower and hung up her phone.

2.6

Yvette's shifts at the cafe brightened when Heather appeared and dimmed again when she left, snatches of conversation arousing flashes of fond memories. Of the day Heather's father had taken them to Underwater World, and they'd held hands in awe of the sharks circling above them, all grey menace beyond a thickness of glass tube. Stingrays, with their ribboning fins and barbed tails, looming shadows gliding by. The sea horses adorned with befuddling ornamentations hovering above friezes of pretty coral. Heather's older brother Angus had come along too, a sullen, spotty teenager interested only in spooking his little sister and her scrawny friend. Despite his efforts, they'd had a fabulous time. There were ice-creams and fish and chips and then the long drive home.

Back at the flat she applied herself to cockroach extermination. She placed baits in strategic corners, left trails of powder along every crack, crevice and skirting board, mashed borax with jam and put dollops in cupboards and under the fridge. Nothing worked. For every roach she killed, another ten appeared to replace it. She considered borrowing Kafka's *Metamorphosis* to develop some empathy but thought better of it.

One morning, as day broke into the room, she noticed a cockroach crawling up the wall beside her bed. And another ambling along a skirting board. She'd thought cockroaches were light averse but this lot were in no hurry to escape back into the dark. And they'd become accustomed to her presence. They were familiar, like cats, wandering up to her inquiringly. Perhaps she'd like to chat?

Had the entire contingent of cockroaches in this wretched building moved into her flat? Or were the other residents plagued with the critters too? She had no idea. Two weeks and she hadn't met her neighbours. No one passed her in the corridor or on the stairs. She might be the only person in the entire block, a single human representative fending off a plague.

She went to the bathroom and glanced at the basin. One of her unwanted housemates was taking an interest in her toothbrush. Revulsion moiled through her. She declared war. She'd bomb the lot of them to oblivion.

It was nine o'clock when she exited the building and marched down several suburban streets to the hardware store. She returned about an hour later with two insecticide bombs.

Reading the instructions, she felt like America: Open every cupboard door, shut all windows and move furniture away from the walls. She had to stay away for eight hours. She scanned her street map and found the nearest library, about half an hour's walk away. She stuffed a peanut butter sandwich and a bottle of tap water into her shoulder bag, set off the bombs and left the flat.

This time when she opened the door at the bottom of the stairwell she was confronted by a barrage of hot air, the concrete car park radiating the sun's ferocity. There was no breeze. Heading north, she walked along the nondescript suburban street, ignoring with dogged intent the brick-and-tile houses with their verdant lawns. She crossed through a park where a few gum trees provided brief relief from the sun and the lawn was as lush as the lawns she'd just passed.

Back on the pavement the heat was excoriating. She crossed the dual carriageway at the traffic lights and walked along an arterial road bereft of shade and lined with a splash of crassly presented car yards, petrol stations, pizza bars, milk bars and tacky discount stores. She ached for the streetscapes of Malta, berating herself for not returning with Carlos. She still could. She had a return ticket from Djakarta to Rome that didn't expire until May. But there was a voice inside her adamant she had to stay. A voice she heeded, convinced it represented the sensible part of her.

She turned down a side street and walked through another brick-and-tile housing estate. There had to be more to Perth than this: she couldn't imagine the man in the palm-reader's prophecy behind the windows of suburbia.

She walked through the library's automatic sliding doors into the resurrecting cool of the air conditioning, determined to occupy the whole day here. She started towards the main room, passing through the foyer where shelves of reference books lined the bottom half of a wall, when among an array of encyclopaedias and dictionaries with dull dark spines, one volume caught her eye. She sensed the book didn't belong there. Glossy white with *Profits of Doom* in bold black lettering down the spine. It was the word 'doom' that first caught her eye, thinking ironically that perhaps the book would explain how she might profit from her circumstances. She pulled the book from the shelf and went through to the back of the library where several armchairs faced a low melamine table.

Ten pages in and her senses came alive. She was right there with the author, Antony Loewenstein, in first Curtin then Christmas Island, with the refugees who had come to Australia by boat. She'd had little idea till now the tragedy those people suffered. It was rapidly becoming unfathomable that she should have managed to remain so ignorant, especially when Malta was geographically in the front line for endless African migrants. Bowing to the demands of her art degrees, trapped inside her obsessive love then caged in a chamber of grief, all her adulthood she hadn't once paid attention to the plight of boat arrivals. Still, she gave herself no shrift.

Large chunks of the narrative slipped by without her full comprehension. Hers was an empathic response. Amongst all the data there was embedded in the narrative the tears of the prisoners, their anguish, their loss of hope. The author was restrained. Yet she could feel his frustration. She read, on and on, slipping outside to eat her sandwich in the violent sun, then heading back to the same seat, to journey on to Papua New Guinea. Here she stopped. There was too much to absorb. She flicked back and re-read the descriptions of interviews with prisoners and the prison staff. Then she requested the use of one of the library's computers and Googled images of both locations.

Curtin was located in one of the hottest places on earth, in a flat plain of scrub and red dust. A high chain link fence fringed with coils of razor wire contained a concatenation of grey demountable buildings. Inside the prison there appeared little shade save for that cast by the buildings and the odd tree here and there. The Christmas Island centre was no better. It was surrounded by lush forest, but the beauty stopped at the fence. Absolutely every feature of all the squashed-together buildings was grey: the roofs, walls, awnings, concrete paths.

As she scrolled through the images, other detention centres appeared on Nauru and Manus Island. Conditions in both places looked abysmal. How could she be sitting here in this cool library, when her status was no different to those people? If anything, those refugees had a greater legitimacy being here than she. Men, women and even children herded in, locked up and stripped of their identities. To be addressed, Loewenstein had noted in his book, not by their names, but by a number, their boat identification number. This was Auschwitz without the gas.

Already forming in her mind was a sketch. But she needed inspiration. She was out of practice, so long had it been since she'd felt creative. She wandered around the library shelves in the non-fiction section and found a small collection of art books. Setting aside her prejudice for all things Antipodean, she fished out at random a number of books on Australian art and returned to her seat.

She laid out the books on the table: *Cubism and Australian Art, Joy Hester and Friends,* a book on Sidney Nolan and another on Russell Drysdale. The Arthur Streeton she soon closed, and the Tom Roberts she set to one side without opening.

With little idea what she was searching for, she skimmed over colour plates and descriptions of the works of Arthur Boyd and Grace Cossington-Smith, Danila Vassilieff, Hester and Nolan. These were some of the Modernist painters whose works challenged the traditional realism staunchly favoured by the Australian-art establishment of the early twentieth century, so said an introduction, the turning point coming late, but that was to be expected. Australia, she had long since decided, had always been culturally backward.

She derived little from Cossington-Smith's work, finding the paintings too soft and cosy, almost quaint for all their post-impressionist technique. Hester's work piqued her interest, portraying intense emotion in brush and ink, her use of expressionist strokes reminiscent of Picasso, the artist's engagement with the news reels of Nazi concentration camps striking an inner bell. Yet she knew she had no capacity for such renditions of human tragedy.

Saving Drysdale's landscapes for last without knowing why, she went on to contemplate the raw emotion of Vassilieff's urban street scenes, followed by Nolan's Ned Kelly series and Boyd's Bride series, savouring each artist's engagement with their subject, impressed with the way the artists conveyed the anxieties, the tensions and the alienation, noting as well the embedded social critique. Yet their expressionist renditions left her aesthetically unmoved.

It wasn't until she opened the book on Drysdale that she felt she'd found a home. His combination of realist and surrealist techniques in his depictions of the outback echoed her own love of O'Keeffe's scenes of New Mexico. Both worked in oil on canvas. Both conveyed a stillness that was stark and evocative.

She was reminded of the day in her first year of university, when one of her lecturers, Dr Faultone, a wild-haired, bra-less woman in her fifties, required her students to research Modernism. The students were to select from three major artists one that best represented their own artistic direction. Dr Faultone insisted that all art was derivative, there being no such thing as absolute originality, even innovators relied on their exposure to various cultural and intellectual currents and pre-existing works. For Dr Faultone's previous assignment, students kept a journal of gallery visits along with their impressions of a range of works through the centuries. Yvette's most memorable entry recorded a moment of epiphany she experienced while gazing at Stubbs' *Whistlejacket* in the National Gallery. She was amazed and a little disturbed that a painting of a horse could arouse in her such an intensity of emotion.

For Dr Faultone's latest task, Yvette had sat in the university library surrounded by art books, discarding the works of artist upon artist, many of whom she had been forced to emulate at high school, succumbing to a mounting frustration, convinced she would never find a single Modernist artist that matched her own aspirations. Until she found and fell in love with O'Keeffe.

Now she'd found Drysdale and through his work gained a speck of appreciation of Australia.

Her senses aroused, imagination sparking, she went to the main desk and asked a librarian if she could join the library. The librarian handed her a leaflet. Yvette soon found she didn't have photo identification. She returned the leaflet to the counter in disgust. You can't fart in Australia without photo identification. She went back to the computer she'd been using and quickly checked her emails, disappointed a second time when she clicked on her inbox and found no word from Malta.

The moment she was back at the flat she opened all the windows wide and propped open the front door then sat out on the balcony. A magenta hue brushed the western horizon, accenting the rigid lines of the high rises on the city skyline. The sky to the east darkened as she watched, revealing the stars, indistinct points of shimmering light in the dusky firmament above the city.

She stared and stared, and as she stared she succumbed to an extraordinary sense of awe, her ordinary reality cracking open, revealing a human tragedy of unconscionable proportions, here, in Malta, no doubt in many lands the world over, millions of little lights dimmed. She'd adopted unquestioningly the view promulgated by the media that people smugglers were to blame, and believed governments' claims that if they didn't impose severe deterrents their nation would be overrun. She'd paid no attention to the plight of millions, held the flimsiest of an understanding of the various causes —war, famine, natural disaster. Now she was beginning to question everything. It was a horror to her and she wanted to face it.

Later, she phoned Thomas and told him in a string of hurried sentences a blow-by-blow account of her day—the cockroach massacre, the book, her inspiration—she was soaring.

'There's a library about five minutes from your flat.'

'I'm glad I didn't know that.'

'Why?'

Why? Hadn't he heard anything she'd said?

'What are you doing tomorrow?' he said quickly.

'Nothing.'

'I'm having coffee with a friend, Dan. He's a lecturer in journalism. Want to come along?'

'Sounds great.'

'I'm meeting him in Northbridge. I'll drive. Come over around two.' And he hung up.

2.7

I t was another hot and breezeless day, the sun burning a dazzling
hole in the vast canvas of the sky. After half an hour of
navigational bickering—which way right, which left and the correct
manner to hold a street directory—Yvette was relieved when Thomas
drove down an open tree-lined street in the evidently trendy suburb
of Northbridge, pulling up outside Café Mocha. Housed in a neo-
gothic building sandwiched between two low-rise concrete
shopfronts, the café exuded cosmopolitan glamour. She admired the
façade, the stucco quoining and the tall and narrow windows, while
Thomas fumbled with the steering lock. She had to repress an urge to
tell him she was sure the car would be fine; they'd be able to watch it
through the café windows.

Inside, the café was cool. Fans whirred in the high ceiling. A long
glitzy counter stretched along the sidewall and sofas accompanied
standard café-style tables and chairs. There were books, magazines
and newspapers for the patrons' edification and vibrant artworks
covered every inch of hanging space—Expressionist in style, desert-
scapes and seascapes, riotous dances of wild flowers beneath blue
skies, thick smears of ochres and cadmiums untamed by white or grey

—overbearing, and yet she was envious of all that paint at the artist's disposal. The paintings taunted her.

Thomas headed for the back corner, where a good-looking man was seated at a table.

The man looked up from his newspaper. 'Hey, Thomas! How're you doing?'

'Good, thanks.' They shook hands.

The man turned to Yvette and smiled broadly. She smiled back. 'I'm Yvette.'

'I'm very pleased to meet you.'

His handshake was firm and she warmed to him immediately. He was tall, suntanned with sandy hair and a friendly open face.

They sat down as a waitress approached, and ordered the coffee and cake special.

'Yvette, that's a French name,' said Dan.

'Yes, it is.'

'Do you have any French connections?'

'Afraid not.'

She caught Thomas stifling a snigger. Then he shot a glance at the newspaper and asked Dan what he thought of the new Prime Minister. Dan rolled his eyes. The two men began to chat about various public figures Yvette hadn't heard of and she soon stopped listening. She hadn't engaged with local politics since she'd arrived in Australia. She was of the view that one incumbent was as bad as another and since she couldn't vote, she had no need to form an opinion. She stared past the other diners and out the window at Thomas's car, wondering who out of the fresh-faced throng that walked by would want to steal a Honda Civic.

She was drawn back to the conversation when Thomas mentioned asylum seekers and the Medevac repeal. Yvette looked at her companions inquiringly.

'Asylum seekers held in off-shore detention did have the right to be flown to Australia for medical treatment,' Dan said. 'No more.'

'Our politicians major in sadism, Yvette.'

'I had no idea.'

'Neither did I until I migrated here.'

'We had boat arrivals in Malta.'

'Australia has a special way of dealing with them.'

'It started with Tampa,' Dan said sourly.

Yvette looked puzzled.

'The children overboard debacle. Weren't you here when that happened?' said Thomas.

'When was it?'

'About eighteen years ago.'

'Um, no.' She was in London, adjusting to her mother's new husband.

'The government of the day made false allegations that refugees had threatened to throw their own children overboard in a ploy to secure rescue and passage to Australia,' said Dan. 'That was when asylum seekers, so-called boat people, were taken to a detention centre on Manus Island for processing.'

'The Pacific Solution,' Thomas said.

Yvette leaned forward. 'Some solution.'

Dan caught her eye. His face wore a solemn expression, the harsh and unfair treatment of asylum seekers clearly an offence to his sense of justice. She liked the man.

'It's getting worse,' he said. 'These people are denied any sort of permanent residency and now even access to Australia for medical reasons. What next? Seems the unenlightened many, or at least the present government, want refugees to live the rest of their days on some remote island that can barely sustain its own people.'

'Dreadful,' she said, struggling to take it all in and falling silent.

'Worse. They closed all avenues of justice.'

'You mean rights of appeal?' Thomas said.

'And any free access to legal representation.'

'Sounds like Guantanamo. Held forever then tried by a military court.'

'Not quite, but might as well be.'

'A kangaroo court then.'

'Welcome to fortress Australia.'

'I heard the government forces refugees to sign a code of conduct.'

'You are kidding?'

'Nope. Anyone on a bridging visa has to comply.'

'What? Thou shalt not spit?'

'Or swear, or annoy. Or be in any way anti-social.'

'We might as well all leave now. That would apply to everyone in the country.'

'Everyone except a saint.'

Thomas looked thoughtful. 'Ethically and logistically brilliant,' he said, narrowing his eyes.

'Worthy of the Adolph Eichmann Memorial Prize,' Dan quipped.

They all laughed, yet Yvette felt guilty. It didn't seem right that she was entirely free to sit here in this café, walk out the door and on down the pavement, work, shop, eat and sleep, all without any sort of censure. 'It's unconscionable,' she murmured, not sure as she spoke if she was referring to the treatment of asylum seekers or her own comparative freedoms.

'It is,' Dan said in reply. 'Those who came by boat are being used as a deterrent.'

'What about the asylum seekers who come by plane?' There must be some. Or plenty.

Neither man seemed interested in responding to her question. There was a moment of silence as the waitress, dressed neatly in bistro black, came with the cake and the lattes, topped, Yvette noticed with a wry twinge, with a flower exquisitely sculpted in brown.

'Is Anthony here or in Kalgoorlie?' she asked Thomas, watching him give his sugared latte a rigorous stir, the froth sliding down the sides of his glass.

'Here,' he said. 'He's spending the weekend at my place.'

'I haven't seen him in ages,' she said.

Thomas didn't reply.

'Is he planning on teaching out at that school when his placement expires?' Dan said.

'Placement?' she said.

'The only way to get staff out to rural schools in Western Australia is through special placements for qualifying teachers.'

'Incentives,' Thomas said, setting down his glass.

'No one wants to go out there.'

'Is it that bad?' Yvette said, spooning the froth on her latte.

'I wouldn't call it bad. But even so, teachers used to be bonded.'

'Bonded? Sounds like slavery.'

'It was in some ways. Hence *Wake in Fright*.'

Thomas laughed. 'Brilliant movie.'

'You've seen it?'

'Anthony's favourite.'

'It is a good film. If you don't mind the slaughter,' Dan said.

Thomas shovelled into his mouth a hunk of mud cake. Dan stirred his coffee and levered the tines of his fork into the slice of lemon cheesecake on his plate.

'So, is Anthony going to stay out there?' he said between mouthfuls.

'I doubt they'll keep him on,' said Thomas.

'Oh?'

'He's crafted quite a reputation.' Thomas demurred, his eyes darting back and forth from Dan to Yvette. He lowered his voice. 'On a school trip to Perth he took a group of students to a strip club.'

'Outrageous,' said Dan. 'They were boys?'

'He sees himself as the Pied Piper.'

'Luring the young to take a leap into the unknown,' Yvette said.

'And he's still employed?!' Dan shook his head in disbelief.

Yvette was astonished that a person charged with professionalism would choose to behave so recklessly. Still, she'd have benefited from the maverick. Instead, in her primary years she suffered Mrs Thoroughgood, whose wrath descended on tender hearts for the mildest misdemeanour. She was a dreadful introduction to Australia.

Thomas slurped the dregs of his coffee and glanced at his watch.

'I better go. I'm meeting him in half an hour.' Something like guilt flitted across his face.

Yvette gave way to disappointment. She had no idea she'd be making her own way home. Not that she minded catching the train. But the thought of entering that flat to spend another evening alone was depressing. Her despondency must have shown on her face. The moment Thomas left, paying his bill on the way out, Dan said, 'You're in Maylands?'

'Yes.'

'I can drive you home if you like.'

She hesitated.

'It's on my way,' he said, standing.

He went to the counter and paid for the two of them, refusing her contribution with a wave of his hand. 'Thanks,' she said, following him outside to his car.

Dan's driving was smooth. She sat back in the passenger seat and relaxed. They headed to Mount Lawley along Beaufort Street, a flat straight road through another uninspiring thoroughfare. The stark light of the Western Australian sun that bounced off concrete and glass gave the whole place the look of an over-exposed photograph.

They were both silent for a while. Then Dan said, 'What do you do?'

Yvette was disconcerted by the question. She didn't know where to take it. She answered tentatively, 'I'm an artist.'

'Amazing! Painting, sketching, sculpture?'

Now she felt embarrassed. 'Um, painting. Or I would, if I had any paint.'

'Did you train?'

'Goldsmiths. I did my Masters at the Royal College of Art.'

'I'm impressed.'

'Don't be. After five years of study I took off to Malta and haven't painted anything since.'

'Why Malta?'

'At first to work in a bar. Then I met a man and my whole life changed.' She explained her story, from Carlos right through to the cockroaches. His interest seemed genuine and keen.

'Are you in a hurry?' he said. 'I'd like to swing by my office. I have something that might interest you.'

'I'm in no rush,' she said, her curiosity aroused.

His office was a featureless rectangle crammed with the paraphernalia of an academic life. He knelt down behind the door and pulled from a bottom shelf a large box. 'I'm not using these. Take a look.'

She knelt on the carpet and opened the lid.

Art materials!

She was quivering like a dog forced to sit before its dinner bowl. She wanted to devour the contents in one gulp. There were tubes of acrylics of every hue, a tray of oily pastels, charcoal, watercolours, bristle and sable brushes of all shapes and sizes, a pack of Derwents, a small bundle of acquerello paper and, most thrilling of all, tucked in one corner, a tray of high-quality oils.

'Are you sure?' she said, amazed by his generosity.

'I'm never going to use them.'

'But...'

'I insist.'

'Thank you so much.'

'Don't mention it. I did a couple of introductory art courses at my local community centre. I bought all the gear then discovered I had no aptitude. I was about to take the box to Vinnies charity shop.'

'You've no idea what this means to me.'

'I think I might. All you need now is paper and some sketching pencils.'

'I have the pencils.' She'd never been without her tin box of assorted pencils. That tin box had for years been part of her miniscule collection of favoured possessions, surviving, along with her pink alarm clock and a green comb, every one of her pre-move culls.

2.8

The sunset muted from crimson to a diffused apricot. Back at the flat, Yvette had arranged her art materials in a row on the sofa. A soft glow infused the room. She gazed at her paints covetously, still stunned by the gift, at once marvelling over the surreal unfolding of her new life in Perth; already filled with chance encounters and good fortune, it had taken on a sort of mythic reality, as if she'd slipped between the covers of a fantasy novel simply through her chosen quest to fulfil a prophecy. She couldn't fathom the cause of the events. That inquiry seemed to her taboo. She absently stroked her chin, before reaching for the charcoal.

Her preferred medium was oil, but she had so far sketched nothing worthy of the concentration and labour required for an oil painting. Besides, she lacked a canvas.

Ideas buzzed around her like bees. At art school she'd gravitated towards precisionism upon her early encounter with O'Keeffe's works, and inspired as well by Sheeler, the portrayal of the industrial landscapes of 1920's modernity then seeming to her apt: London's cityscape had changed with the millennium. There was the Dome, the Eye, the Gherkin and Broadgate Tower. Precisionism went with the cool indifference of the modern corporate world. Yet what had once appealed to her—the clean lines, the exactitude, the at times photographic quality of her work—now seemed sterile and devoid of emotion. And here, reverberating around the walls of this drab grey flat were the moans and cries of all those who'd passed through Curtin and Christmas Island. She would never be an Expressionist painter—that would be going too far in the opposite direction—but she had to find a way to convey the raw dark emotion, the images that ferried her way like boats on Acheron.

She looked up. Something small and black scuttled down the kitchen wall. She switched on the overhead light and opened cupboards, drawers and doors to find the cockroaches had survived their Armageddon and taken up their stations throughout the flat.

She groaned. She was a prisoner in this concrete cell, trapped in an underworld six storeys high. She was a modern day Persephone. And, she noted with bitter irony, she first came across the Queen of the Underworld shortly after she'd met Thomas. In a pub one night they'd been listening to the 'Persephone' track by The Cocteau Twins on her iPod, sharing the earpiece. She'd mispronounced the name, (she thought the word rhymed with telephone) and Thomas, after sniggering to himself for a humiliatingly long time, corrected her. Per-seph-oh-nee, he said, then sniggered on for even longer, before giving her the gist of the myth. She couldn't have known it then that he'd install her in his own pestilent hell.

Later, unable to sleep, she spent the whole night sketching, occasionally looking up to check on the occupiers' movements.

2.9

Her creative upwelling vanished with daylight. After a shower and breakfast she packed away her art materials and cleaned the flat, leaving for Leederville before the sun had begun scorching the day.

At work she was dreamy and distracted. When she wasn't serving, she wandered around the café absently wiping tables. Heather didn't appear and she was surprised to find herself disappointed. She viewed the diners, mostly women and retired couples, not an eligible-looking man among them. She couldn't imagine meeting a half-decent man in here. She wasn't likely to meet a suitor through Thomas's network, and as for Heather, she seemed too matronly for girls' nights out on the pull.

And when a mother walked in cradling a newborn baby, Yvette's longing for a child of her own returned with force.

Towards the end of her shift, two plump, middle-aged women sat at a table near the counter. Yvette tidied the kebab wrappers, listening to their conversation.

'You should try it. My aunt met the love of her life through Love Station.'

'Yeah? I bet she had to sieve through a load of creeps before she met him.'

'What have you got to lose? It's free.'

'Aw, I dunno.'

'Everyone's doing it. These sites are filled with profiles.'

After the women left, she cleared their table. The *West Australian* was folded open at the personals column. There, below a string of chat lines and massage services, was a large listing for Love Station. She glanced over at the counter. Pinar was standing beside the till, chatting with a customer. Yvette tore out the page and stuffed it in her trouser pocket.

On her way back to the flat she went to the library, the one five minutes away that Thomas had mentioned. This library was smaller and there were few visitors. She was able to secure a computer session without a wait.

Ignoring the corpulent, balding man seated to her left, she logged on and found the Love Station website. Joining was free, as the woman in the café had said, so she filled out the registration form and scanned through the other profiles. There were thousands of hopefuls of all ages. Kind, fun-loving forty-something women without ties seeking adventurous, sincere gents for romance. There must have been hundreds like that. The financially secure seeking the well groomed. Good sense of humour essential. The generous looking for loyal, the natural looking for fit. Already she was composing a profile in her mind.

The man beside her shifted in his seat so she leaned forward, placing her shoulder bag on the desk, hoping it was between his line of sight and her screen.

She filled out her details in the fields. She found a photo attached to an old email, taken in Malta, and uploaded it. She looked good in that photo, suntanned, round lips spread in a comely smile, hazel eyes lively and inviting, wavy copper hair cut short. What sort of man was she looking for? Must have artistic interests. She didn't want to be more specific.

She clicked submit then scanned her emails. There was nothing of interest, nothing but junk, nothing from Malta. Nothing.

The fat man, whose presence beside her was making her feel sleazy, rose laboriously from his seat and walked away. She sat back with relief and placed her bag on the floor at her feet.

Ten minutes later she clicked back to her profile. There were thirty-two hits. She was flabbergasted. She had no idea she'd be so popular.

With anticipation moiling in her belly, she scanned the photographs and immediately eliminated half the contenders; men too old, too fat, too showy, too geeky. She examined the others more closely. Three computer programmers, a welder, a pig farmer, four public servants, two science teachers, a lawyer and a real estate agent ended up on her reject pile. She doubted any of them knew a thing about art.

The remaining three seemed promising: Frank, a fund manager from Applecross with an interest in Renaissance portraiture; Dimitri, a professional photographer from Cottesloe; and Lee, a music teacher from Scarborough, who made no mention of visual art but music was close enough. She wondered how these men would view her.

Doubt shimmered briefly in her mind, doused by an upsurge of excitement. Two weeks and all she'd managed were a few outings and dinner at Thomas's place. Time was running out. She knew it was crazy to attach so much significance to the words of a palm reader, but some irrational part of her thought otherwise, determined as ever to have its way. So, she reasoned, if it *was* preordained that she'd meet the father of her children before she was thirty then she mustn't be obstructive by isolating herself. A heroic figure in a black polo neck wasn't about to abseil down to her balcony with chocolates, red roses and a declaration of eternal love. She needed to be out and about meeting men.

2.10

She met Frank in London Court. She was standing beneath the clock watching a throng of city workers and tourists wander up and down the narrow thoroughfare of small shops and cafes. All the buildings had mock Tudor façades, replete with dovecotes, gabled rooves and weathercocks, crenelated towers and wrought-iron gates, and gargoyles, shields, crests and statues. Nothing, it seemed, was missing from that homage to an Elizabethan history Australia never experienced. An elaborate and expensive folly, but one undeniably attractive. At the first stroke of seven a gathering of tourists gazed at the clock above her head. She looked up as four mechanised knights moved around the clock face.

Frank was considerably shorter and older than his photograph suggested. Even at a distance of about fifteen metres Yvette knew he wasn't her type. The closer he got, the stronger the feeling became. He looked swanky in a loud open-necked shirt, beige trousers and patent leather shoes. With his hair swept back from a clean-shaven face, he had a rakish look about him. His face lit when he recognised her as the woman in the profile. 'I'm pleased to make your acquaintance,' he said, with a contrived chivalrous bow. At that moment she pictured him, an extra from the pageant of London Court, in a powdered wig, frilly collar, doublet and hose.

'Shall we?' He escorted her by her elbow back to his sports car, shiny and red with a plush interior.

As they headed towards his favourite restaurant, her mind raced faster than his driving. What was she doing with this man? For all she knew he was a lecherous creep using internet dating for easy sex.

The restaurant was set in a swathe of manicured lawns and carefully arranged plantings of native grasses, overlooking the sublime estuarine waters of the Swan River. The setting immediately brought to mind the original name of the Swan River, the Derbarl Yarrigan, so named by the Nyoongar people, the place of the fresh water turtle. The river was later renamed by Dutch explorer Willem de Vlamingh, Yvette recalled with irony, after the preponderance of black swans. Facts beaten into her class by Mrs Thoroughgood, who had a twisted sense of white dominion, an unvoiced yet discernable ethnocentric hatred of all migrants, and a palpable disdain for the Aboriginal custodians of the land, all of which she conveyed with sleight. For Mrs Thoroughgood, swans were eminently superior to turtles. No doubt swanky Frank felt the same.

Inside the restaurant, the tables were occupied by expensively dressed couples murmuring conversations over softly glowing candles in ornate jars.

The *maître d'* led them to their table and handed them each a menu before walking away.

'Have whatever you want,' Frank said, sweeping a limp hand above his menu.

Yvette chose modestly, *goujons* of chicken with steamed vegetables and mash. He chose the lobster, commenting that unlike his Irish forebears, he would never suffer a diet of potatoes.

Once the waiter, a thin and serious young man, had come and gone, Frank explained that his wife had died of a heart attack last year and he'd been lonely. Now he felt he'd recovered from the loss and was ready for romance. He reached across the table for her hand.

'You don't seem the sort of woman that's only after a man's money,' he said, staring hard into her eyes.

'Of course not,' she said, shocked he should even suggest it. She pulled away her hand and took a large gulp of the Sancerre he insisted she should try because it was French. She didn't bother telling him she'd visited France many times. Keen to divert his attention, she asked him about his interest in Renaissance portraiture.

'I'm a collector.'

Figures, she thought. 'Fascinating,' she said. 'But why that period?'

'Good resale value. Art from that period doesn't devalue.'

'What sort of portraiture? Originals or reproductions?' She couldn't imagine anyone as crass as Frank being in the multimillion dollar fine-art market. She pictured in his house a reproduction of the *Mona Lisa* in a chunky faux gilt frame above the fireplace. Perhaps that was unfair. A Holbein then.

He looked offended. 'I have a Goya and a Botticelli.'

'Blimey,' she said. But his claim did nothing to shake her scorn.

When the food arrived she paid close attention to her every bite, riding out the ordeal making small talk.

Once the meal was over, he made a show of paying the bill then offered to drive her home.

When they pulled up outside the flats he peered out the window.

'You're renting here?' His tone was judgemental.

'Yes,' she said, suddenly defensive.

'Well, it's been lovely.'

'Thank you.' She opened the door.

He kept his hands on the steering wheel. He made no attempt at a kiss, not even a handshake. Instead he said, 'Dating wealthy men isn't the pathway to riches you know.'

She slammed the door on his remark and marched across the car park. How dare he judge her circumstances! Ostentatious twat!

2.11

The following evening, undeterred, she was seated in Café Mocha, looking out for a swarthy thirty-something man with a shaven head, if Dimitri's photo was honest. He appeared twenty minutes after the arranged time of six, decked out in black: leather jacket, T-shirt and jeans. He seemed flustered. Noticing her sitting alone at a table by the window, he quickly regained his composure and walked towards her wearing a charismatic smile.

'Yvette,' he said, taking up the other chair. 'Sorry I'm late. Just finished a photo shoot. Damn model couldn't hold a pose.'

She gave him an understanding smile. He was handsome in a burly way with dark eyes and a sensual mouth. He seemed intriguing.

'Have you ordered?' he said as a waitress approached their table.

'No.'

He took the menus and passed one to Yvette. The waitress stood over them, the cleavage of her bosom heaving above her tight blouse.

He scanned down the list of main dishes. 'I'll have the fettuccine con broccoli,' he said, shooting Yvette an inquiring glance.

'Vegetarian lasagne.'

He flicked over the menu card. 'And a bottle of house red.'

The waitress returned with the wine. Dimitri poured, holding up his glass to Yvette before taking a swig. Buoyed by the wine, he launched into a detailed account of his day, of his creative frustrations and photographic successes. Several times Yvette opened her mouth to speak, hoping to break into his monologue, but without success. The food arrived and he was still talking.

Then at last he leaned back in his seat and acknowledged her, as if for the first time. 'So, tell me about yourself.'

'I paint,' she said, convinced this remark would kill any further conversation about her.

'Walls?'

'Hardly.' Suddenly wanting to impress him, she added, 'My Masters focused on Precisionism.'

'Sheeler?'

'And O'Keeffe.'

'Ah, now you're talking. My favourite piece is Red Canna.'

'I thought it might be,' she said with a slow smile.

His eyes wandered across the room. She followed his gaze to the waitress leaning over a customer ordering from the menu, her bulging cleavage almost spilling out of her blouse.

'Beautiful name, Yvette,' he murmured, returning his gaze to her face. 'Are you French?'

'No.'

'Pity.'

'Why?'

He didn't answer.

Yvette cut into her lasagne. She ate quickly, swallowing her discomfort with every bite.

Dimitri, it seemed, had latched on to her artistic tastes. When they were about halfway through their food, he pointed in her direction with the tines of his fork and said, 'You must be a sensual woman to be into O'Keeffe.'

'There's more to her than just the flowers.'

'Yeah, maybe. But what courage and audacity to convey female sexuality through flowers so explicitly.'

'I think you're exaggerating. It's all in the eye of the beholder.'

'Ah, but there is always the artist's intent.'

She avoided his gaze after that and they finished their meal in silence.

When Miss Busty cleared away their plates, Dimitri's eyes never left her cleavage. He asked for the bill then followed her to the counter with his wallet. Yvette sat up straight, irritated and anxious to leave.

Outside, young couples with gay expressions strolled by beneath the limbs of small trees. Dimitri stood to one side, letting a woman holding the hands of two small children shamble past before he turned to Yvette. 'Would you like to take a walk?' Without waiting for a reply he took her hand and they strolled to Russell Square.

The park appeared empty except for two figures embracing beneath the vast canopy of a large fig tree. Dimitri led Yvette across a swathe of lawn to the play equipment and invited her to climb up a ladder to a platform leading on to a wobbly bridge.

She gazed in the direction of the couple, wondering what she was doing here with this lascivious stranger, when he pulled her to him, wrapped an arm around her waist and kissed her hard. Then he pressed his body to hers, grinding his loins, groaning. She felt the hard lump of his manhood and struggled to repress a gasp.

'God, I fancy you,' he said. Without so much as a 'May I?' he slid a hand beneath her skirt, pulling at her knickers. 'You are adorable,' he murmured in her ear, his hand pressing up between her legs. She was aroused, in spite of her misgivings. Yet before she had a chance to decide she didn't want him, he'd unbuckled his trousers.

He thrust and squeezed and thrust and squeezed, moaning, 'Honey, oh, oh,' over and again, until his ohs and his honeys merged into one long whooooaaah.

And she was free of him.

'Wow. Did you feel that?'

She said nothing.

'That was intense.'

'Really?' she said, straightening her clothes, feeling a sudden rush of self-disgust.

They headed back to the café. Dimitri paused beside a silver hatchback. 'Here's my car.' He pulled his keys from a trouser pocket. 'It's been nice. We must do this again sometime.'

'Absolutely,' she said, but what she thought was absolutely not. Dimitri belonged in her pantheon of self-centred men she had known. His ego more precious to him than his Nikon.

2.12

Lee, the music teacher, was no better, although she thought he might have been at first. The day they met, she'd found him charming. He was medium in height with a light build, cropped black hair framing a genial face. They'd strolled up James Street on their way to a café, chatting happily. He told her he was half-Chinese, half-Portuguese; his mother married a businessman from Hong Kong. He'd asked her where she was from, took an interest in her family and her past and when she supplied him with carefully crafted vignettes he interjected here and there with a polite comment. He'd seemed a sensitive and well-mannered man.

Two dates in and he was lounging on her sofa in a green polo top and a pair of loose track pants. He'd been there since he arrived that afternoon. It was a bum note in his symphony of charm. A full hour had passed and he'd done nothing but recline with his hands behind his head, talking to her about how superb last night's school concert turned out to be, how accomplished the ensemble, the orchestra, the quartet and the solos. She concluded that his tender gestures, cupping her hand in his, stroking her cheek, smoothing her hair, were practiced behaviours. He was a man adept at getting what he wanted by the most pleasant means. And once he had, or thought he had achieved his aim, complacency held sway.

Her weak affections for Lee took a farewell bow as she asked him to leave, conjuring by way of excuse a throbbing headache and mumbling that she needed an early night.

She'd been right all along, you can't force fate. Yet, left with no one to soothe her longing, her thoughts wandered back to Carlos.

Dearest Carlos. Dear Carlos. No. Hi Carlos.

She pictured him watering the plants in the courtyard. The stone staircase winding up to the bedroom, their bedroom, with the four-poster bed and the rocking chair and the window overlooking the flat roofs of the village. Her heart was still bound to that house. Only a small part of her, that skerrick of common sense and the instinct of self-preservation, had escaped. Were her belongings still there? She thought of retrieving them. She didn't expect he'd ship them to Australia on her behalf. More likely he'd use them to tempt her back. She wondered where he was. At home planning his next adventure? There was no phone in his house, he never answered his mobile and he didn't use email. She'd already sent three letters. He wasn't the sort to reply.

With her elbows on the table, she rested her face in her hands and gazed in the direction of the kettle. She thought about working on a sketch but felt too bleak to try. There had to be a man out there, a man capable of eclipsing Carlos. That palm reader had looked too fey to be a charlatan. Mustering her resolve, she refused to give up hope.

A cockroach meandered across the kitchen bench.

2.13

Her mother phoned the following afternoon, as she did once every week, partly to find out if Yvette had heard from Immigration. Yvette told her she hadn't.

'Met any nice men yet?'

'No, Mum. Not yet.'

Yvette couldn't bring herself to tell her mother she'd been doing online dating. She was certain Leah wouldn't approve. After her second husband had died, Leah remained a widow, concentrating her affections upon her grandchildren and her cat.

'I saw Terry the other day,' she said lightly.

'Did you speak to him?'

'Not really. He was in a hurry. He looked preoccupied.'

'Oh well.'

'You should have married him, Yvette. It would have saved all this waiting.'

Yvette said nothing. She listened with forced patience to her mother's update on the progress of the forthcoming agricultural show and Debbie's run-in with her son Peter's current teacher over a low grade for his geography project. 'Keeping busy?'

'Yes, Mum.'

She said her goodbyes and hung up her phone.

2.14

The following evening, Yvette adjusted the fall of her short black skirt and slipped on the loose batik top she'd bought in Bali. She brushed her hair and applied a thin smear of tinted balm on her lips. Thomas was due at the flat any minute. He'd been attending an acting course and the tutor was having an end-of-semester celebration at his house in Subiaco. The Honda Civic was having clutch repairs so Thomas had arranged for his friend Rhys to drive them there.

In response to a soft knock, she swung open the door. Thomas and Rhys stood side-by-side, dressed like twins in plain Ben Sherman shirts and chinos. Thomas kissed her cheek and Rhys, small and thin with short mousy hair, a dimpled chin and an overbite, offered her the limp handshake she'd anticipated. They were early so she suggested a cup of tea.

Ignoring Rhys hovering near the sofa, Thomas followed Yvette to the kitchen and leaned against the bench. Looking past him at Rhys, still standing as if he needed permission to sit, she said, 'Please, sit down,' and he did.

She flicked on the kettle. 'How's it going?' she said quietly.

'Better, I think. Anthony strays but he keeps coming back. He says no one else satisfies his intellect.'

'There's hope then. Excuse me.' She went to open the cupboard door nearest his face. He moved away and joined Rhys on the sofa.

'What do you do, Rhys?' she called out.

'I'm studying for a certificate in small business.'

'What for?'

'I want to open a model and hobby shop.'

'Good for you,' she said encouragingly. 'Tell me, how did you two meet?'

'In the stairwell. I used to rent a flat on the ground floor.'

Yvette succumbed to a sudden rush of repugnance, comparing herself to the sorts of tenants that lived in this block. 'Where are you now?'

'Back with my parents in Inglewood.'

'The ancestral home?'

'Yeah.'

She set down on the coffee table three mugs, a jug of milk and a bowl of sugar.

'Milk?' she asked Rhys, catching his eye.

'Err, yes please,' he said, blushing.

'Sugar?'

'No, err, no thank you.' He took the mug from her hand and knocked his elbow on the armrest, spilling tea on the floor.

'I'm so sorry,' he said, wincing.

'Don't worry. The carpet's absorbed worse.'

She felt unexpectedly sympathetic. He was artless and unsophisticated. She was pleased he'd come; Thomas seemed a little less intense in his company. And having lived his whole life in Perth, Rhys was bound to find his way to Subiaco without a hitch.

Rhys drove a dark-blue sedan. Yvette was sitting in the back behind Rhys, relieved she didn't need to navigate. Heading for a route that circumvented the city centre, Rhys swung the car into Beaufort Street. The setting sun cast a redemptive glow on the lacklustre flat-roofed buildings. They waited in the right-turn only lane at a set of traffic lights.

The lights changed.

'Walcott Street,' Yvette said, reading a street sign.

'Walcott Street?' Thomas said, puzzled. 'Don't we need Vincent Street?'

'Woops,' said Rhys. 'I took a wrong turn.'

He slowed, indicated and swung the car back down the street, narrowly missing an oncoming vehicle. Thomas stiffened.

Two right turns and they drove down Vincent Street.

'I need to take a left somewhere up here,' Rhys said. 'Yep, this is it.'

Charles Street. Yvette watched the approaching city lights.

'I don't think this is the right road,' Thomas said. 'We don't want to end up in the city.'

'I'll turn off,' said Rhys, heading up a slip road to a roundabout. 'We'll be able to cut across the freeway.'

He changed lanes and exited down another slip road. The road swept in a wide arc, entering the Mitchell Freeway. Even with her limited knowledge of Perth, Yvette knew they needed to head across the city centre towards the ocean, then veer south to Subiaco. Which meant they did not want the Mitchell Freeway.

'Damn!' said Rhys. 'Which way are we heading?'

'North,' she said. 'The city lights are behind us.'

'I'll take the first exit.'

'That'll be the Vincent Street exit,' Thomas said.

Before long they were back at the Charles Street intersection.

'We've been here before,' she said wryly.

Rhys indicated right.

'Don't you need to turn left?' Thomas said.

'That's what I did before. I'll turn right this time.'

'But we've come at the intersection from the opposite direction,' she said, thinking Rhys couldn't navigate his way round a figure-of-eight slot-car racetrack.

'I'm sure there's a way across the freeway if we head up here.'

He swung up the slipway to the freeway roundabout again.

This time he took a different exit, veering in a downward arc. The camber seemed strange.

When they entered the freeway Thomas yelled, 'Wrong way, turn back!' as three lanes of cars raced towards them with flashing headlights.

Thomas gripped his seat.

Rhys braked hard, threw the gear stick into reverse and screamed back up the slip road, chased by a roaring semi-trailer blaring its horn.

One laborious three-point turn, three times round the roundabout and Rhys chose another exit.

Now they were heading south on the freeway.

Yvette groaned.

Thomas stabbed the air frantically. 'Take the next exit! Riverside Drive.'

'No. That'll take us into the city.'

'But we're about to cross the river!'

They had to stay on the Kwinana Freeway for about five kilometres until the next exit. Thomas could scarcely disguise his exasperation. Speaking between locked teeth in a hissing monotone, he fed Rhys's every manoeuvre. 'Now stay in this lane. The exit we need is up ahead. See it approaching. Now indicate. Yes this *is* the right road. Up here.'

'But ...'

'Yes, yes, we do need to get back on the freeway.'

As they crossed back over the river, approaching a sign for Riverside Drive, Thomas shouted, 'Take this exit! And turn left.'

Flustered, Rhys headed down the slip road.

'Left! Left!'

Rhys veered right.

'Oh no!' Thomas covered his face with his hands. 'We've missed the turn!'

They were on Riverside Drive, heading straight for the city.

Rhys braked and steered the car towards the narrow hard shoulder flanking the central reservation.

'What are you pulling up here for?'

'I need to see the street directory.'

'You can't stop here!'

'You don't need a street directory,' Yvette said, struggling to suppress a laugh. 'The sunset is behind us. That's west. That's the direction we need to go.'

Thomas was shaking his head. Rhys switched on the interior light then rifled through the directory. When he found the right page he pored over the map. Eventually he said, 'You're right. I need to turn around.' He started the engine, made a U-turn at the first opportunity and managed to take the Subiaco exit at the roundabout.

'Now, just keep going,' Thomas said.

Reflections of city lights danced on the river. To her right, King's Park was a dark swathe of native bush blanketing Mount Eliza, so vast for a few moments she lost all sense of her location. Sitting in the back seat of the car, bearing witness to the most ludicrous navigational experience of her life, she couldn't resist imagining that a battle of competing fates was occurring over the course of her life, Rhys and Thomas unwitting agents of Hope and Doom. She had no means of discerning which was which.

Thomas directed Rhys the rest of the way to Subiaco. They were nearly there when the car spluttered, slowed and came to halt beside a small park.

'What's wrong?' she said.

'I think we've run out of petrol.'

'Oh. My. God,' Thomas muttered under his breath.

'It's okay. I've got a petrol can in the boot,' Rhys said with surprising nonchalance. 'Any idea where the nearest petrol station is?'

'We passed one back there,' 'Yvette said, pointing behind her.

When they were standing on the pavement, Rhys took out his wallet and searched inside. 'Err ... You don't have any cash I could borrow?'

Thomas caught Yvette's eye. She shrugged. He reached in his back pocket for his wallet and extracted a five-dollar bill.

'Do you want us to wait here?'

'We'll walk the rest of the way,' Thomas said. 'I feel like some air.'

At the end of the first street, Yvette said, 'I thought Rhys knew his way around Perth.'

'Fair assumption.'

'He should stick to remote-control cars.'

'He'll be U-turn Rhys forever more.'

Thomas sniggered, holding his hand to his mouth. Yvette laughed along with him and soon they were both doubled over, wiping tears from their eyes. It was the first time she'd seen Thomas relaxed and happy since she'd arrived in Perth. She hoped for his sake it marked a U-turn in *his* life. He needed to move on from his obsession with Anthony. Maybe find someone else.

Before long they passed an imposing flat-roofed building of pinkish-brick that bore down on the surrounding houses. Yvette read the sign out the front: 'King Edward Memorial Hospital for Women'. Now guilt passed through her like a deluge, as if the building itself were admonishing her and she'd no right, no right at all, to enjoy even the simplest of pleasures.

They crossed the road and the railway line and went down a side street.

Thomas stopped outside a quaint, weatherboard cottage set in a compact garden filled with ornamental plants. She followed him to the front porch. A suave-looking man dressed flamboyantly in a Chinese silk jacket and fisherman's pants swung open the door upon Thomas's rapid knock and greeted him with an effusive embrace. Then he took Yvette's hand in both of his and looked straight into her eyes. 'Welcome,' he said with theatrical sincerity. 'I'm Anton. Come on through.'

The living room was spacious with polished floorboards, leather sofas and an open fireplace at one end. Filled with anticipation she looked around at the other guests. Her quest uppermost in her mind, she ignored the women and scrutinised the men. The majority were unappealing. Some were too short, some too fat, others too raucous or shy. With unflagging optimism she persisted, mingling here and there, exchanging brief niceties, heading to the kitchen, where a clutch of women in flowing dresses giggled inanely, and through to an enclosed veranda out the back.

Immediately, she saw him, standing in a group of men gathered beside a table laid out with a buffet of finger food. Dashing, in tight high-waisted pants and an open-neck peasant shirt, thick and long fiery red hair loosely pinned back in a ponytail at the nape of the neck. He towered above the others. His eyes, a pale haze of blue, caught hers. She edged closer. There was a mystique about him, not the demonstrative charisma of Carlos, all bombast and camaraderie; here was someone gentle and serene. He turned to her with interest and smiled.

She smiled back. 'Hi. I'm Yvette.'

'Pleased to meet you,' he said in a soft accented voice. 'I'm Varg.'

'Varg. Hi Varg.' Varg? He was a Viking then, standing at the helm of a longship, bearskin for warmth, hair blowing back behind him beneath a horned helmet, a battle axe in one hand and a pewter mug of mead in the other. An image at once absurd and intoxicating.

He held her gaze, eyes searching, lips turned up slightly at the corners. He had an angular face, strong jaw and heavy brow. She felt herself floating. The room emptied, the others taking their plates and glasses elsewhere.

They chatted. In five minutes she established he was single, a carpenter from Norway with aspirations to become a professional actor. He had an air of the thespian. His graceful manner put her at ease. He asked where she lived. She described the flat, minus the cockroaches. He listened attentively.

'Do you eat meat?' he said, taking a plate. He selected a few titbits from the buffet, arranging them neatly. She didn't, not for one moment, question his sincerity. Just what she may have looked for in a man he revealed in perfect measure.

When he offered to drive her home she was thrilled. She found Thomas chatting to Rhys in the living room as she followed Varg to the front door. 'See you later,' she said breezily. She didn't wait for a reply.

Varg unlocked the passenger-side door of his white Celica. 'Now, where do you live?'

She told him as she sat back in her seat. His driving was smooth. He headed straight to her flat with unfaltering ease. She finished telling him the story of U-turn Rhys as he pulled into the car park. He looked up at the flats without judgement.

'Can I have your phone number?'

She wrote it on the back of an old receipt.

He walked her to her door, kissed her cheek and turned to go. With the key in the lock she looked up at him and said, 'Fancy a nightcap?'

He smiled and followed her into the flat.

2.15

The cockroaches were retiring from their nocturnal activities in the soft light of dawn. Yvette stepped outside to clear her head, inhaling the cool morning air. Sunlight glistened on the roofs of cars, the long shadows cast by houses and trees shortening even as she watched. A sweet afterglow infused her; still wrapped in Varg's presence, transfixed by his smile. He'd been as attentive in her bed as at the party. Before he'd left—it must have been about two, something about having to be up early—he invited her to a concert at the Fremantle Town Hall on Friday night. That was a week away and there was every chance she'd spend every hour of it mooching, the day stretching before her like the sky, empty to the horizon. She needed to keep busy, needed a distraction. Then, in the steely blue light, surrounded by the grim concrete of the balcony, images of Curtin flashed before her and she felt an unexpected welling of creativity. She could work on a painting, one that would convey some of the stark oppressiveness that Loewenstein had described. For that, she needed photographs.

She showered, dressed in an old T-shirt and shorts, plopped her thumb drive into the side pocket of her shoulder bag and went out. She had no idea if the local library would be open, but she'd find out soon enough.

Down on the pavement her strides were purposeful. She reached the library five minutes after opening and walked past the reception desk and the stacks of non-fiction books to the computer terminals. She glanced back at a librarian wheeling a trolley of books and pointed at a terminal with a look of inquiry on her face. The woman nodded so Yvette sat down.

Minutes later, she walked out of the library with her thumb drive loaded with images of Curtin. Heading home she called in at the photo processing shop on the corner of her street and then ducked into the Vinnies next door, where she found three canvases of Australian landscapes, none painted with flair.

Back in the flat she laid out on the table a line of five photos, three depicting the detention centre from an aerial point of view, a concatenation of dismally grey shacks behind the strict lines of chain-link fencing and razor-wire coils. How would Sheeler have approached the subject? A bird's eye perspective accentuating the overlapping planes of the iron roofs? A geometric simplification of the cluster of demountable buildings positioned in pairs like pinned butterflies, with their conjoined breezeway bodies covered in grey Colourbond? She could use a three-point perspective of the site to accentuate the height of the overhead lighting poles. Or a ground level face-on O'Keeffe-style treatment of a single pair of demountables.

She went and sat out on the hard concrete of the balcony floor. Out there in the stark light, each of her artistic ideas seemed geometrically enticing, yet she wondered how she'd incorporate a moral engagement with the subject. She sensed the problem she had lay in the sterility of the approach. Yet she was determined to proceed.

She began a sketch, then another, tracing lines and shading

shapes, drawing closer to the subject in her mind until she was standing outside the high fence, staring in at the buildings in the intense heat.

After hours of trying, fending off a mounting dissatisfaction, she took her sketchbook inside.

2.16

For the whole of the following week, Yvette was by turns swayed by artistic frustration, restlessness and the yearning promise of Varg. Now she was standing outside the Fremantle Town Hall, a neo-classical mock-stone building with Corinthian pilasters, pediment windows and heavily moulded architraves. This was her first visit to Fremantle and she was delighted to be surrounded by an abundance of fine old buildings, all of them at least two-storeys high. Even the train station, a stone building with an impressive redbrick and stone façade, had an air of grandeur so lacking in the suburbs of Perth, and an authenticity absent in faux Tudor London Court. In King's Square, giant fig trees offered that welcome respite of shade. As daylight began to fade, streetlights illumed the church that presided over the square. Built of limestone in a simple gothic style with a row of arched windows over the nave, a church not out of place in a Cotswold lane. Altogether it was a delightful scene, enhancing the anticipation stirring in her belly.

She waited. She watched people passing by in all directions, some bustling along, others sauntering up the town hall steps. She thought he was late. Then she thought he'd stood her up. How long would she give him before she headed back to the train station? Not that much longer, she decided. She felt a rush of relief when at last Varg appeared out of the melee. He was dressed in the same high-waisted pants and loose-fitting white shirt. He glanced in a parked-car window, flicking his hair, cascading in long and full locks, from his face. Then he saw her and smiled.

She caught her breath.

He dodged a gaggle of youngsters climbing the steps, bent forward and kissed her lightly on her cheek. 'You look stunning,' he said and she was pleased she'd chosen to wear the slinky black dress she'd found in one of her numerous trips to Vinnies.

He guided her through the entrance hall and on into a small, high-ceilinged room where a gathering of fresh-faced and tanned men and women were chatting enthusiastically around a large wooden table. Music, a high-pitched female voice accompanied by piano, spilled from the main stage located in an adjoining room.

'Hey, Varg!' said a man with short black hair and a full beard.

'Francois.' Varg shook the man's hand and smiled warmly at the others.

'Pull up a chair.' Francois shunted his own chair to one side.

Feeling awkward, Yvette sat beside Varg. She had no idea their first date would be so public. When Varg introduced her to the gathering, one by one she smiled and shook hands, forgetting each person's name the moment she greeted the next.

Varg settled into conversation with Francois. Yvette listened, avoiding the gaze of the fair-haired woman opposite, who kept trying to catch her eye. Varg was discussing his role in a Nativity play to be performed at a nursing home. Varg was to play Joseph. 'Anton's insisting I wear a wig,' he groaned.

'A wig?' Francois laughed.

'He says no Joseph he'd ever directed had red hair.'

'He has a point.'

'Can you see me in a wig?'

Francois laughed again.

'He's too picky.' Varg turned to Yvette. 'Don't you agree?' She hadn't a clue what to say. Before she came up with an answer, Varg had turned back to his friend. 'And, he keeps changing the script.'

'You're joking. It's a Nativity play.'

'I know. He'll have rewritten the whole thing before opening night.'

'What a fuss pot.'

'Worse. He keeps cutting my lines. He's reducing my character to a monosyllabic simpleton.'

'Poor Joseph,' Francois said.

'Poor me. Anton reckons the new version is more subtle.' There was a sarcastic tone in his voice. He tilted his head from side to side in a girlish parody of Anton. 'It leaves space for the audience to ... ponder.'

'Maybe he's right,' Yvette said, seizing a chance to include herself in the conversation.

Varg shot her a blank stare. 'What do you know about acting?'

'Only that acting goes far beyond words. A character is portrayed in tone, intonation, mannerisms and nuances of body language.'

'I'll rise to the challenge I'm sure.' He turned back to Francois. 'But I preferred the script the way it was.'

An enthusiastic applause in the other room was followed by a twangy guitar accompanying a droning male voice. She was glad she was seated away from the brunt of it.

Varg continued talking to his friend. The man on her right was engaged in a private exchange with the woman beside him. Yvette was largely ignored, save for the fair-haired woman opposite, who seemed as keen as ever to gain her attention. Yvette steadfastly avoided looking in the woman's direction.

Towards the end of the evening, after much bonhomie and Yvette's half-hearted attempts to include herself somewhere, anywhere in the merry flow, Varg left the room and the fair-haired woman, now drunk, eased her way round the table and sat on Varg's chair, gripping the side of the table to steady her descent.

She reached for Yvette's hand. 'Yvette,' she said intently. 'You're beautiful.'

'Thank you,' she said, struggling to sound polite.

'Varg is special you know.' The woman put her arm around Yvette's shoulder. Then, placing a hand over her heart, she thrust her chest forward and said ceremoniously, 'On behalf of all the women of Perth, I wish you every happiness.'

'Thank you,' Yvette said again. She was mystified. Was this woman nuts? Maybe she was an old girlfriend.

Outside, Varg suggested they take a walk. He folded her arm into his and led her down a narrow side street lined with the Georgian and Victorian gothic buildings she so adored, and on past trendy-looking cafés. Patrons filled all the outdoor seating, the air rich with garlicky cooking smells. A cosmopolitan atmosphere reminiscent of European cities pervaded the streets. Yvette was enchanted. She knew from Mrs Thoroughgood's weekly history instruction that Fremantle was famous for its maritime history. She hadn't realised the town had such style. Fremantle glowed civic pride from every façade. Perth took on a fresh significance. She was no longer alienated by the dead plains of suburbia.

They strolled down to a small sandstone building of chunky unevenly-cut stone, squat and proud on its clipped lawns, and on through the tunnel beneath to a short strand between low harbour walls. The water was dark. Waves slapped lazily on the shore. Harbour lights flickered and the ocean-infused air blew in on a soft breeze. Imagined embraces of passion and love glided through Yvette's mind.

Varg turned and cupped her face in his hands. 'Yvette,' he murmured. He searched her eyes. He seemed about to say more, then hesitated. A man and his dog walked towards them. His hands fell and he stood back.

'Shall we go?'

Yvette did her best to hide her disappointment.

2.17

She was pushing a trolley down the canned-foods aisle of her local supermarket, her heart swelling to Maria McKee's breathless ohs and pleading heavens spilling from a hidden sound system in as mellifluous a voice she'd ever heard. The desperate longing of the song perfectly matched her mood. She could scarcely believe she were capable of such slushy emotion. She was an embarrassment to herself. The only redeeming feature of the song was that it wasn't sung by Bonnie Tyler.

Yvette hadn't heard from Varg since he dropped her back at her flat after the concert in Fremantle last week. A swift drive through the suburbs and she'd spent the whole journey swooning, reading into his silence a passion commensurate with her own. When he pulled up outside her flat he leaned across the console, kissed her cheek and told her he'd call her soon. She was ecstatic. She floated up the stairs to her flat thinking she'd at last found a truly respectful man.

Now she went to the checkout with two tins of diced tomatoes, an onion and a small block of generic cheese. All she could think of was that she had to get back outside as fast as possible in case Varg phoned.

Her love-struck state dissipated the moment she opened the front door of the flat and her phone rang. Convinced it was Varg, it had to be Varg, she dropped her bag of groceries at the door and scrambled through her shoulder bag for her phone before he rang off.

She pressed the receiver to her ear and heard her mother's voice.

'Still not heard anything?' Leah said. The same question, every time. And each time she asked after Yvette's residence application, Yvette felt a twinge of anxiety, this time coupled with an avalanche of disappointment.

'Not a word.'

There was a pause.

'Debbie's had a bit of drama,' she said. 'Peter was taken to hospital yesterday.'

'Is he okay?' Yvette was concerned in the detached sort of way she felt for anyone come to harm. Her nephews were strangers to her.

'It was only a broken finger. He collided with a cricket ball.'

'Oh dear.'

'Last week of school too. Rotten luck. What are you doing for Christmas?'

'Spending it with Thomas I think. I haven't really thought about it,' Yvette said quickly. 'And you?'

'Going to Debbie's as always. She's threatening to roast a turkey.'

'I thought you liked turkey.'

'I do. Only last time, she left the cooked bird uncovered on a bench and by the time we came to eat, it was flyblown.'

Yvette didn't know whether to defend Debbie or share in her mother's revulsion. 'She won't make that mistake twice.'

'I know. I'm bringing my meat cover.'

'Oh, Mum.'

She wondered then if Leah talked to Debbie about her in the same way.

2.18

L ater, after snacking on cheese and some sticks of celery that had been languishing in the crisper all week, Yvette sat down on the sofa. Her earlier anticipation stabbed by her mother's call and replaced with doubt, and she read differently his hesitation on the beach, his silence in the car. He wasn't going to call.

She flicked through her sketches. Then she toyed with her tin pencil box. Stamped on the lid, between a capitalised 'Mars' and a lower case 'Staedtler' was a cameo of a Roman soldier in profile. Apparently the manufacturers wanted to impart the message that their pencils were all it took to conquer a drawing. The hinges squeaked as she opened the lid. Perhaps this once that Roman figure would be right.

The evening wore on. A line here, some shading there, crosshatching part of a side wall, adjusting the angle of the fence, staring sunrise into one of her photos wondering if she ought to shine a desk lamp on the side of a cereal box until she had the effect she was after and not mustering the will to do it.

There was nothing wrong with her execution but with every stroke of her pencil she sensed it wasn't enough. Somehow she needed to find a way inside the compound, portray the breadth of emotion of the inmates. Yet her entry was barred, her training and her predilection for precisionist art preventing her from accessing the reality inside the fence. All she could produce, felt herself capable of producing, was the front cover of a detention-centre procedures manual or a glossy advertising brochure.

She carried her dwindling self-confidence to bed.

She was in Carlos's house. Only he wasn't there. Dustsheets covered the antique furniture. Cobwebs hung in corners. She was in the courtyard. The pearlescent light of the moon illumed the bedraggled pot plants in its centre. Somewhere in the house she heard a door creak. She climbed the stone staircase to the bedroom. With every tread she entered a thick choking fear. She pushed open the door and shivered in a sudden rush of cold air. Sitting in a rocking chair was a voluptuous young woman wearing a scarlet ball gown. Her feet were bare. Her hair long and thick and black. Yvette seemed to know her. The woman stared with wild, trance-like intensity at the four-poster bed with its crumpled sheets. Sensing her presence, the woman turned to Yvette and screamed, 'No!' It was a murderous scream. Yvette absorbed the scream with horror. It was then Yvette saw that the woman's wrists were chained to the arms of the chair.

She woke with her legs tangled in the bed sheet. She yanked the sheet from under her left thigh and sat up, hugging her knees.

The room was a dim grey. She slipped out of bed, went to the kitchen to make tea then stepped outside, inhaling the fresh air. Dawn glowed mellow. A car beeped its horn somewhere below. Before long the rooftops glinted in the early morning light, the curtain raised on another bright and sunny day.

Deep in her was a space black as pitch, a dark dreamscape no sunshine could disperse.

And out of that space burst the woman in her dream, the face, the screaming face, lips opened wide, the whole of that fleshy cavity contorted. The torso rigid, hands rearing, wrists and forearms straining at the chains that bound her to the chair. It was a confronting image, one that repelled as much as compelled her.

She went inside.

In an hour she'd sketched out the form. For now it didn't matter how the chains would track around the wrists. No, she told herself censoriously as her precisionism came to the fore with issues.

She leaned against a wall one of the canvases she'd found at Vinnies. Opening Dan's art box she automatically grabbed the oils. She hesitated. Acrylics would be better.

She hadn't attempted a painting like this since her last year of high school. Then she'd approached her coursework with all the resentment of a headstrong teenager coerced into producing an expressionist work in acrylic. Plastic, quick dry, one level up from poster paints. She'd always been a medium snob. For her, oils were supreme, requiring skill and patience. To be a master painter was to be an oil painter. She'd carried the attitude stoically right through her years at Goldsmiths, culminating in her Masters—the Shelton with Sunspots: Gender, Modernism and the Urban Landscape. It was a topic that matched her skills and creative ideals.

How many isolated hours had she spent on the Goldsmiths campus, determined and aloof as though she had to prove herself to herself at any expense? Her only friend at that time was Josie, a bright and enthusiastic redhead with boundless energy and a passion for Matisse. Josie had the studio space next to hers. She would stride in to comment, purposefully interrupt, steer Yvette away for a coffee. Looking back it was Josie who'd kept her from the brink of burnout.

They'd shared a house in Hackney with two other artists, cooked together and went for long walks through Hampstead Heath. It was Josie's parents' house in Kew that provided Yvette with cosy Christmases and Easters. And when Yvette completed her Masters it was Josie who enticed her to Malta.

Now she had no idea how to manage the wayward stirrings of her creativity. She obliterated the Australian landscape beneath a layer of gesso and as she waited for the canvas to dry it stared blankly back at her. Holding the sketch in one hand she fell to quiet desperation. How would she transpose that intense form?

All her confidence fell away. She'd spent too many years being precise and now she couldn't let go. All of her artistry fell away. She dare not even stroke the canvas with the tip of her brush.

Her inhibition took her by surprise. And she was four again, with an unsteady hand and an uncertain eye. She stared into her hiatus. Perhaps she needed direction, a life-drawing class, a mentor to guide her. Someone like Josie. Yes, someone exactly like Josie.

Deflated, she put away the canvas and the sketchbook and went out and sat on the hard balcony floor.

2.19

Christmas decorations were sparkling throughout the mall and an overly adorned Christmas tree standing in the centre of the main thoroughfare assaulted Yvette's unfestive mood as she walked by. Tinsel draped window displays, and lumbering from glitzy shop to glitzy shop, a man in a Santa suit ho ho'd, ringing his bell. Even the café had silver tinsel arcing along the counter front, in cultural collision with the Turkish delicacies piled on platters beside the till.

Pinar greeted Yvette in her usual appraising way and asked her to clean the coffee machine.

A steady flow of customers occupied an otherwise tedious four hours.

Towards the end of her shift, when she'd relinquished any hope of seeing Heather, her friend, strikingly dressed in a flowing emerald skirt and matching blouse, entered the café. She took her usual seat by the windows that overlooked the car park and caught Yvette's eye with a friendly wave. Trapped behind the counter, Yvette returned Heather's smile as Pinar went to her table.

There was an unexpected rush of customers. A harried-looking mother with five boisterous children ordered chips and soft drinks while ignoring their demands for everything else. A group of six men wanted extra-large kebabs and iced coffees to go; and an elderly couple, who took forever to make up their minds, settled on baklava and flat whites.

More grannies, more mothers, more kids and thankfully, not a love-hearted latte among them.

When at last she removed her apron, Heather approached.

'Sorry I didn't get a chance to chat,' Yvette said.

'I could see you were busy.'

In the mall, 'Jingle Bells' played cheerily on. A clutch of excited toddlers jostled around Santa. Yvette followed Heather into the glaring daylight and they stood in the shade of an awning. The car park, a mass of metal and glass on tarmac, radiated heat like a kiln.

'Christmas in Australia?' Yvette said. 'It's bizarre.'

'Beach and barbecues and the start of school holidays.' Heather chuckled. 'Not exactly Hogmanay is it?'

She had a flash of memory, something wholesome and sweet. 'Do you remember our Christmases when we were kids?'

'Sure do.'

'I adored going to your place. Especially after Christmas Day. All those presents!'

'It was guilt,' she said drily. 'My father making up for the absence of my mother.'

'I never knew why she wasn't there.'

'Neither did I. She walked out on us when I was six.'

'That must have left a hole.' She paused. 'You had a terrific dad though.'

'Yeah. He's great,' Heather said with a measure of warmth. She rummaged through her shoulder bag and took out her car keys.

'Your back yard was a playground,' Yvette said, caught in the reminiscence. 'Swings, slippery dip, a swimming pool.'

Heather looked off into the distance. 'We had a ball.'

'Heaps of balls.'

'Of all sizes.' She returned her gaze to Yvette. 'I never did see your place.'

'I wasn't allowed to have friends over.' She winced inwardly, her mind belted by an unbidden image of her father in a frothing rage, hurling her Christmas presents down the back steps of the veranda. The anguish she felt watching that little girl gather her presents off the lawn. Little wonder her mother preferred to keep her and Debbie in a domestic fortress, the drawbridge shut fast. She recoiled at the thought of walking in her mother's shoes, choosing for the father of her offspring a Vesuvius of a man, spewing his bilious guts at any time.

They hugged. Heather's embrace was strong and lingering. 'Happy Christmas, Yvette,' she said as she pulled away.

'You too.'

Heather was about to head to her car when a thoughtful look appeared in her face. 'Do you still sing?'

'Sing?' She'd forgotten the afternoons when they'd stand in front of Heather's bedroom mirror, hairbrushes in hand, opening their lungs to Whitney Houston playing on the radio. 'I do a bit,' she said, cautiously. 'Not very well.'

'I'm in a choir. The Cushtie Chanters. We meet every Saturday in Fremantle. I thought you might like to come along.'

A choir? Straight away she thought of her nephews Simon and Peter, and Debbie's motherly pride. Resistance pinged in her guts. 'I'd love to,' she said with forced warmth.

Heather handed Yvette her business card with the address for the choir neatly scribed on the back.

'We start at two. I hope to see you there.'

2.20

It was the summer solstice and after a long morning toying with the idea of dipping one of Dan's brushes into a splodge of acrylic paint in an effort to break through her hiatus, Yvette slipped on a summer frock, grabbed a cold bottle of water from the fridge and left the flat. In the northern hemisphere, pagans of yore had cavorted, revelled and wassailed through winter's deepest night. Here in Australia she wondered what went on, two hundred, three hundred years before now, before the whites took over?

Heading into Perth, she walked the scalded streets to the station, a half hour later alighting the train to venture into the festive melee of the city, determined to purchase herself a Christmas present to compensate for the anticipated disappointment she'd feel upon opening the pre-loved Christmas paper from her mother. Through all of her ten years away, Leah sent her a small gift, one year a tea towel and a pair of oven gloves, another an apron with 'I Love Bermagui' plastered across the front, and always wrapped in what Yvette presumed was the wrapping paper she'd received from Debbie the year before.

The air was unusually still for midday and it must have been at least a hundred degrees. Surely Malta was never this hot? Or had her tolerance for heat inexplicably diminished? The air was cooler in the shade of the plane trees that lined the street. Beyond, the aggressive brightness rendered every building sharp and distinct. In this oxymoronic setting, Christmas had lost all meaning, all warm fuzzy associations of a freezing day at Grandma Grimm's house back in England, with aunties and uncles and cousins everywhere, with cheers and chatter, mince pies and *vol au vents*, and the smell of roasting turkey. Her Christmas spirit was as empty as a wizened walnut shell. Yet she had to summon a modicum of enthusiasm for Christmas for the sake of her soul.

She wandered into Myer's department store, relishing the air-conditioned cool, and her spirits lifted, rising further with the ascent of the elevator and a crooning Bing Crosby dreaming of white Christmases, with glistening tree tops and sleigh bells in the snow. Bing knew how she felt.

As she neared the women's clothing department she garnered her resolve, scanning the racks for special offers and searching to the bottom of the bargain bins. She found a thin scarf and a T-shirt among the marked down mark-downs and went to the checkout, stoically ignoring the woman in front of her clutching a giant teddy bear under one arm, the other struggling to hold a basket overflowing with apparel.

On her way down the escalator she felt reluctant to head back into the heat. So she took the next escalator down to the basement and walked around the racks of suits and shirts. A young man with neat fair hair was replenishing a display of novelty boxer shorts in red and green satin with ludicrous 'Jingle my bells' motifs. As she approached he turned to her. 'Can I help you?'

'No.' She felt confused and couldn't fathom why she was even in the store.

She went back up the escalator and exited the store through sliding glass doors as Brenda Lee rocked around the Christmas tree, with no expectation of a flurry of snow but maybe at least a sea breeze. Her head spun for a moment. She walked quickly towards the shade of the awnings of a nearby arcade, narrowly avoiding colliding with a man in a suit laden with gift-wrapped parcels in bulging shopping bags.

Back in the flat, Yvette opened the sliding door as wide as it would draw and stepped outside. The sun was high in the western sky. The rows of jacarandas in the street below were a feast of blue-lilac. Directly beneath the balcony, in the garden of the neat suburban house next door, a large gathering was whooping up a shivaree of pre-Christmas celebrations. Even six floors up, she could pick out children's squeals and sudden rushes of laughter. Heading for the front door, she went back inside, wincing in the sudden gloom. She propped open the door with a sandal, allowing the stale air of the corridor—at least it was cool—to waft through the flat. She went back to the kitchen and was about to flick on the kettle when, in an isosceles of light on the scuffed vinyl floor, a cockroach caught her eye. She made to stamp down her bare foot but thought better of it. No doubt the critter and his cronies had festive plans of their own. With a swirl of defeat rising in her belly she decided to leave them to it.

She'd reached her threshold of endurance in this entomological flat share but she hadn't a clue what do to do about it. The cockroaches had made it clear they were not about to move house, so it was down to her, but to where, how, and how would she afford it? She doubted Pinar would give her more shifts at the café and her casual wage wouldn't cover any rent.

And she wasn't about to fly back to her mother's farm.

She felt suddenly queasy, which she tried to ignore, but the bilious wave rose inside her and she ran to the bathroom.

Back in the living room she sat on the sofa and stared blankly at the drab-cream of the opposite wall. She knew without needing to visit a chemist or a doctor what that vomit meant. She was pregnant. She couldn't be certain as she hadn't had a period since her abortion, but she felt that vague sense of self-containment. She hadn't thought falling pregnant again would be so easy. Only counting back the weeks she realised she had no way of knowing which one of her recent liaisons was the father. Two days after Dimitri the prurient photographer had seduced her in the park, she'd slept with Lee the music teacher. It had been a lacklustre tryst and he'd turned his back to the wall the moment he was done but conception had nothing to do with pleasure.

She didn't even know how to contact either man. The day after she'd met Varg she'd discarded all evidence of the men's existence. She couldn't even recollect their surnames. She supposed she could track them both down through Love Station but it hardly seemed worth the effort. Why bother? It would be sure to bring her more trouble. She didn't like either man and recoiled at the idea of negotiating the terrain of shared custody.

Now she hoped Varg wouldn't phone. She'd slept with him as well, invited him into the flat that first night, and he too might be the father, she could have claimed he was the father, hoped with the might of Demeter that her offspring had red hair, but the pretence would have been unendurable.

Little wonder that palm reader had looked at her strangely the moment she'd released Yvette's hand. She'd met the father of her children, that much was true, and the prophecy was fulfilled, but what about her? Twenty-nine years old, stuck in Australia on a holiday visa, here in this scummy flat with few friends, about to be a single mother to a child with a triptych of possible fathers. She had to summon all her resolve not to feel cheap.

She wondered if the Department of Immigration would look more favourably upon her status if they knew she were about to give birth to an Australian? Would that be exceptional circumstances? Did they have exceptional circumstances? Or would her baby be allowed to stay but her, the mother, deported? She couldn't face finding out.

All she knew for certain was she would avoid telling her mother until it was too late for her to advise a termination.

2.21

An hour later and she had scarcely moved. She contemplated taking a shower when her phone rang. It was Thomas. After the ritual exchange of how are you, he invited himself round after dinner.

'About eight okay?' He sounded ebullient. Before she had a chance to tell him that was fine he hung up.

He arrived about half-past eight carrying his violin case and a bottle of wine.

'Sorry I'm late,' he said, kissing her cheek.

He set down the violin case just inside the door.

'Aren't you going to serenade me?' Yvette said.

'I've just had an audition.'

'Fantastic,' she said enthusiastically. 'For an ensemble?'

'For a gypsy folk band.'

'I won't have heard of them.'

'The Romanas.'

'How did it go?'

'First rehearsal next week.' He was grinning.

'That's great.'

'I'll let you know when we perform.'

She took the bottle from his grip and went to the kitchen, pulling open one of the drawers and rummaging through the contents for a corkscrew before realising she needn't have bothered. The bottle had a screw-top lid.

They sat out on the balcony. A light breeze cooled the air. Beyond the haze of the city, stars shone down from their lofty heights in a clear moonless sky.

'I have something to tell you,' Yvette said, but Thomas wasn't listening. He was gazing at the city skyline.

Without turning he said, 'Would you like to come to my place for Christmas dinner?'

'Thanks. Will Anthony be there?'

'I believe so.'

She took a sip of her wine. It was surprisingly good.

He continued staring off at the skyline, the fingertip of one hand idly gliding round the rim of his glass.

'Have you seen Varg again?'

'No.'

'I thought you two were an item.'

Yvette looked into her glass and said nothing. She had profound misgivings confiding in Thomas but he'd find out soon enough. Yet, now was not the moment.

She relaxed somewhat after a second glass of wine. It occurred to her she shouldn't be drinking but couldn't bring herself to stop.

They chatted for a while about the great Australian way of life, exchanging a long string of light-hearted insults before agreeing that the culture wasn't that bad.

'You were lucky you came by plane,' he said shooting her a wry look.

'It had occurred to me.' His remark triggered images of razor wire whorls and miserable demountables. She shooed them away.

They were silent for a while. Yvette made out patches of slow-moving high cloud that blacked out the stars. Then Thomas took a succession of quick gulps from his glass. 'I better go. Thanks for having me.'

'You're always welcome.'

She followed him to the door. They exchanged goodbyes and he made to walk away.

Consumed by a sudden desire to confess, she stood on the threshold and blurted, 'I'm pregnant.'

He swivelled round to face her. 'What?!'

'I said, I'm pregnant.'

'I heard you, but how, I mean ...?'

'I'm not sure.'

'Huh?'

'Never mind.'

'And?'

'And what?'

'Are you going to keep it?'

'Of course.'

'But you'll be a single mother.'

'So?'

'You're crazy.' His face had turned to stone. 'Are you going to tell Varg?'

'No.'

'No?'

'I don't know if it's his.'

'How come?'

'Don't ask.'

'Are you sure you know what you're doing?'

'Yeah, in fact I do. Besides, when you know a thing is right ...'

'When it comes to matters of the heart,' he said bitterly, 'there is no right.'

'I agree. But it *feels* right.'

'I'm glad one of us is able to trust their feelings.'

'Stop judging me.'

'I'm trying to save you ... from yourself!' He sounded exasperated. She hadn't expected censure from him.

'I don't need saving,' she snapped. 'I know what I'm doing.'

He shook his head and blew through his lips. Then he walked briskly down the corridor without a backward glance.

His reaction stung. Besides, she knew what she was doing. She was following where life led her. That was how she'd always lived her life. Besides, it was Thomas who invited her to Perth to live in his cockroach-infested flat. Thomas who invited her to that party. Why now try to rescue her from the very fate he'd been instrumental in manifesting?

She closed the door and made for the balcony, where she slugged the rest of the wine.

2.22

Christmas Day and outside the air was still and the morning sun did its usual dazzling and baking. Down on the streets, there wasn't a car or a pedestrian in sight. The neighbourhood was silent. No kids on bikes. No washing hanging in back gardens. The whole of Maylands was hushed. Not even a fly disturbed the peace.

She went back into the relative cool of the flat. This time of year, when families and friends unite in celebration, she felt so separate, her own family foreign to her. Still, she picked up her phone and called her mother.

'Merry Christmas, Mum,' she said cheerily.

'Merry Christmas.'

'Thanks for the present.' Another tea towel and, of all things, a nutcracker.

'Oh, that's all right. Hope you like them. I didn't know what to get you.'

Anything except a ruddy tea towel. 'They're great,' she lied.

'Well, I better go. I'm off to Debbie's shortly. Pity you're not here.'

She felt a twinge of longing, of missing out, mingled with relief.

For once Leah didn't ask about the progress of her application.

The Immigration department were having a rest from the horrors they inflicted at a pen-stroke.

She knew her mother had left Australia in the nineties without any intention of coming back. If she had even considered the possibility of returning she would have made sure they had all become citizens. Yet Yvette couldn't help a pang of resentment.

It had been cold and murky that first Christmas back in London, Yvette's first family gathering at Grandma Grimm's. In front of the bay window Grandma Grimm had crammed a needle-shedding Christmas tree, tinselled and baubled and sprayed white with fake snow. Uncles stood about smoking chunky cigars and telling lewd jokes. Aunties gathered in the kitchen to gossip over sips of advocaat. Cousins she barely remembered or hadn't met before giggled and scampered, hovered looking bored or bragged and swaggered like their fathers. After the turkey and the pudding they gathered round the old upright piano. Aunty Iris punched some chords and the rest of the adults formed a circle in the middle of the living room and made enthusiastic attempts at 'Knees-up Mother Brown' and the 'Hokey Cokey', while the older cousins rolled their eyes and stroked their iPhones.

Yvette had a great time. To her, the Grimms were a family united. She wasn't to know the tensions and strains, the feuds and the fights, in all, the violent rip that sucked at the family psyche. She was innocent, the mind of the child adept at storing bad memories in the darkest corners. Leah lavished the Grimm-family story upon her years later, in those months after her father left, ensuring Yvette developed an unwavering loyalty to her and an unequivocal animosity towards him. At which point Yvette never again saw any member of the family Grimm.

She was due at Thomas's at twelve. She put into a shopping bag a bottle of sparkling Chardonnay, and the large plastic tubs of potato salad and coleslaw she'd made last night.

Leaving the roaches to party by themselves, she slammed shut the front door and walked down the carpeted corridor and the six flights of concrete stairs passing no one. There were no cars in the car park.

The streets were deserted. Walking past the neat frontage of one dwelling upon another, she imagined there'd been an exodus, and she, the last remaining human of the suburbs, was left to fight an apocalyptic battle with the cockroaches.

When she reached Thomas's flat she was relieved to hear muffled voices and a radio playing somewhere. Before she knocked, Anthony flung open the front door and spread his arms wide. She was thrown for a moment by his effusive 'Ah, Yvette!' He kissed her firmly on her lips then took her hand, pressing it between his own. 'So good to see you again.'

'And you.' Anthony was exactly as she remembered him, slight of build with wispy fair hair, a little shorter than he wore it in London, haughty eyes and a mouth drawn into a small smile, pulling slightly more to the left. He had the same effete manner, accentuated today by his outfit, a paisley-printed silk chemise cascading over loose ivory pants.

'Yvette. Yvette. Yvette. It's been too long.' He steered her into the room. Laid out on the coffee table were small plates and napkins, bowls of peanuts and pretzels, champagne flutes and an opened bottle of sparkling wine. The room was uncommonly tidy and smelt faintly of patchouli oil.

Thomas called out from the bedroom. He appeared moments later straightening his shirt. 'I was just getting changed,' he said, blushing.

'I brought some goodies,' she said, raising the shopping bag. She put the bag on the kitchen bench and removed the contents. Anthony bustled up beside her. 'Fridge,' he said abruptly, handing Thomas the bottle and the coleslaw.

'Fridge?' said Thomas, pointing at the potato salad.

'No. Bench. Better warm. The flavours are more ...' he kissed his fingertips, 'present.'

He opened one of the drawers and pulled out a sharp knife. Then he deftly split and de-seeded three avocadoes and mashed them in a glass bowl. 'Lemon juice, garlic, a little chilli, a pinch of salt,' he chanted, holding the last syllable of each phrase. He squeezed the juice of a lemon and tossed the squashed skin into the sink. 'Tut, tut. You don't belong in there,' he said, plucking out a pip with his fingers. Yvette watched, amused. Then, with a knife hovering over four cloves of peeled garlic, he looked up at Thomas and said, 'Where did you buy this?'

'Coles.'

'Never, *never* buy garlic from Coles.' Anthony waved the pointy end of his knife in Thomas's direction. 'It's kept in cold storage until the flavour turns bitter.'

'I'm sorry. I had no idea.'

'We'll survive,' he said, rolling his eyes. His reprimand, though playful, carried with it certain malice. He winked mockingly in Yvette's direction. 'Shall we?' he said, gesturing at the coffee table.

'I'll be one moment,' Thomas said. With focused intent he arranged olives and crackers, strips of carrot and celery, and cubes of cheese on a platter.

Anthony sat cross-legged on the floor and poured the wine. Yvette joined him, taking up a space on the other side of the table. She took the glass he proffered. Through the adjoining wall, next-door's pop music reverberated in dull, muffled pulses. Once Thomas had sat down, choosing the straight-backed chair beside his music stand, she raised her glass.

'Merry Christmas.'

'To absent families,' Anthony said.

'Absent? I thought yours lived in Perth.'

'They're camping on a beach near Margaret River. Parents, three sisters, their husbands and a mob of nieces. I'm driving down tomorrow.'

Yvette glanced at Thomas as a look of anguish appeared in his face.

'Respite from the heat and the dry of Kalgoorlie,' she said positively. Then, keen to steer the conversation elsewhere for the sake of Thomas, she asked him how he'd enjoyed last night. He'd gone to the Fremantle Town Hall to listen to Kavisha Mazzella's women's choir, *Le Gioie Delle Donne*, sing Italian folk songs.

'I know Kavisha,' Anthony said, under his breath.

Thomas held her gaze. 'Captivating,' he said dreamily, 'And poignant. The hall was packed with a mixed crowd, but I was surrounded by Italian migrants. The woman seated next to me clutched a white handkerchief to her bosom and muttered to herself "Oh Mamma, Oh Mamma" through the whole performance.'

Yvette reached for a pretzel. 'Memories of home,' she murmured, suddenly aware of Thomas's Jewish heritage. The only son of an Orthodox mother, he'd struggled with guilt his whole adult life, over his lack of faith and his sexuality.

'It fascinates me what motivates people to emigrate,' said Anthony.

'There's no single reason,' Yvette said, glancing at Thomas again, who looked tense. 'Everyone has their own circumstances.'

'Other than sun and sand and the great Aussie dream.' He directed his gaze at Yvette. 'So, what were yours?'

She reached for another pretzel and dipped it in the guacamole.

'Delicious,' she said between mouthfuls.

'Thank you, dear heart.'

'I see what you mean about the garlic though.'

'I'm surprised you didn't know.'

'I took it for granted. In Malta, garlic is always fresh.'

'You haven't answered my question. Why leave Malta and come here?'

'England is too cold and too grey.'

'You see? I told you. It's always the same. The good old lucky country.' He dipped a celery stick in the guacamole and waved it in her direction. 'And your parents? Why did they come here?'

'Is this an interrogation?'

'Just curious.'

'As you say, they wanted a better life.'

'Did they get one?'

'Not really. My dad worked in a factory and my mother was a cleaner.'

The muffled sound of the pop music next door droned on annoyingly. Yvette took a large gulp of her wine and grabbed a handful of olives. Anthony's eyes never left her face.

'You don't strike me as the offspring of a factory worker and a cleaner, if you don't mind me saying. There's always been something, dare I say, more cultured in your manner.'

She bristled. 'Is that so?' she said, returning his gaze with a measure of contempt. 'Well, I got an education.'

'Ah, of course. That explains you a little more. Here's to education.' Anthony raised his glass.

Thomas, who had been tapping his arm rest and looking nervously back and forth from Anthony to Yvette, darted forward and grabbed a handful of pretzels. He didn't appear to want to add to the conversation so Yvette shot Anthony a cold stare and said, 'So, tell me, how do you find the bandit and bordello life out there in the wild west? I expect you fit right in.'

'Ha. Touché.' Anthony laughed. 'No bandits or brothels these days, although the legacy is there, sort of ingrained in the locals.'

Thomas was now tapping his fingers rhythmically on his thigh.

'Do they still mine?' Yvette said.

'God, yes. The Super Pit is still going. As the name suggests, it's a massive open-cut gold mine. And just across the highway from my house.'

'You can see it?' she asked.

'No. It's over the crest of a rise. But there's a background drone sometimes. When the wind blows from the east.'

'As it does,' said Thomas.

'As it does.'

'And dust?' she said.

'Yes, even more dust.'

Thomas slurped back the rest of his wine and went to the kitchen. He returned moments later and laid out a seafood platter and a bowl of salad greens along with the coleslaw and potato salad.

'Fabulous!' Yvette said.

'Thanks.' Thomas gave her a cordial smile.

The conversation meandered along as they ate. Thomas engaged Anthony in an exchange about wild flowers and a visit they'd made to Wave Rock. Yet the atmosphere remained strained.

After lunch Yvette thought about leaving, hesitating when Thomas removed his violin from its case and adjusted the music stand. Following a brief and intense few moments of string tuning, he launched into the piece he'd been learning since Yvette arrived in Perth, Sibelius' *Valse triste*, in D minor—an adorable piece but a dubious choice for Christmas Day. His body seemed rigid, thighs pressed together, head frozen to the side, a look of pained concentration on his face. Altogether there appeared not one jot of pleasure in his manner.

Anthony plucked a volume of Byron's poetry from a bookcase and flopped into the armchair where he flicked through the pages, making intermittent pretences at reading a stanza here and there. Yvette wandered about the room. A single Christmas card leant against a hard cover of Jean Genet's *The Miracle of the Rose*. The front of the card, embossed and speckled with glitter, displayed a bucolic Christmas scene. Inside, in shaky cursive, Thomas's mother sent all her love and best wishes. She must miss him, her only son.

Sunshine streamed in through the window. Thomas played a last few wistful notes before setting down his violin to draw the curtain. He then moved on to play some equally melancholic tunes. Anthony now seemed engrossed in a poem so Yvette lay down on the floor and closed her eyes.

Christmas at Josie's parent's house was nothing like this. Their semi-detached home, set well back from a leafy street in Twickenham, had large bay windows, at that time of year festooned with decorations, the lights on the Christmas tree winking reds, yellows and blues at the darkness of the day. The house was a haven of genuine yuletide cheer, no accoutrement overlooked, from holly wreaths and mistletoe to novelty Santa napkin rings. Josie's mum, a plump and homey woman who oozed benevolence, would pass round mulled wine, homemade sausage rolls and devils on horseback, before inviting the family to the table to feast on roast turkey and Christmas pudding. Josie's dad, a tall and portly senior lecturer in English, would carve, and Josie's siblings—two older brothers and a younger sister, all as charming as Josie—would ready themselves for the cracker pull. Then came the Drambuie and the mince pies, the nuts, the chocolates and even Turkish delight. Yvette pictured Josie, bedecked in seasonal red, throwing back her head and roaring with laughter at her dad's attempt to convey *Corpse Bride* in charades. Present opening was the only time Yvette felt apprehensive, but not over the exchange of gifts—she always gave them a bottle of good French wine and they gave her something carefully chosen: one year a box of oils, another a book on Dadaism. It was the well-meaning inquiry as to whether she was missing her family and what they were up to right there and then in Australia. Yvette was always evasive.

Now she wondered what on Christmas Day the prison guards offered the detainees at Curtin.

2.23

Boxing Day and Yvette was clasping a mug of tea out on the balcony in the cool of the early morning. The solitude, the vacuum left by yesterday's company and memories of other Christmases, and she'd woken wondering if she was doing the right thing bringing a child into the world, knowing she could never be like Josie's mum. She knew that her last chance to have a termination was fast approaching. She reassured herself that she wasn't having a baby to gain permanent residence, that no part of her, not even lurking unseen in her depths, held such a corrupt motive. She was bonded to her unborn child like a barnacle to a rock. Giving birth had become imperative, a seed she'd planted in her psyche like a farmer experimenting with a new crop. And she knew with all the conviction of fate that the pregnancy was preordained. Therefore, she reasoned, it was her destiny and changing course now would lead to a lifetime of punishing loneliness.

Still, she felt restive.

She stood up and leaned against the balcony wall. The family in the suburban house below were in their backyard again. Women were arranging tables and three men were leaning over a barbecue.

Looked like another celebration. Up until then, Yvette had been annoyed she'd been rostered on at the café. Now work seemed the better of the two locales. At least there she could pretend to be gainfully if precariously a part of this nation, and she didn't want to spend a single moment more than she had to in this squalid little flat.

At the sight of the party preparations below, it occurred to her to host her own celebration. She would invite all of her Perth friends, which amounted to only a few, but even so, she wanted to prove to them and to herself she could throw a decent party. It would be her eve of New Year's Eve party. Competition for the cockroaches. She left the flat feeling buoyed by the thought.

2.24

'We are the reckless,' Yvette sang, following the lyrics of 'Daughter' playing on her new CD player, another Vinnies score, as she sashayed her way to the kitchen. 'Olive anyone?' she called out, pretending she could be as carefree as her guests were taciturn. So far her party had all the *joie de vivre* of a wake and it was all she could do to hide her displeasure.

'Sure,' said Rhys, plucking an olive from the bowl.

Dan, and his boyfriend Barry, a tanned and toned man with short hair and a moustache, sat quietly together on the sofa sipping champagne. Thomas was staring despondently at the carpet. Something had passed between him and Anthony on their way in and he hadn't recovered. Anthony, elegantly dressed in a light-blue suit that loosely covered his slender frame, a trilby hat tilted over his pallid face shading his eyes, his mouth arranged as always in a pert ironic smile, had the enigmatic hauteur of a character from the silent-movie era.

'I'm ninth generation Australian, or seventh depending on which side of the family I follow,' he said, putting on an Aussie drawl. 'They were migrants too. One of my ancestors came out on the Second Fleet, for having a forged one-pound note in his possession.'

'And Australia has never recovered,' Dan said sardonically. They'd been discussing the Australia Day celebrations to be held at the Burswood Entertainment Centre, a multicultural extravaganza featuring scores of Perth's migrant communities, and Anthony had chimed in with his usual flippancy.

Thomas raised his face to the others, snapping from despondency in a single breath. 'Will indigenous Australians get a look in?'

'For sure,' Dan said.

'Invited to cavort about to the sound of didgeridoos, no doubt,' said Anthony.

'They could stage a massacre,' Thomas said with a laugh. 'The custodians' revenge.'

'In keeping with *The Chant of Jimmy Blacksmith*. That would fit right in with my year tens.' Anthony grinned and slapped his thigh.

Dan looked at him reprovingly. There was an awkward silence.

Thomas and Anthony, seated in chairs on opposite sides of the living area, had started to flash conspiratorial looks at each other. Yvette was annoyed with both of them for being so ill-mannered, especially Anthony. In the little time she'd lived here even she knew the contentiousness of his remarks. And how could Thomas allow himself to be an accessory to Anthony's poisonous badinage?

Rhys, who had said little all evening, leaned forward in his seat, apparently inspired by the banter to add his own witty remark. 'Do the boat people have a spot?'

Anthony's eyes sparkled. He shifted to the edge of his seat and said in a low, dramatic voice. 'I can see it now. Ten short men, dressed in black, running on stage and crouching down pretending to be a boat pitching and rolling in a storm.' He stood, removed his jacket and walked to the end of the sofa, turning abruptly and taking command of the room. 'And then Varg Axenrot ...'

'Varg?' Yvette said doubtfully.

'The very same.'

'Why Varg?'

'Because he's a head and shoulders taller than the rest of us. Now don't interrupt or I'll lose my thread.' He flicked a censorious hand in her direction then went on. 'Varg appears on stage in his peasant shirt and high-waisted pants and makes his way to the man-boat.' He paused, casting a cantankerous eye around the room. 'Then he steps aboard.' Anthony raised his left leg and made an exaggerated step. Thomas started snickering. 'He's standing at the helm with his hand to his forehead. The boat starts pitching and rolling then lists heavily to one side.' Anthony swayed. 'Then the starboard men tumble on the portside men, leaving Varg flailing on the floor of the stage.' A long pause to maximise impact. Thomas and Rhys were both grinning.

'What happens next?' Rhys asked.

Anthony shrugged as if the answer were obvious. 'The men simulate waves by doing the worm dance.'

Thomas laughed loudly.

'The worm dance?' said Rhys.

'The very same.'

Thomas took control of his laughter to explain.

'And of course Varg worms his way to the front of the stage,' Anthony said.

At this point Thomas doubled over, clutching his belly. 'Do it, do it!' he gasped.

'What?'

'The worm dance.'

'You have to be kidding.'

Yvette was uneasy. She'd just glanced at Dan. He wore a face of granite.

Anthony bowed, sweeping his hands wide. 'The perfect school play, don't you think?'

'You can't be serious,' Dan said between his teeth.

'Of course not. It's just buffoonery.'

'Fun? You think that was fun? You're barbaric.'

'Oh, come on,' Anthony said, annoyed.

Dan stood abruptly and motioned to Barry to do the same. 'Yvette, I'm sorry. We must be going. Thanks for inviting us.'

'Please, don't go.'

'I'm afraid of what I might do if I don't.' He picked up his jacket and walked to the door. 'All the best with your painting.'

'Thanks.'

At the door, she kissed them both goodbye and thanked them for coming, catching Dan's gaze with a shoulder-raised smile.

'Yvette,' Anthony said, the moment she closed the door. 'What are you painting? Do tell.'

'Nothing, really.' She went across the room to the CD player and pressed play, not caring if they heard the same tracks twice. Then she went to refill glasses.

'Not for me,' Thomas said, covering his glass with his hand.

'Me neither darling. We better be going too.'

Anthony gave her a weak hug before fetching his jacket. Thomas kissed her cheek, mumbling in her ear an apologetic 'See you soon,' and Rhys scurried out of the door ahead of them.

She was dismayed by their sudden departure. This had to be the worst party she'd ever hosted, eclipsing even the time Carlos threw a party in the month before they'd left for Bali, and she had imprudently invited Josie.

Josie had never liked Carlos. She'd warned Yvette to keep away from him the very first time he'd entered the bar where they both worked. It was about six months into her stay, and she was about to fly back to London, when Carlos breezed in, all grand gestures and camaraderie. He sat on a bar stool with his arms resting wide apart on the counter and caught her eye. Four beers later and he was taking her home. Before she left the bar, Josie had grabbed her arm with a hissing, 'He's no good.' But five years of strict self-discipline and study had left her hankering for adventure like a long-stabled filly released in an open field. She was all frisky, heels a-kicking, ready to gallop off full pelt.

Four years with Carlos and she'd developed a taste for spliffs and sniffing white powders. She'd resigned from the bar, moved in with him and tinkered with simple jewellery making to keep occupied while he was away doing business. Many times Josie had told her Carlos was dangerous. She didn't want to hear it. She knew. She knew he was a womaniser and a crook. She didn't care. She also knew she was going through a phase. That she'd never fully let herself go, there remained the onlooker, fascinated with the lifestyle she found herself in. Josie didn't see things that way.

At that last party Yvette told Josie she was pregnant. They were standing by the pool surrounded by sparsely clad sylphs with glossy hair and smart-suited men with swanky attitudes and brash mouths. The air was redolent with French perfume. No sooner had the words left her lips, she realised she'd made a mistake. Josie wasted no time telling her under no circumstances to go through with the pregnancy or she'd be tied to that ne'er-do-well for life. Then she left and Yvette hadn't seen her since.

Now she couldn't understand Josie's or for that matter, Thomas's attitude. What right did they have to dictate what she did with her body?

A short while later there was a light knock on the door. It was Heather.

'So sorry I'm late.'

They hugged on the threshold and Heather handed her a bottle of red.

'I'm pleased you made it. The others have left.'

'Oh no! Am I *that* late?'

'They left early. Long story. Come on in.'

She'd invited Heather two days before, the last on her guest list. She'd been uncertain about the social mix and when Heather had explained a prior engagement, fully expected her not to show up. Now she was here Yvette was unsure where to take the conversation. Fortunately Heather took the lead. 'How was Christmas?' she said, following Yvette to the kitchen.

'Okay, and you?'

'The same as ever. Dad was in his usual dour Christmas mood and Angus lounged about in a half-drunken stupor all afternoon.'

They both laughed. Yvette filled their glasses and they sat down on the sofa.

'Help yourself,' she said, gesturing at the food.

'Thanks.' Heather sat back in her seat. 'Must have been hard not being with your folks again.'

'Not especially. Mum spent the day with my sister's lot.'

'You don't sound that close to your sister.'

'Debbie? Ten years separation has taken its toll.'

Heather didn't speak. Her face took on a reflective expression. She sipped her wine.

'You don't have children?' Yvette said, stating what seemed obvious yet she couldn't be sure.

'No. Not yet. My ex-husband wasn't inclined.'

Yvette was strangely relieved. 'How long were you married?'

'Three years.'

'What went wrong, if you don't mind me asking?'

'Nothing. He came out.'

'Oh.'

It occurred to her it was fortuitous the others had left. Not that any one of them might have been Heather's former husband. What would Heather have made of her coterie of gay friends? Certainly she wasn't the sort to hold a grudge against an entire group, but nevertheless Yvette was relieved Heather hadn't met Anthony. She glanced in the direction of the balcony and spied a cockroach ambling towards the kitchen cupboards. She groaned.

'What is it?' Heather looked concerned.

'A cockroach.'

'He's out early.'

'He'll be the scout. Do cockroaches have scouts? All I know is this place is infested.'

Heather grimaced. 'They're disgusting.'

'I know.'

'Have you tried an insecticide bomb?'

'Didn't seem to make a difference.'

'They're tenacious buggers.'

'You're telling me.'

They were silent for a while. Yvette stared into her glass.

'Are you okay?' Heather said softly.

Yvette sighed. 'I have to get out of this place. It's driving me nuts.'

'I can imagine,' Heather said, looking around.

'It isn't just the roaches. I feel like a prisoner in here.'

'I have to say, it is rather, um, cell-like.'

'Trouble is Heather,' she said, succumbing to an urge to confide, 'I can't afford to rent anywhere on what I earn and I don't want to go back to my mother's farm.'

'No, don't do that.' She seemed thoughtful for a moment. Then she said, 'Would you like to stay with me?'

'With you?'

'I have a spare room. Angus is staying with me at the moment but he's moving on soon. So help me.' She raised her eyes to the ceiling with a playful shake of her head.

'Where do you live?'

'Fremantle. When do you need to be out of here?'

'Yesterday.'

'Can you hold out till Australia Day? Angus should be gone by then.'

'I think I can manage a few more weeks.'

'Then it's settled.'

'How much is the room?'

'Nothing. I couldn't charge you rent.'

'But ...'

'No buts. You are my oldest friend. It's the least I can do.'

'Heather, thank you. Thank you so much.'

'I take it you don't have a car.'

'No.'

'Then I'll swing by and help you move your things.'

'I could catch a train.'

'I won't hear of it.'

Yvette felt heady. Heather, she told herself, was the nicest, warmest, kindest friend she'd ever encountered.

III

THREE

3.1

She leaned against the balcony wall one last time, resisting an impulse to rest her elbows on the scalding cap of concrete. A shimmering haze rose from the rooftops, the city skyline indistinct in a sandy murk. She turned her face to the east, the wind sweeping back her hair. She heard a car roar up the road somewhere below, the screech of brakes and a few loud honks. Stupid goose, she thought, narrowing her eyes as she imagined a domed head of slicked-back white hair and a clapping beak. Her bare arms were stinging so she pulled back into the shade.

Australia Day was affecting her mood. The anniversary of the arrival of the First Fleet when this land was invaded and conquered, and its indigenous peoples oppressed, a day of white-fella flag waving, righteous congratulations and back-slapping celebrations, the sort of day relished by Mrs Thoroughgoods and an entourage of blokes and sheilas. Today Yvette couldn't help identifying with the indigenous peoples, not that she knew any. For her it was a day of complete alienation. After all, that was what she was, an alien. Some creepy, be-tentacled freak barred entry after having dropped in from outer space.

She wondered if any of those asylum seekers stepping out of their ramshackle boats and landing in detention could ever view Australia as a haven. Doubtful. Deported to malaria-infested islands and locked in detention centres and left to languish for years and even decades in demountable buildings and tents, how could they hanker to belong here, to commit their hearts, minds, bodies and souls to this place? Like her, they would be questioning why they even came here.

The heat and the glare became too much so she went inside, closing and locking the balcony door before going to the bedroom and the bathroom scanning for missed items. Then she opened all the kitchen cupboards. They were empty. Not a cockroach in sight.

Heather was due any minute. Dressed in a loose cotton shift that vaguely hid the small bump of her belly, Yvette stood by the door with her meagre possessions that were packed into the three small boxes, the canvas holdall and the blue travelling bag, all stacked at her feet. Her canvases were leaning against the edge of the sofa.

She heard footsteps approaching in the corridor and opened the door before Heather knocked. Heather was garbed in a loose berry-red frock with cream brocade around the neck and the short-sleeve cuffs. She had a way of seeming regal without the pretentious airs. Yet her outfit was too smart for house moving. She surmised Heather must be on her way elsewhere. They hugged and she breathed in a musky scent.

'Is this all?' Heather said, looking down then glancing around the flat.

'I'm a light traveller.'

'So I see.' She bent to lift the box nearest her feet. Yvette followed her downstairs with another.

Two more trips up and down the stairs and they stood by the car, panting. Sweat beaded on Heather's brow. 'Ready?' she said, opening the driver-side door.

Yvette swung open the passenger-side door to a blast of hot air and braved entry into the car's vinyl-infused interior. At least now they were away. Australia Day, she thought, would always be the anniversary of the day she left that rotten flat. She glanced up one last time as Heather pulled out of the car park. It's all yours, she said to the cockroaches.

'Thanks Heather,' she said.

'Don't mention it.'

Heather turned into Beaufort Street and they waited at the next set of traffic lights. It was clear from her demeanour she knew where she was heading.

'How does it feel, being back here?' she said, once they'd got through the stream of traffic.

'Weird.' As though her past crowded around her, a jostling throng of memories, of school, home and Heather's place. 'I've always remembered you,' she added.

'Same. It was lonely for a while, after you left.'

It had never occurred to Yvette that she'd been missed. She thought of Josie back in Malta and wondered if she, too, felt that loss. Maybe it was easier for the one who leaves, than the one left behind.

Forty minutes of light-hearted observations and fond reminiscences and Heather parked in a narrow, tree-lined street outside a charming brick cottage with a façade rendered in cream and a red-tiled roof, the house tucked behind a neatly clipped hedge. Yvette was immediately confident good fortune had provided her with the ideal place to bring a child into the world.

'I have something to tell you,' Heather said as she unclipped her seat belt. 'Angus hasn't quite moved out. He's sleeping on the couch. You might say, he's in transit.'

Then Yvette saw, parked in Heather's driveway that ran down the side of the house, an old bus, gaily painted in green and red horizontal stripes. To get to the front door, they had to pick their way past spanners, wrenches, screwdrivers and pliers scattered in a wide arc around the front end of the bus. Laid out higgledy piggledy on the small square of lawn were the old bus seats, and up on the porch sat a small fridge and a two-ring gas cooker. Lengths of pine and sheets of Masonite leaned against the side wall of the house.

Inside, the house was spacious, airy and cool. All the rooms to the left and right of a wide hallway had wooden floorboards. Heather showed Yvette into the last room on the left. They both set down a box and after giving Yvette's arm a quick squeeze, Heather turned to go back outside. Yvette started to follow but Heather told her not to bother. 'Go put your feet up,' she said and soon Yvette heard the fly screen clap shut.

A double bed took up much of the room. Beside the door there was a wardrobe and a matching chest of drawers. Centred in the far wall, a small desk. A tall window overlooked a neat garden of native shrubs and small trees. She sat on the bed, made up with a lusciously patterned maroon and turquoise quilt, when Heather returned and set down the last of her things.

'I'll go and make tea,' she said. 'How do you take it?'

'Heather. I need to tell you something too.'

Heather paused in the doorway. 'No you don't. I already know.'

'How?'

'That you're pregnant?' With a cupped hand she made a sweeping curve over her belly.

Yvette gave her a sheepish look. 'I should have told you.'

'You were about to.'

'I mean before.'

Heather gazed at her sympathetically. 'How far gone are you?'

'I don't know exactly.'

'You haven't seen a doctor?'

'Not yet.'

There was a pause.

'And the father?' Heather said quietly.

Yvette wasn't sure what to say. How would Heather take the divulgence? 'I wish I knew,' she said.

She needn't have worried. Heather's 'oh dear' contained no censure.

3.2

A week later and Yvette was sitting at her desk. The room was dark, the only light an Anglepoise lamp shining its circle of light on her sketch of the deranged woman with the screaming face. The work hadn't progressed much past her initial effort. She still felt far from translating the sketch into paint. All week she'd been pampered by Heather, who brought early morning cups of tea to her bedside, baked savoury slices and quiches, prepared stupendously zingy salads for dinner, and whipped up wholemeal cakes for snacks. She'd even driven Yvette to work a few times and hung around for her to finish her shift. Perhaps that's why Yvette hadn't been feeling creative. Suddenly, her life had become soft as feathers.

She clasped her hands behind her head and arched her back. Angus was in the kitchen strumming his guitar. She tuned in to his melodic ramblings and smiled. He'd never be an Eric Clapton, his playing more a pastiche of song snatches. She had barely known Angus when they were growing up. He had his own interests and friends and remembering all their squealing and cavorting in Heather's back yard, his little sister and her friend must have been to him an irritation he was forced to bear.

The strumming stopped and the fly screen door squeaked open. Soon she heard the murmur of voices coming from the backyard. She put down her pencil and tiptoed across the hallway.

The kitchen was large with patterned tiled walls. Cupboards and shelves were crammed with all the paraphernalia of a good cook. An old oak table took up the centre of the room. Cooling on a wire rack in the table's centre was the date and walnut loaf Heather had made before she went out to visit a friend.

Yvette stood by the back door. Angus was talking over the fence to their neighbour, Viktor, a welder who'd emigrated from Serbia in the eighties to work in the shipyards. The day she moved in, Viktor had invited Angus over and he returned with a lemonade bottle filled with plum brandy. Viktor had a still. He had a wife too but Yvette had yet to meet her. Viktor, a pro-Milosevic Serbian from Belgrade, was a wizened old man with a thin mouth, a large nose and piercing blue eyes. He'd look terrifying if he allowed his face to drop its smile. So far she hadn't seen him wearing anything other than what appeared to be his work clothes. He would entertain Angus with stories of his old life in the Balkans and Angus would entertain him with tales of driving trucks across the Nullarbor. No doubt with the help of a glass of plum brandy that never emptied.

Angus was no doubt telling Viktor about his fascination for the German explorer, Leichhardt, judging by the sprawl of notebooks and paper on the kitchen table. Heather had explained while preparing dinner last night that her brother's interest had been kindled when he saw *Travels with Dr Leichhardt in Australia* in the window of a second-hand bookstore in Fremantle. He'd come back with it tucked under an arm. Apparently, within the time it had taken to head home he conceived an entire screenplay.

'A documentary?' Viktor said.

'No, no. A drama. A mystery.'

'You are a talented man, Angus.'

'Thanks. And the story is great. Leichhardt disappeared in the mid-nineteenth century during an expedition across central Australia.'

'By himself!'

'No. He had men, horses, bullocks and mules. They were last seen in the Darling Downs.'

'Where's that?'

'Near Brisbane.'

'Didn't get far then.'

'Oh, they did.' Angus sounded defensive. 'Remains have been found near the Tanami Desert on the Western Australian border.'

'Really?'

Yvette sensed Viktor was humouring him.

Angus seemed oblivious. 'A brass plate among other things. No one knows if it belonged to Leichhardt, but I believe it did.'

'Not much of a film though, eh?'

'I'm going to reconstruct what I think happened. Some say the party died of thirst. Others that they perished in a bush fire. But I think they were massacred by Aboriginals.'

'Yes, that makes for a good ending. Well, best of luck with it my son.'

Yvette thought Angus's preoccupation with Leichhardt was obsessive. She doubted he had the talent or the skills for scriptwriting, but she humoured him. When she'd tried to suggest the project might be a touch ambitious, his eyes darkened and his face took on a sort of petulance. He growled at her to leave him alone. So she did. She didn't suggest he read the copy of Patrick White's *Voss* she'd bought at Vinnies one time. Or that he might research other screenplays already written, and performed.

Last night, on her way to the bathroom, she'd caught him standing before the bedroom mirror reciting lines, shifting first one way, then another, tilting his head, raising an eyebrow, pointing his chin forward. He was a tall, thickset man, with a helmet of dark hair framing a long rectangular face. Puckered lips, eyes set deep beneath an arch of eyebrow that barely paused above his stubby nose, and his face carried a look of Munch-crafted alarm, rendering his current efforts even more ludicrous. She had to stifle a laugh as she walked by.

Then she censured herself. What right did she have to ridicule his aspirations? She was behaving like Anthony. Angus might lack talent but at least he was trying. She had to respect that. Besides, he was Heather's brother.

And, to his credit, after months of unemployment Angus had managed to acquire a part-time job at a Mr Muffin franchise in Canning Vale. At last he could raise funds for his trip. He had to wear a blue uniform and a Mr Muffin cook's hat. He went to work in a sour mood and came home with a headache and a box of leftover muffins.

Angus was busy. He had his guitar, the screenplay and his job. Heather was either at work, out seeing a friend, or in the kitchen cooking up a feast. While they were doing all that Yvette frittered hours and hours of her days sketching faces. She'd probably have been more productive had she taken up whittling.

3.3

At work the following day, Yvette was feeling surprisingly light-hearted. It was another bright summer's day but the sea breeze had come in early and there were wisps of high cloud to the north. With the school holidays over, the café was quiet and there wasn't a discounted Santa toy or box of Christmas cards in sight. Yvette set about cleaning tables, tidying the counter and serving the few customers that trickled in from the mall.

At the end of her shift, Pinar drew Yvette aside. She gave her a knowing smile and said, 'Are you having baby?'

'Yes.' There was no denying it.

Pinar's smile fell away and her face took on a troubled look. 'Yvette, I am sorry. I let you go.'

Yvette stared at her, open-mouthed.

'Your husband take care of you. Yes?'

'My husband?'

'This your last shift.'

Yvette was stunned. It was an old-fashioned perspective on domestic life she thought had faded out of existence along with cross-your-heart bras, wrap-around housecoats and Doris Day's 'Secret

Love'. Its last gasp had to be when, back in the eighties, Scottish belle Sheena Easton sang 'Morning Train'. She hoped Sheena earned a lot of money singing that crap. Enough to support her comfortably for the rest of her life.

Pinar couldn't really believe the dependent-woman-cosseted-in-domestic-bliss myth. She ran her own café. No, Pinar was using the pregnancy as an excuse to get rid of her. She didn't like working as a waitress but she was always polite and courteous. Perhaps her distorted love hearts were the real cause.

Whatever the reason, now she had no job.

Heather was waiting for her in the car park. She opened the passenger-side door and gave Heather a quick smile before getting in.

'How was your day?' Heather said as she pulled away.

That was all it took for the tears to roll. After sniffling and wiping her eyes Yvette managed to fight back the flow and tell her.

'Oh dear.' Heather paused. 'Because of the baby?'

'I thought I'd manage a few more months, but that stupid cow told me my husband could look after me.'

'Ouch.'

'Now what'll I do?'

'There's Centrelink.'

'I can't claim benefits.'

'Why ever not? It's nothing to be ashamed of.'

'Heather, I need to tell you something else.'

'Again?' Heather glanced at her with an ironic smile.

There was no avoiding the truth, yet in the telling Yvette succumbed to more shame than she thought herself capable of feeling. 'I'm an illegal immigrant,' she said softly.

'What?! How can that be? You grew up here.'

'We never became citizens before we left.'

'So this time you came on a holiday visa.'

'I'm trying to get in under family reunion.'

'Do you fit the criteria?'

'No. My father is still alive. I don't even know why I bothered filling in the form.'

'You really could do with a husband.'

'I can't bear to think about it. I'm hoping when they find out I'm having an Australian baby they'll let me stay.'

'Were the contenders Australian?'

Yvette explained she had no idea. Dimitri was obviously Russian, Lee half-Portuguese half-Chinese and Varg Norwegian.

'Ah ...' Heather let out a soft chuckle.

Yvette was baffled by Heather's easy acceptance, and at once relieved her friend didn't judge. For she was surely judging herself, cowering beneath a welter of shoulds; she would have undone time if it hadn't been zipped up and fastened in place like some diabolical ligature.

3.4

It was Saturday. Angus was at work on his screenplay. There were pages of writing scattered across the kitchen table. Looked like he'd be working all afternoon. With every passing day of her pregnancy she had less time for the larrikin, who, ever since that single petulant growl, had fused with the image of her father that she carried in the deeps of her psyche. She stood in the doorway and watched him for a while, before grabbing her shoulder bag off a chair.

'See you later,' she said breezily.

'Where are you going?'

'Choir.'

'Have a good time,' he said, without looking up.

She walked purposefully through the front door, letting the fly screen swing shut of its own accord. She stepped down from the porch and picked her way across the garden. She didn't allow her thoughts to wander. Last night over dinner Heather had invited her to choir. She recoiled, determined to pursue nothing, no matter how tenuous, that had any association with her sister. She endured Heather's gentle cajoling, steeling herself against her friend's 'It'll do you goods' until she realised there was no reason she could provide that didn't sound craven. She relented, assuring Heather she'd see her there.

The narrow streets, the houses all huddled together, the picket fences and wrought-iron gates—soon she felt a spreading calm. She adored Fremantle's quaint cosmopolitan vibe. She was at one with the area. Other than the cockroaches, enormous in size, there was nothing to dislike about it. Especially today, when tufty clouds scudded across the sky and a fresh breeze blew in from the ocean.

She passed the newspaper-reading, latte-sipping lunch crowd seated outside the cafés at the end of Wray Avenue then crossed the road and headed down South Terrace. Walking by the heavy edifice of the Fremantle Hospital she looked the other way. Beyond, it wasn't until she passed the next block that the streetscape settled back into the old and the higgledy-piggledy that was Fremantle's colonial heritage.

The Cushtie Chanters rehearsed in Scot's Hall, a Presbyterian church adjoining Fremantle Markets. Built of creamy limestone with contrasting russet-brick quoining on the narrow buttresses and window mouldings, the church was solid and imposing, as if built to withstand a Scottish winter's icy north wind.

She was early. The door was ajar so she entered.

The hall was large with a raked ceiling and bare floorboards. Light filtered in through windows set high in the walls. At the far end there was a stage, more a raised platform with a wooden lectern set to one side. At the other end, a trestle table laden with mugs, jars of tea, coffee and sugar, a jug of milk and an urn. She went over to a row of wooden chairs lining the far wall and sat opposite the entrance door.

Women of all ages and shapes drifted in, some with children. A thicket formed over by the urn. Chatter and laughter echoed round the walls. One woman came in through a door near the stage, glancing at her watch. She was tall and thin with long fair hair and dressed in loose-fitting jeans and a colourful short-sleeved shirt. She scanned the room then stood by the entrance door greeting women as they appeared. She had a commanding yet edgy manner. Yvette stared in her direction, hoping that one of the women filtering in would be Heather.

The chatter and laughter soon became a hubbub. The tall woman, who was clearly in charge, closed the door and walked to the centre of the hall. She raised one arm and called out, 'Okay everyone. Gather round.'

The chattering diminished and the women flocked around her. The door opened but it wasn't Heather. Quashing the misgivings darting about inside her like midges, Yvette joined the others.

'For the newcomers,' the woman said, raising her voice, 'I'm Fiona. Welcome to the Cushtie Chanters. If you haven't paid, it's five dollars.' She looked at a heavyset woman with cropped grey hair standing at the front. 'Sue, could you pass round the hat?'

There was a rummaging through pockets and bags and the clink of coins. Yvette withdrew a five-dollar bill from the pocket of her jeans and waited for the hat to pass her way.

Fiona kept talking. 'We'll start by forming three groups; tenor, alto and soprano. If you're new and you don't know where your voice sits, join any group.' She looked around, her gaze settling on Yvette. Feeling awkward, Yvette struggled not to blush.

The choir members strolled towards the stage end of the hall and formed three huddles. Knowing her vocal range couldn't reach heights or depths, Yvette joined the altos, standing behind the hat-bearing woman, Sue, who turned to her with a smile.

The door creaked open. Yvette glanced over and was relieved to see Heather walk in. She caught her eye. Heather's face lit with affection. She came and stood beside her, triggering in Yvette a warm glow.

'Hi,' she whispered. She squeezed Yvette's hand. 'So glad you didn't change your mind.'

Fiona called out from the front, 'We'll start with "Inannay". It's an indigenous lullaby. Anyone heard The Tiddas's version?'

There was a murmur of yeses.

Fiona turned to the sopranos. She sang the verse and chorus solo.

Her voice was thin with an operatic inflection, exaggerated mouthing released on a breath, no doubt an ethnic interpretation a world away from the ancient language of the song. Then she raised her hands and with a sudden downward sweep of her arms and a rhythmic nodding of her head, led the sopranos through the song. Satisfied she moved to face the altos.

Yvette sang along, quietly at first, then opened her throat and relaxed into the flow of the harmony, sensing her own voice blending and merging with the others. The air resonated with their voices. And she found herself swept along by every rise and fall. She'd forgotten how good it felt. She was swelling inside. She was a child again, in Heather's back yard, performing a routine they'd devised using the slippery dip and swing set as props, singing their little hearts out to 'The Best Things in Life Are Free'. She was Janet Jackson, Heather Luther Vandross, until they were forced to swap roles because Yvette couldn't reach the high notes.

Fiona turned to the tenors and once satisfied, conducted the whole choir with a look of intense concentration. They sang through the song three times and moved on to rehearse two more songs. When they finished, a look of admiration softened Fiona's face. 'Well done,' she said and the choir members, all smiles and laughter, broke ranks and wandered to the back of the hall.

Yvette followed Heather to the queue forming by the urn.

Searching for something to say she glanced down at Heather's dress, taking in the rich shades of brown and cream, the embroidery and the elegant cut.

'You wear such lovely clothes.'

'Ingrained in me since childhood.' Heather paused. 'Do you remember how Zoe Fullman always got picked to write on the blackboard?' Her response brought to the fore the threads of their shared school life, the years they endured of Mrs Thoroughgood's vicious spite. An image of Zoe Fullman, all smug and precocious, came immediately to mind. 'Teacher's pet,' she replied.

'I hated her, for no other reason than that she was pretty.'

'I always thought that was why Mrs Thoroughgood chose her.'

'Me too. She was the bane of my life. Stupid I know.' She paused again. 'Did you see her out of school? She wore the finest dresses.'

'I don't remember.'

'I do. I was jealous. I didn't own a pretty dress. Not one. Clothes were not my father's forte.'

'I'm sorry.'

'Don't be,' she said with a laugh. 'I'm making up for it now.'

Yvette stood beside her friend, feeling the strength of her character, trying to imagine growing up without a mother. She could only wonder at what possessed Heather's mother to leave. Did Heather blame herself for her mother walking out? Children have a remarkable propensity for self-blame, a propensity designed to eclipse the unconscionable possibility that mum or dad are weak and fallible. Or horrible. Poor Heather.

They shuffled forward, Heather now in conversation with one of the altos. Before long they reached the urn.

3.5

Having forgone a tattered *National Geographic*, Yvette flicked through an old copy of *Vogue*, before tiring of that as well. She was in the waiting room of a nearby doctor's surgery, located in a dilapidated weatherboard house. It appeared nothing had been done to the décor of the room since the seventies. All the walls were papered with repro-paisley wallpaper, tan, grey and washed-out orange against an off-white background, wallpaper that clashed horrendously with the ancient loop-pile carpet of deep-purple swirls. The reception area was crammed into what must have been the former kitchen, accessed by patients through a high serving hatch. A series of posters pinned to a wall beared down on waiting patients with bold warnings of the consequences of imbibing and injecting and gorging on junk food. On a rack nailed to the wall beside the hatch was a selection of pamphlets on a range of health matters, from anorexia to diabetes.

Yvette was seated between a doddery old man and a plump mother whose sniffling child scrambled about on the floor at her feet. Yvette ignored the child. Hers would never turn out like that.

And she was surprised to find she was filled with a placid

acceptance of her lot. Never mind the paternal contenders—what a self-absorbed bunch they were—the course of her life would turn out fine. Fate was no bad thing. As well, she was awash with the unconditional kindness and support afforded by Heather who had insisted she seek medical attention.

Yesterday, while munching through the breakfast of bacon and eggs Heather had cooked for her, Yvette complained that she couldn't afford the doctor's fee, whereupon Heather whipped out her wallet, extracted two fifty-dollar bills and thrust them into Yvette's hand saying, 'That should cover it.' Yvette had been too overcome by her friend's generosity to decline. Heather had even made the appointment.

Tired of glossy photos of nubile women draped in designer clothes, all pouts and come-hither eyes, and not keen to return to images of endangered animals in equally striking poses, she went to the wire rack and rifled through the leaflets, extracting a bi-fold on the Fremantle Prison, which clearly didn't belong there any more than *Profits of Doom* had belonged in the reference section of that library on the day of her cockroach blitz. She returned to her seat and read the pamphlet blurbs, slipping into reverie; in her imagination an army of beleaguered convicts in ragged slops lumbered limestone boulders in the blistering heat. Then she heard her name.

She put the pamphlet back in the rack and followed the doctor to one of the rooms in the front of the house. The doctor was a crone of a woman, her long white hair, parted in the middle, drawn away from her face and clipped in place by two carved wooden combs. Her face was weather-beaten with a pair of beady brown eyes, a hook nose and sparrow-beak mouth. Dressed in a grey blouse and straight black skirt she looked half public servant, half witch.

Yvette sat down on the edge of a wooden chair beside the desk and with a quiver of trepidation explained the purpose of her visit.

The doctor observed her closely. 'When was the date of your last period?'

Yvette thought back. 'About twelve months ago.'

The doctor looked puzzled.

'I had a termination last April and I haven't had a period since.'

'Can happen. Why do you think you are pregnant?'

'Morning sickness.'

'When do you think you conceived?'

'About the middle of November.'

'We'll date the pregnancy from the first.' She scribbled a note on Yvette's new-patient file. 'And the father?'

'I'm not sure.' Yvette felt the colour rise in her cheeks.

She detected in the doctor's face a wry smile that faded as quickly as it appeared. The doctor wrote out a request for a blood test and told her she didn't usually ask for an ultrasound at this stage but since they had no real idea how long she'd been pregnant she requested one as well and told her to return once she'd had the tests.

After paying at the counter, Yvette left the surgery clutching the two forms. The appointment had left her uneasy, her placidity replaced by harsh reality, her circumstances yanked into the brilliant light of the day.

3.6

Angus was in the back garden when she returned. As she tramped down the hall she could hear him chatting to Viktor. Heather, it seemed, hadn't arrived back from work. She sat on her bed, knees drawn to her chest. An ultrasound? The receptionist at the doctor's surgery told her the cost was a hundred dollars. A hundred bucks to have her uterus scanned when women have been having babies for millennia before that technology had come along? She screwed up the referral having reasoned away the need.

Then she reached into her shoulder bag for her phone and ran a finger over the keypad. She had to call her mother. She hadn't been in touch since she moved to Heather's place and had been ignoring Leah's calls. Told herself she was too busy. Now she felt she had no choice. She dialled the number.

Straight away her mother asked if she had any news. She said she didn't. Then she listened with no interest to her mother's blow-by-blow account of Debbie's latest confrontation with Simon's music teacher and how sweet and unsure of themselves the boys had looked in the choir at the folk festival. Leah said she was sure Peter forgot the words to one of the songs. Yvette made polite introjections, thinking she'd never tell her mother she'd joined a choir.

At last Leah turned her focus back to Yvette.

'How's the flat?'

'I've moved to Fremantle.' She braced herself for the reply.

'What do you want to live *there* for?'

'It's changed since the America's Cup. You know that.'

'Nowhere can change *that* much. It was, and always will be, filled with Italians.'

What could her mother possibly have against Fremantle's Italian community? Yvette felt her own irritation rise; Leah still hadn't mellowed her prejudices. Was this a veiled attack on her choice of men? Leah had been almost accepting of Carlos in her letters, assuming he was Maltese, which was somehow acceptable since Malta was a former British colony, but as soon as Yvette mentioned his nationality, Leah never mentioned his name again.

Yvette knew Leah would never condone the exotic mix of ethnic possibilities on the paternal side of her grandchild, which lent her predicament a new if perverse appeal.

'You'd better give me your new address,' Leah said.

Yvette told her, adding, 'I'm staying with Heather.'

'That Scottish girl?'

'She's been incredible.'

There was a moment of silence. Then her mother said, 'Terry's been looking for you.'

'Really?' She didn't want to hear it.

'He asked after you in the post office and the newsagency.'

'Why?'

'Why? Because he still *cares* for you.' That inflexion again.

Yvette didn't answer. She was struggling to accommodate Leah speaking to her this way, as if she were still eighteen. She felt herself pulled back to a younger self as she pulled in the opposite direction, determined to be who she was. Yet another part of her sensed, albeit dimly, that her mother wanted for her a lesser catastrophe than the one she was bent on fashioning for herself.

'You could do a lot worse,' Leah added as if in agreement.

There was no easy way to do this. 'Mum. I'm pregnant.'

'Pregnant?'

There was a long pause before the inevitable questions.

'How far are you?'

'About four months.'

'Why didn't you tell me?'

'I'm telling you now.'

Leah said nothing for a while. Yvette pictured the down-turned mouth, the stern eyes beneath a furrowed brow. 'Well, congratulations,' she said at last, with little warmth in her voice. 'And the father?'

'Um ... Does it matter?'

'Of course it matters!'

'I don't know.'

'How can you not know?'

'There's a choice of two.' Which sounded a lot better than three.

She heard her mother sigh. 'And this is what you want?'

'Yes.'

Her question filled Yvette with doubt. Something she'd never let her mother know. She'd burrow her way into it like a worm.

'At least now you've solved your immigration problem,' her mother said, with a cool, pragmatic air.

'You think so?' Yvette said doubtfully.

'You've told the authorities, haven't you?'

'No.'

'No? Why not?' Her voice rose in exasperation.

'I want to wait until I hear the outcome.'

'Be it on your own head,' she said in a low voice and hung up.

Yvette reeled. To her mother she supposed she would always be an insufferable disappointment.

She had never been able to ascertain if beneath her mother's harsh exterior there lurked a caring heart. It was why, when Leah had left London with Yvette's stepfather and sister ten years before and settled in Cobargo, Yvette stayed behind. She wanted to make her own decisions. She wanted then what she wanted now, to be out from under her mother's influence. Then she'd thought half the world would be just about beyond earshot. Besides, she'd had an offer from Goldsmiths. Art school was her way of rising from the narrow aspirations of her parents. And she was not without talent. She'd duxed her final school year in art, her paintings hung in all the school stairwells, one even finding its way into the office corridor, bearing down victoriously on the school roughs waiting outside the headmaster's door.

Her mother had tried to persuade Yvette to go with them, insisting that as a child Yvette had loved Australia. Yvette didn't know where her mother got that idea. Not the heat. Not Mrs Thoroughgood's cruelty. Nor her father's tornado of a temper. Maybe her mother selectively recalled the flush of Yvette's face, the gleeful smile she wore, when she came home from Heather's place.

When they arrived back in England and spent that first Christmas at Grandma Grimm's, Yvette felt deep in her core a cultural resonance. She would stare out the upstairs bedroom window looking down on snow-covered gardens, the very cells in her body fibres in the fabric of the place. Encoded in her DNA were the houses, the garden sheds, the leafless trees, the half-light of winter, the accents, attitudes, television, food, and all of it made perfect sense.

She wasn't to know the tribulations that lay ahead, that she was to attend one of England's roughest underachieving schools, its pupils, all two thousand of them, roared to order by an ex-military sergeant garbed in gown and water-board. He instilled terror in all but the most hardened sort. He made Mrs Thoroughgood seem almost affectionate. But he had no influence on the bullying, the malice, the threats. Coming from Australia, skinny and timid and cursed with an Aussie accent, she was a target from the first day. Words flew from the tough girls' mouths like bullets from a machine gun. Girls with peroxide blonde hair, mean faces and scarred wrists. She survived the six years. She retrieved her southeast London accent. Defiance grew in her like jam in a pressure cooker and when her mother announced they were to return to Australia, it erupted in scalding splats across every inch of her faith in her family.

3.7

Early-autumn sunshine shafted through her bedroom window, a sea breeze causing the shadow of the paperbark in Heather's back garden to dance on the opposite wall. Yvette made a mental note to suggest to Heather that she move the block print to avert fading. She turned onto her back and gazed absently at the ceiling, placing both hands over her belly, feeling the heat from her palms on the taut skin around her navel. And a quiet triumph pervaded her despite her apprehensions. In under a year she'd replaced the fruit of one man's seed for that of another. For the first time she thought of Carlos as part of her history. She could conjure his image without craving his presence, and Malta, that island filled with the artefacts of the underworld, at once glorious and grotesque, was set free. She'd even lost her compulsion to check for messages from Josie on Heather's laptop, relinquishing her disappointment that Josie hadn't been in touch since her arrival in Australia. Still she craved her friend's forgiveness, which had left her untypically hanging like a door loose on its hinges, flapping back and forth in a fickle breeze.

Her triumph dissipated the moment the fly screen door snapped shut and she heard the steady throb of chords, meandering, then what had become for her an annoyingly twangy prattle. She was anxious for Angus to move out, tired of shoving his doona aside when she wanted to sit on the living-room sofa, tired of his lackadaisical attitude. Angus was condemned in her mind as nothing but a wastrel with delusions far in excess of his abilities. His presence in Heather's house made her recoil and it was as much as she could do to be polite.

She kept her contempt hidden from Angus, with whom she remained civil, and especially from Heather. She didn't want to appear to her friend ungracious. Besides, she had no idea the strength of their filial bond. It was impossible to gauge with Heather at work, shopping, visiting friends or otherwise rarely at home.

Before long, the strumming stopped. Footsteps tacked across the kitchen floor and the fridge door opened and closed. Hearing that sound she was hungry again. Which left her no choice. She joined him in the kitchen.

He was bent over his script. 'Leichhardt had an incredible drive you know.' He straightened, clenched a hand and punched his chest. 'I feel it, here in my gut.'

She stifled a laugh. The fool had no idea where his organs were.

'Writing this script,' he went on, 'it's as if I'm becoming the man himself.'

'Wow,' she said, but what she thought was *good grief*.

'I'll have to take the part. I don't think an actor would do him justice.'

Could he think of nothing else?

She went to the fridge and pulled out a container of the frittata Heather had made last night. She cut a hunk and levered it onto a plate, grabbed a fork from a drawer and turned to see Angus gazing at her.

'That bump of yours sure is growing.'

'Thanks.'

'I must set to work on the script while there's still peace in the house.'

'I thought you were moving out?'

'All in good time.'

She tried not to contemplate the thought that he might never leave.

She noticed the local newspaper, tucked under a pile of opened envelopes at the end of the bench. She picked up the paper and took her plate to the table, taking up the chair furthest from Angus. Ignoring him was an effort. She forked a chunk of her frittata and opened the newspaper, keeping her eyes firmly on the print, scanning all the articles from the first page: old-age pensioners celebrate opening of new senior's centre; school kids raise money for cancer; street crime spike in Hamilton Hill; local men's group determined to fight on for the rights of fathers. She quickly turned the page, casting an indifferent eye over all the adverts, then the TV guide, the 'What's On' page and even 'Trades and Services'. Arriving at the penultimate page she stopped, short of sport, to read the small ads.

She had to find a job. With the pregnancy came additional expenses. She'd need a cot, a pram, baby clothes and nappies. She scanned the ads. Cleaner, cleaner, cleaner—nope. Bookkeeper, gardener, dog walker, and, finally, something she could do—junk-mail delivery. The only requirement was a passion for keeping fit. She went back to her room and called the number.

The following afternoon, leaflets, fliers, and glossy brochures from Coles and Woolworths advertising the week's specials were piled on Heather's kitchen table. She had to collate the junk mail herself. She'd been allocated South Fremantle, with a junk-mail drop of about one thousand. She made two cents per leaflet. Today's delivery amounted to a hundred dollars. When the distributor, Kylie, a jolly woman in her thirties, had dropped off the leaflets, (something she generously offered to do when Yvette explained she had no car), she told Yvette she was lucky: it was a bumper week. Heather had tried to talk her out of it before she left for work that morning but Yvette was resolute. Angus had stared in disbelief at the leaflets, mumbling an annoyed, 'I suppose I can write on my lap,' before tramping to the living room with an arm full of his Leichhardt script.

Four hours later, Yvette crammed the folded junk mail into two large shoulder bags. With a rough outline of a route and a gut full of determination she left the house.

She reached the end of the street and already her shoulders were tense. She could head left down to Marine Terrace or right and up to the end of the next street and down the other side. She headed up the hill.

It was a punishing ascent. At the crest she crossed the road and worked her way down, passing, over on the other side, blocks of units with letterboxes out front, all huddled together in low brick walls. Damn! On her side, on about every third letterbox was a No Junk Mail sign. She loathed junk mail, a crass form of advertising, a useless waste of paper and therefore trees, but delivering this heavy bulk she couldn't help resenting every No Junk Mail sign she passed.

By the time she reached Marine Terrace, her bags felt no lighter than when she'd started. After that, she turned every corner and went up every street, her bags emptying, her heart filling with resentment and humiliation. She could think of at least five ways she'd rather keep fit, swimming, dancing, tennis, yoga, the gym, anything but this. It occurred to her that at least detention-centre detainees had all their basic needs met, a thought she slapped away before it had a chance to take hold.

3.8

When she returned to the house, Angus was in the living room, a luxurious space, with walls of terracotta red, the damask of the sofas in complementary sienna, strong colours tempered by cream curtains, cushions and rugs. The room was a sanctum, sullied now by Angus slumped on the sofa with a can of beer, his eyes fixed on the television.

An even greater abhorrence unfolded on the screen. A close-up of a careworn woman, the voiceover telling viewers she'd just given birth to a premature baby and they both faced deportation to Nauru. *Nauru*. That hellhole! Yvette wondered what Dan would have made of it; at once troubled by her own lack of engagement, her initial interest dwindled to chaff drifting at the bottom of an empty sack of grain. The few morsels of *Profits of Doom* she'd managed to retain had faded into the background of her awareness. What happened to the burst of illumination she'd experienced that day? Even her initial creative fervour after the night of her troubling dream had abated. Artistically, she still found herself in a space between her old precisionist ways and something new, but her mind was hazy and unstructured. She left Angus undisturbed and dumped her bags in her room.

She found Heather in the kitchen, dicing zucchinis. Behind her, onions sizzled in a frying pan. 'Smells delicious,' Yvette said, sitting on the chair nearest the bench.

'Cheers honey.'

'Can I help?'

'Stay where you are. You look exhausted.' She scooped the zucchini into the pan and gave the contents a stir.

'I've never done anything so gruelling,' Yvette said. Which was true, she wasn't given to hard labour.

'Does it pay?'

'I made a hundred bucks,' she said with a surge of unanticipated triumph.

'I make that in an hour,' Heather said benignly. Adding, 'I'm sorry. I didn't mean ...'

Yvette deflected the rancour that rose in her defence. 'That's okay,' she said. 'The annoying thing is I'm a graduate. I have a Masters for heaven's sake. But of course, painting doesn't pay.'

'Unless you paint walls.'

'In cream.'

They both laughed.

She watched Heather crack eggs into a bowl. The steady rhythm of the fork chinking against glass, the sight of the fresh herbs, the mound of grated cheese, the tomatoes and salad vegetables laid out along the bench, it was all so consummately homey.

'You could teach,' Heather said reflectively.

'I don't think I'd be good at it. Besides ...'

'I meant in the future. For now you are stuck.' Heather poured the eggs in the pan. With her attention on the omelette she added, 'The mother of Angus's daughter is a teacher.'

'I never knew he had a kid!'

'Hasn't he mentioned her?'

'No. But then, we haven't talked much.'

'He's the silent type. Doesn't give much away.'

Yvette found the remark an odd assessment of Angus. He was a gas-bag in his exchanges with Viktor. She let Heather's belief pass without comment, keen to find out more about his offspring. 'How old is she?'

'Amy? Five. Cute little thing but we don't see much of her.' Heather left the stove, a look of sadness fixed in her gaze.

'That's a shame.'

'It is.'

'Where is she?'

'The mother, Julie, has custody. She's in Adelaide.'

'A bit far.'

'He's moving over there as soon as he's fixed up the bus.'

Angus started to make sense. Heather had never displayed to her brother anything but a diffused goodwill, accommodating his presence on her sofa with tolerance and sympathy. The whole time she'd been here, Yvette found her friend's attitude towards him astonishing. Even with this new insight into his character he still hadn't shifted far in Yvette's estimation. All along she hadn't doubted the Leichhardt script would come to nothing, yet at least now she could see that perhaps it didn't matter. The script was his way of coping with his loss. He was a little less a wastrel, a little less delusional. He'd become to her a larrikin with a wound and she made a mental note to regard him with a measure of respect.

3.9

A week later and she couldn't motivate herself to move a muscle. She'd returned from her second and this time self-funded visit to her doctor an hour before and gone straight to her room and to her bed. At the surgery, after a humiliating few minutes explaining how she hadn't managed to have an ultrasound, a further ten minutes enduring cold-hand prods and the icy pad of the stethoscope pressed hard here and there, the doctor-witch told her with considerable enthusiasm that she was having twins. Twins. Not one but two tiny foetuses sloshing about inside her. The doctor had been delighted, just about bouncing in her seat with vicarious jubilation as if those foetuses were her own progeny.

Yvette was as ebullient as a fish-hooked mullet. She pictured Thomas in his tiny unit surrounded by old books and half-worn clothes, at one with his violin in an altogether different world that spoke of serenity and ethereal heights. She pictured Josie, slapping paint on another canvas in wild abandon or behind the bar in Malta, laughing gaily as she served a throng of merry-making tourists. Thomas and Josie were free to be who they were and do as they wished. She couldn't help thinking she'd been served a double dollop of misfortune, her freedom curtailed by the burden of carrying twins and the uncertainty of her immigration status. So much for prophecy; she was suspended in the troposphere, with no idea where she'd fall.

Several hours passed before she managed to rouse herself. Then she sat up and flicked through a holistic-healing magazine that she'd taken from the pile in the living room. Heather was in her room, meditating. Yvette could hear the dulcet tones of Tony O'Connor through the wall. Angus was in the kitchen, at work as ever, and with the evening meal cooked and eaten, Yvette was leaving him to it.

She closed the magazine and stroked her rounding belly. After her doctor's deplorable revelation the bovine resignation she'd grown used to that rendered her impervious to her vicissitudes had disappeared, leaving her at the mercy of her misery that surrounded her like a dark haze.

A sudden burst of the setting sun reflected off a neighbour's shed and shafted through the window. She lay back down. Tony O'Connor stopped chiming through the wall. A remarkable quiet consumed the house in his absence. She let her mind drift. She was almost asleep when her phone broke into the hush.

'Hey, Yvette.' It was Debbie. 'Mum told me. How are you?'

Something in Yvette reared defensively. 'Oh, I'm fine.'

'Sorry I haven't phoned before. But you know how it is, husbands, kids and all that.'

'That's okay,' Yvette mumbled.

There was a brief moment of silence.

'Well, hey. Congratulations.'

'Thanks.'

Yvette could have tried to sound more affectionate, opened up to her sister a little. But she didn't open up.

Her sister went on. 'You'll need a lot of support. Especially being so inexperienced.'

She expected Yvette to respond to that? The woman was infuriating. Then Debbie launched into a vivid description of both of her natural births, ending her vignettes with, 'Well, I guess it helps to have a loving husband by your side.'

'It does,' Yvette said, thinking Debbie's insensitivity was, once again, incredible.

'If there's anything I can do.'

'I'll let you know.'

'The least I can do is offer advice.'

There was no stopping her. Advice spilled from her mouth like a galloping horse.

'Will you breastfeed?'

'Of course.'

'Good. Then get in touch with nursing mothers. They really helped me with my first.'

'I will. Thanks.'

'I better go,' she said, adding with a nervous laugh. 'Alan doesn't like large phone bills.'

3.10

The following Saturday, after an idle morning spent separating clothes that no longer fit from those that for now she could wear, she grabbed her shoulder bag, marched down the hall and closed the front door firmly behind her, bidding Angus, spread-eagled under the chassis of his bus, a casual see-you-later as she picked her way over the bus-junk scatterings on the path.

The walk into Fremantle was pleasant, a cool breeze dampening the sharp heat of the sun. Once again she admired Scot's Church and she felt exalted, almost religious for a moment.

She pushed open the side door and entered the stale warmth of the hall. Fiona greeted her as she passed. A gathering of choir members were chatting over by the urn.

Yvette glanced around and saw Heather talking with Sue, whose sturdy frame looked formidable in a clingy T-shirt tucked into tight jeans. Heather caught Yvette's eye and waved. She returned the greeting. As Heather's gaze slid away, Yvette admired her friend, that earth mother look of hers, the long russet dress, shoulders draped in a patterned silk scarf. She exuded self-assurance and easy charm. A magnificently self-contained woman not given to sudden rushes of emotion, yet not inhibited like Leah and without the rigid attitude. Heather's bountiful goodwill and tireless conviviality were, she decided, little short of saintly.

Heather walked over, nodding hellos to the others as she passed. When they hugged, Yvette wanted to nestle her whole being in her friend's embrace.

Heather pulled back and looked at Yvette closely. 'You don't seem that happy.'

How did she do that, see beneath the surface so astutely? Yvette gave her a weak smile and said, 'I'll be fine.'

Heather gave her hand a quick squeeze.

Fiona called the choir to attention and, for the benefit of new members, launched into the same preamble about finding your voice as she had that first time Yvette had come. Sue passed round the hat.

'I have some disappointing news and some exciting news.' Fiona looked around. 'Which first?'

'Get the bad news out of the way,' a woman called out from the back. Yvette glanced at her, taking in the long and sun-bleached hair, the suntanned face, the full lips and warm brown eyes.

'Okay, Fran. Our application to perform at the next Fremantle Festival has been unsuccessful.'

There were murmurs of disappointment.

'Don't be disheartened. The organisers have been flooded with applications.'

'I bet Kavisha Mazzella's choir got a spot,' a woman in a green beret said churlishly.

'Yes, they did,' Fiona said, turning to the woman, 'and that's to be expected. They've been doing this a lot longer than we have.' Fiona looked concerned. It seemed she wouldn't allow disharmony to take hold in the choir. 'We're sure to be accepted next year,' she said, 'and that leaves us plenty of time to rehearse.

'And the good news?'

'We've been invited to perform at the Fairbridge Music Festival.'

There were some cheers and hoorays.

'Where's Fairbridge?' Yvette whispered to Heather.

'South,' Heather said quickly. 'In the country.'

With a commanding, 'Now let's make a start,' Fiona took up her place at the foot of the stage.

The choir formed three groups in a wide arc. Yvette joined the altos, standing beside Heather at the back. Sue, Fran, and the woman in the green beret stood in front of them. The choir began with the lullaby, 'Inannay'. Yvette remembered the song but felt tentative. The choir sounded polished, the harmonies perfected, riding the emotion of the song, blending and rising and falling like an ocean swell.

She tuned in to Heather's voice, clear and distinct, and projected her own, keen for her voice to merge with her friend's and hers alone, as if in the resonance of their two voices their souls would merge, and all Yvette's childhood memories, too often brought to the forefront of her mind since she came to Perth, would melt away.

Then in a burst of illumination she pictured Heather's childhood. And her heart went out to her friend. Snared in her own past she had too readily overlooked Heather's, the brutality of her mother's sudden departure, the loss and the hardship she must have borne. Yvette felt an opening. It might have been the first time she'd experienced empathy. And she recognised in Heather's keenness for her friendship, and her respectful reserve, the stamp of those early years.

3.11

Outside, the sky had clouded over and there were spatters of rain. The moment choir practice had finished Heather rushed off to see a client. Left alone on the pavement, Yvette's life seemed suddenly empty. The rain began to fall heavily, so she headed to Myer's department store for shelter.

Browsing aimlessly, she wandered downstairs and found herself in the men's department. There, as she stood by a row of smart shirts, she had to fight off a craving for a meat pie. It was her latest impulse, one she found revolting and certainly emanating from the beings inside her, leaving her wondering what sort of uncouth blaggards she was spawning. Then, as the craving faded, she felt an all-consuming urge to sit down. Breathless, she walked on a few paces and clutched the edge of a table display of novelty underwear.

A middle-aged man in a suit was fastidiously arranging cellophane-wrapped ties on a rack nearby. He glanced in her direction and seeing her distressed, rushed over. 'Are you all right, madam?' he asked politely.

'I just need to sit down.'

He darted behind the counter, wheeled out a swivel chair and beckoned her to sit. 'I'll fetch you a glass of water.' He headed off, returning moments later with a glass of ice-cold water, a napkin and a shortbread finger biscuit on a small plate.

Yvette sipped the water. 'You are so kind,' she said, and noticing his name badge, added, 'Gordon.'

His face lit with interest as if in calling him by his name she'd broken the spell of formality. 'You are most welcome,' he said graciously. He had a florid sort of face, with a generous mouth and kind brown eyes. She was drawn by the theatricality of his manner, the ironic intonation he applied to even the most ordinary of sentences. She took in the silvery-grey of his hair, the creases about the eyes. He must have been about sixty.

'What might madam be looking for? Perhaps I can help.'

'Please, call me Yvette.'

'Yvette. An unusual name.'

'My mother wanted to call me Jane. But Grandma Grimm, that's my father's mother, said, "Oh not plain Jane!"'

'Yvette Grimm.' He paused and said reflectively, 'Names can be such a curse.' Then he covered his mouth with his hand. 'Oh, I'm sorry. I didn't mean ...'

'It's fine.'

'You see, I was almost Gerard Card.'

They both laughed.

'Thankfully my father insisted on Gordon.'

He glanced at his watch. 'Is that the time? I must leave at four on the dot. I have an appointment.' A look of concern flashed in his face. 'Will you be all right?'

'I think so.'

'I don't like to rush you. Are you sure you're fully recovered?'

'Yes, I'm fine. An appointment is an appointment. You mustn't be late.'

'It's a rehearsal.'

'You're a performer?'

'No. I'm directing a play I wrote.'

'My friend is an actor.' As she spoke she realised she hadn't seen Thomas since her eve of New Year's Eve party and felt a pang of remorse. She really had to stop turning off her phone and ignoring her messages.

'Is she?' Gordon said with interest. 'Stage, film or television?'

'He, and strictly amateur.'

'Perhaps he'd like to audition for a part.'

She felt a twinge of uncertainty. 'I'm sure he'd be delighted,' she said, 'And your play is called ...?'

'"Trouble and Strife." It's a Restoration comedy.'

'Sounds fascinating.'

'Why don't you play a part too?' He looked straight at her.

She gave him a coy smile. 'I can't act.'

'Of course you can. And I have the perfect role for you.' He placed a hand over his heart and said with false tragedy, 'Penelope Pinchgut.'

They both laughed again.

'I'll think about it.'

'Oh, do. *Do.*'

He reached into his breast pocket and handed her a business card.

She stood and thanked him for the water and the biscuit, then she wandered through the other departments with no intention of buying anything and on outside. The rain had stopped and whorls of steam rose from the pavement, the whole milieu glistening in the sunshine.

3.12

She strolled home past Fremantle Oval and on to Fothergill Street where the narrow pavement follows the curve of the imposing wall of Fremantle Prison. Beyond the wall was a vast four-storey limestone building. She recalled the brochure she'd read in her doctor's waiting room saying that the convict barracks were built by the convicts themselves in the eighteen-fifties using limestone quarried on site. Backbreaking work carried out by those unfortunate souls, wrenched from their families for the most trivial of misdemeanours.

The brochure had gone on to explain that the prison had been the primary place of incarceration in Perth ever since, notorious for hangings, floggings, escapes and riots, but now that the inmates were moved to a new maximum security prison in Casuarina, the site had gained World Heritage status, and conservation groups and government bodies had turned the prison into a tourist destination. Hence the glossy bi-fold. It must have been a matter of considerable state pride. She'd wondered at the surgery what it was about people that they should want to visit places where horrific things had happened, tourists in shorts and straight socks snapping photographs;

coach loads marvelling over cell sizes. It was a grotesque happenstance. Cultural curiosity of that sort should at best be solemn and reverent, at worst a horror invoking experience. Now, as she passed by the prison, she thought it ironic yet inevitable that incarceration should dominate Australian heritage. Better to preserve the memory, she thought, than raze the buildings for another stadium-size shopping mall.

She crossed the road and went down an embankment towards the back entrance of the Fremantle hospital, taking a shortcut through to the streets of South Fremantle.

Angus was sitting on the front porch when she cornered the street. As she approached he stubbed out a cigarette. She felt a stab of contempt for him and her mind swayed, another part of her self-remonstrative. She was too judgemental, too quick to condemn. And she recognised in an instant her mother's view of her father.

She rounded the hedge, noting the absence of tools and bus detritus, and before she entered the garden she steadied her thoughts.

'How was your day, sweetheart?' he said, following her inside.

She wished he wouldn't call her sweetheart. She knew the word had no substance, a word conjuring romance and intimacy, neither existing between them.

She sat at the kitchen table. Angus leaned against the bench, hands spread wide, and stared out the window.

'I wonder what Leichhardt would have made of this place.'

'Relieved after all that desert.'

'Yes, but the desert fascinated him. The quest, the adventure, the discovery.'

He really could talk of nothing else. Curious, she asked him how the script was progressing.

'Extremely well. Almost finished in fact.' He paused. 'There's only one problem.'

'What's that?'

'I need to get the setting exactly right.'

He turned to her abruptly, his eyes deep pools of hopeful

delusion beneath his bushy mono-brow. 'The desert is calling me. Leichhardt is calling me.' He turned back to the window. 'And I'm gonna heed that call.'

She wanted to cry out in exasperation and urge him to go all at once. The magnificent unreality of the script had taken on another almost insane reality.

'And your bus?' she asked lightly, feigning a casual engagement.

'All packed up and ready to go.'

The front door creaked open and Heather entered the room. 'Angus?'

'I'm off.'

'Don't you want dinner first?'

'I'll get something on the road.'

They held each other in a warm embrace. Yvette looked on. Why couldn't she and Debbie be like that? She suddenly found herself cold-hearted cast in Heather's light.

'Safe travels,' Heather said, uncharacteristically pensive.

'Don't worry about me.'

Yvette looked away with a twinge of remorse. Now he was leaving she almost regretted not making more of an effort to get to know him.

Yet when she watched him head down the hall the farewell smile she wore belied the churning of the most powerful will that ever was, the will of a mother protecting her young: wily, cautious, ready to kill. It came as no surprise that before he closed the door behind him out trailed her memories of her father.

3.13

That evening, when the sun had set and a soft breeze blew in through an open window, Yvette sat on the empty sofa, relishing the comfort of the house free of Angus. For a few minutes she fell into a doze listening to Heather's meditation music spilling from her room across the hall. Then she stood up spontaneously and before she changed her mind she phoned Thomas, seizing the chance to reconnect, wanting above all to gather her friends around her and extract some fun from life. After a brief exchange about her new life in Fremantle, choir and how wonderful Heather was, she told him about her encounter with Gordon and the play.

'I mentioned you and he thought you might like to be in it. He even has a role for me.'

'For *you*?'

'He wants me to be Penelope Pinchgut.'

'Penelope Pinchgut?' he scoffed. 'He's taken that name from Wycherley's play, *The Country Wife*.'

She had no idea Thomas knew a thing about Restoration comedy but she wasn't surprised.

'Are you interested?'

NINE MONTHS OF SUMMER

'Sure.'

She suggested he come over the following night and then she phoned Gordon.

It was eight in the evening when she answered Gordon's rapid and light knock. He kissed her cheek as she ushered him through to the kitchen. With Angus gone and Heather visiting her father in Rockingham, the house, for the first time, was hers. Thomas was seated in the kitchen with Anthony, who was up from Kalgoorlie for the weekend and had tagged along. Out of curiosity, he'd said. At the sight of him seated cross-legged on a wooden chair, a flash of alarm appeared in Gordon's face before he quickly replaced it with a smile.

Anthony was staring at Gordon, an airy smile lighting his face. 'I'm delighted to make your acquaintance again,' he said without proffering his hand.

'Likewise.' Gordon averted his gaze.

Yvette was bewildered. That Gordon and Anthony had met before was a shock, as if her existence in Perth had just tightened its belt. She glanced at Thomas, who maintained an impervious smile.

'Tea?' she said, pouring water in the kettle.

'No, thank you,' said Thomas.

Anthony shook his head.

'Thank you, I will,' Gordon said. 'No sugar and just a dash of milk.'

Yvette gestured and he took up the chair at the head of the table, immediately pulling from a manila folder copies of his script.

'Shall we get straight to it? I don't have an awful lot of time.' He passed Thomas a script. Anthony, seated at the foot of the table, leaned forward and held out his hand. Gordon hesitated then slid a copy across the table in Anthony's direction before setting another on the table in front of the vacant chair beside him.

Thomas leafed through the pages. Gordon was observing his face. Yvette turned to fill the kettle, catching a glimpse of a cockroach scuttling across the kitchen floor and disappearing under the fridge.

When she turned back, Anthony was riffling through his copy of the script with raised eyebrows, his mouth set in an expression of disdain. Yvette could hardly bear to look at him. Neither could Gordon, who was perched on the side of his seat, purposefully facing in the other direction.

The kettle boiled. She made Gordon his tea in one of Heather's best cups and handed it to him then took up the vacant chair.

'Thank you,' he mouthed.

There was a long stretch of silence. They were all watching Thomas, who sat over his script as if in pose with his elbow on the table, his head resting in a hand.

'Interesting,' Thomas said at last, pushing the script to one side.

'I thought you might like to take the part of Thidney Thornthwaite.' Gordon sounded tentative. 'He's a somewhat rakish bachelor,' he added. 'A merchant from London.'

'Who speaks with a lisp,' Thomas said.

'Yes.'

'Fascinating.' Yvette detected a note of derision in Thomas's voice.

'You can manage a lisp?'

'Of courth he can lithp,' Anthony said.

Gordon ignored his remark and addressed Thomas directly. 'Well, I'm sure he'd suit you better than his cousin Mr Spitzer. He's a university student from Bath. A forthright young man who pronounces his esses with a rasping spit like Daffy Duck.'

'Really?' Thomas frowned.

Anthony emitted a disingenuous yawn. What, for heaven's sake, was he playing at? She felt fiercely protective of Gordon, although she wasn't sure Gordon had seen the yawn; at least, there was no reaction in his demeanour. He sipped his tea then caught Yvette's gaze. 'Perfect,' he said with a smile that faded as it appeared. Then he turned to Thomas. 'Thornthwaite wants Spitzer to marry the gullible Penelope Pinchgut.'

'That's me,' Yvette said, with a faltering laugh.

'And there's Mrs Fanny Bunn, a matronly widow and Penelope's chaperone. She disapproves of the marriage proposal and is suspicious of Thornthwaite's motives.'

'Sounds like a good farce,' Yvette said encouragingly.

'Oh, you'll love it Yvette. It's filled with innuendo, *double entendres* and a great deal of posturing.'

'I'm sure it is,' said Thomas with a measure of warmth, shooting Anthony a sidelong glance.

'There'll be lots of mincing walks and sparring,' Gordon went on, glancing at her again with a wink.

She smiled then turned to Anthony in time to see a look of malice flashing into his face. 'Thornthwaite doesn't need a lisp,' he said dismissively.

'Oh, but he does.' Gordon shifted in his seat.

'You already have rasping Spitzer. Why have two male characters with a speech impediment?'

'It's a comedy.'

'Seems a little overdone, if you don't mind me saying.'

'My word!' Gordon was visibly rattled.

Anthony shrugged and tossed his copy of the play in Gordon's direction. Yvette was flabbergasted. The man had no grace at all.

Flushed, Gordon gathered up the scripts. 'Incredible!' he muttered and made to leave the room.

'Let me show you out,' Yvette said spontaneously, eager to steer Gordon away from the upset Anthony had caused, at once anxious to distance herself from her friends' behaviour and reinforce her affection for her new friend. For an inexplicable reason she found him compelling. Once in the hall, she closed the kitchen door and led him into the living room.

'I'm sorry, Gordon. Anthony can be tactless sometimes. He didn't mean to ...'

'Yvette, I didn't realise you had artistic leanings.'

'Oh that,' she said, following his gaze to her sketch pad open at a rough drawing of the room. 'It's nothing.'

'You're an artist?'

'I suppose I am.'

'What medium?'

'Oils. Although I'm not sure the fumes would be good for the babies.'

'Babies? You're having twins? How marvellous.'

'Thank you.'

'Are you working on anything special?'

She sighed. 'I'm having a hiatus.'

'What's the problem?'

'I have ideas that require a shift of my skill set.'

'Ah.' He nodded slowly. 'I know what you mean.' He shuffled his folder under his arm, took a quick breath and said, 'Would you like to come to my studio?'

She hesitated.

'I'm no expert but maybe we can share some ideas.'

She shoved away her pride. How would she know if he had anything to offer if she didn't accept his invitation? Besides, it provided another opportunity to spend time in his company. 'I'd love that,' she said keenly.

'Would you? Shall we say Tuesday week at two? That's my afternoon off.'

He made to leave and as they stood in the hall she handed him the pen and notepad Heather kept on a tall and narrow table, and he wrote down his address.

She held open the front door and he reached for her hand. 'I'm so pleased you are coming. I feel connected to you. I don't know why.'

She looked into his face. His eyes were moist, his mouth loose.

'I sense that too,' she said, feeling another overwhelming rush of compassion. As he turned and walked away she wanted to gather him up for safekeeping. So strange were these feelings, she could only attribute them to the pregnancy.

She closed the door and went back to the living room for a few moments to collect her thoughts. Then she closed her sketchbook, switched off the light and joined the others in the kitchen.

'Has he gone?' Thomas said.

'He's gone.'

'Good,' Anthony said. 'The man's an amateur. He should stick to selling suits.'

'That's unkind.' And unwarranted. She couldn't understand why Anthony was so bent on dismissing Gordon's play. No, more than that, on dismissing the man altogether.

'He's being honest,' Thomas said. 'Scriptwriting is much harder than people think.'

Yvette said nothing. She despised Anthony then. And she was dismayed with Thomas for siding with what amounted to a shop window of a personality, dressed all dandy and fine, shocked now she was seeing right through to the back of him, where the vermin, scarcely hidden, were on the march. She said little of consequence after that. There was no way she'd tell either of them she was delivering junk mail. The ridicule would have been insufferable.

Before long Thomas announced their departure and she saw them to the door.

Anthony wandered to the car. Thomas lingered, heading slowly across the garden before turning back and asking if she'd seen Varg. She told him she hadn't.

'Have you figured out who the father is?' he said in a low voice.

'No.'

'What are you going to do?'

'Have the babies.'

'Babies?'

'Didn't I tell you? I'm having twins.'

He gasped. 'You're going through with it then?'

'What choice do I have?'

'I've never thought of you as a mother.' He looked her up and down. 'I mean, you always seemed too independent.'

'People change, Thomas.'

'Maybe.'

'It isn't a betrayal,' she said in an attempt to strike at the cause of his attitude.

'What?'

'My being pregnant.'

'I never see you. You never call.'

'I know. I'm sorry,' she said. 'I'm having a hard time.'

'Aren't we all?'

End it then, she wanted to say but couldn't give it voice.

He kissed her cheek and told her he'd call her soon.

3.14

The following Saturday afternoon, when the sun was still strong in the sky, the ocean breeze barely cooling the air in what seemed to Yvette an eternal summer, she decided to go into Fremantle for choir by bus. She waited at the shade-less bus stop at the corner of the street, gazing at the bleached grasses of the neighbours' front lawns, the gnarly flaking trunk of a paperbark nearby and the pendulous arms of a peppermint gum down the road. She watched legions of bees harvest the sweet nectar of a bottlebrush across the street. And she looked back at Heather's house, the neatly hedged front garden, the smart cream of the walls, the windows shaded from the sun's ferocity. Her phone emitted a few sharp rings then went silent. She didn't bother checking to see who'd called. She knew it was her mother.

The bus was late.

She alighted opposite Scot's Church and crossed the road, looking up at the grey cone of the spire, the ring of arched windows beneath, the broad A of the main roof, the triptych of arched windows in the main wall. As she neared the side door she heard singing. She wanted to go in and walk by all at once, feeling in her guts a resistance to the commitment and the sense of belonging to the community that the choir gave, along with a yearning pull of her heart.

She opened the door. Heather was standing at the back of the altos, striking in a purple outfit that swayed as she sang. Yvette watched her for a few moments, taking her in, the shroud of her friendship, and she stood by her side.

Heather held out her hand. 'It's just the warm-up,' she whispered.

Yvette sang along until the song finished. Then a hush descended, the singers waiting patiently for Fiona to speak. There was a murmured conversation occurring between her and a woman at the front. Yvette tried to dodge heads but failed to see who Fiona was talking to.

At last Fiona spoke. 'Sorry about that. Sadly, Norma can't go to Fairbridge. So I have a space in the altos if anyone is interested.'

'Fairbridge?' Yvette said to Heather.

'Isn't it exciting?'

'We have a few more weeks to practice,' Fiona said. 'So don't be shy.'

Heather nudged Yvette's arm. 'Go on.'

'Me?'

'You have a beautiful voice.'

Surely she was joking, yet she kept nudging so Yvette put up her hand. Realising Fiona couldn't see her, Heather called out, 'Yvette wants to do it.'

'Yvette?' Fiona peered about. Seeing Yvette with her hand still raised, Fiona smiled. 'Terrific. Thank you.'

Yvette sang heartily now, buoyed by Heather's comment and by the energy, the unison of voices, the uplifting songs. And the thought of performing at Fairbridge gave her something to look forward to. Another chance to shake off the darkness that had held her in its thrall with the will of Cerberus ever since she'd come back to Australia.

During the tea break, Fiona handed her the song lyrics she'd need to learn. 'Thanks so much,' Fiona said, smiling at Heather as she walked away.

'I can't believe I'm going to perform in a choir at a music festival,' Yvette said, dismissing straight away an image of her nephews.

'You'll be fine.'

The other altos gathered round to welcome her. Sue smiled warmly and held out her hand. She had an authoritative demeanour and Yvette imagined she might be a schoolteacher. Heather introduced the woman beside her as Beth. Beth had the slightly troublesome air of the committee aficionado. She was a proud-looking woman, the sort that presses her jeans; the green beret she wore commando style replaced today with an equally formidable cotton headscarf. Yvette smiled politely and shook her hand.

Heather gestured again. 'And Fran,' she said. Yvette smiled into Fran's brown eyes. Fran smiled back, an open-mouthed smile revealing perfect white teeth, striking in her deeply tanned face. In fact, all of her exposed skin was tanned. She must spend all her days on the beach.

Another woman was standing behind her. She was thin and petite, almost frail. 'And finally, Karen,' said Heather. In a flowing hippy dress and purple leather thongs she didn't look like a 'Karen'. She was more like a 'Sky'.

Straight away the conversation centred on Yvette's pregnancy, when she was due, my she was big, Heather disclosing the twins, Yvette shrinking inside from all the well-meaning comments and the barrage of questions and vignettes, mostly from Sue and Beth who were both grandmothers. Fran had two sons but thankfully refrained from describing her births. Karen recommended a water birth before wishing her good luck and slipping away.

Yvette warmed to all the women, without any sense she'd be cultivating deep friendships. But there was a sense of solidarity among them, knowing in a few weeks they would be drawing strength from each other on stage.

3.15

Gordon's house in East Fremantle was one block from the bus stop. She alighted the bus and walked along the narrow pavement, checking the house numbers, ducking to avoid a low bottlebrush branch when she reached his front gate. She could see from the frontage that his house was a duplex, an old brick home with sash windows and a bull-nose veranda all around, sliced down the middle to form two dwellings.

The front door was ajar. She hesitated, by turns apprehensive, curious and drawn to this endearing gentleman, and drawn closer by Anthony's animosity. She didn't expect to gain artistically from the visit; she was convinced he could offer her little in that regard. He represented a possibility, of what, she had no idea, and aimlessly exploring possibilities seemed to constitute her life here in Perth. She was adrift, a rudderless dinghy floating along with the currents, while her progeny that grew in her womb and the Department of Immigration determined her destiny.

She rang the doorbell and heard it chime somewhere inside. 'Come on in,' Gordon called. She opened the fly-screen and entered a compact vestibule leading on through an open door to a small and elegantly furnished living room. Two wingback chairs were set at an angle before a circular Persian rug. Between the chairs a pile of hardcovers were neatly stacked on a repro Queen Ann table. There was a small television and a CD player angled towards each other on a low oak dresser. A standard lamp with a voluminous burgundy shade replete with long tassels was positioned at the end of a tall bookcase filled with carefully arranged paperbacks. Light filtered in through narrow Venetian blinds tilted against the sun. Hanging on the biscuit-coloured walls were a series of watercolour and acrylic paintings of scenes of Fremantle, the harbour, the café strip, the markets—all of them vibrant and surprisingly good.

Gordon entered the room through another door and bustled towards her, a tea towel draped over his arm. 'We're in the kitchen,' he said, kissing her cheek. 'Follow me.'

The kitchen was light and airy. Taupe cupboards, modern in style, lined one wall and half of another. A glass sliding door opened out onto a paved area leading to a rectangle of lawn edged with clipped native shrubs. In front of the window, also facing the garden, two wooden chairs were set before a narrow table covered in plastic. The table was laid in an orderly manner with an assortment of paper and sketching pencils. Gordon's studio.

Realising she'd forgotten even her tin pencil box, she said with an apologetic smile, 'I didn't know what to bring.'

Gordon folded the tea towel and placed it beside the draining board.

'Yourself,' he said. 'And as you can see, I'm well-equipped.'

She laughed. 'I don't like to come empty-handed.'

'Now, now Yvette. That might be going a little far.' He waggled a finger at her in mock disapproval, then chuckled with a look that suggested he thought the remark perhaps too risqué.

She sat on one of the chairs.

'What's your background?' she said. 'Artistically speaking.'

'I'm naïve. Came late to my creativity, then found I loved it. So I signed up for every evening class I could find. And you?'

She cringed inwardly. 'Goldsmiths and the Royal Academy.'

'Then I'm privileged to be seated by your side.'

'I don't think academic training is any better than any other pathway. Think of Séraphine Louis,' she said. 'Or Henri Rousseau.' She could scarcely believe those words had come from her own mouth.

'I thought I was no good and never would be but I'll never forget the day my tutor upon hearing my complaint stood over my shoulder and admonished me by saying, "Of course your work is not that good, but if you persist it will be." I really was naïve.' He emitted a self-deprecating laugh. 'I thought art was a gift you either had or hadn't, not a set of fine skills that took years to acquire.'

His story impressed her, at once innocent and insightful. 'What's your preferred medium?' she said, deciding to take his artistic abilities seriously.

'I find acrylics give the artist freedom of expression.'

'Hence Expressionism.'

'I'm not into isms,' he said. 'For me, a painting should convey emotion.'

'Or an idea.'

'Or an idea. But not an inert one. Art is about passion. Like acting or singing.'

'I've never been good at expressing passion.'

'First you have to find the passion within.' He gave her a sympathetic look. 'Then learn to draw from the well.' He hesitated and went on. 'You don't have to use acrylics. Many famous expressive artists worked in oil. Like Kandinsky and Chagall.'

She found it curious he should cite those two Russian artists over, say, anyone Australian. Both used colour and line expressively, to convey rather than portray, creating impressions and abstraction. Somehow Gordon seemed to her more a realist, an assumption reinforced when he said, 'Shall we make a start?' then placed three objects on the far side of the table: a large conch shell, a single red rose and a bust of Mozart.

'Still life?' she said doubtfully.

'I call it life drawing in lieu of a nude.'

He sat beside her and selected a pencil, wasting no time roughing in the shapes. She studied the objects and made a start, glancing at his work from time to time, impressed with his fluid style, a flourish here, cross-hatching there, deft flicks and careful strokes interspersed with speculative pauses.

An hour later he put down his pencil.

'Let's have a break,' he said. 'You must be getting hungry, eating for two.'

'Three.'

'Oh yes, three! Well, bless me!'

He boiled the kettle and carefully arranged slices of cake on dainty plates. Then he warmed a teapot, swirling boiling water around before tipping it out. He added loose tea from his tea caddy, re-boiled the kettle and gently poured in the water. He hesitated, added a little more water, pulled on a knitted tea cosy and turned the teapot around three times. It was the way Grandma Grimm made tea. Yvette was transported back to a time she so dimly recalled, before her family had left for Australia, of sitting in her grandma's kitchen, breathing in the smell of frying bacon, strong tea and suety puddings, and drying washing hanging above the stove.

'You're a marvel,' she said.

'It's just a little something,' he said, waving a hand in her direction. He passed her a plate, a fork and a linen napkin then watched her eat.

'Do you like it?'

'Yummy,' she said between mouthfuls.

'I made it myself.'

'You are so domesticated.' Then, curious to know more about him, she said, 'Do you live alone?'

'Sworn bachelor.'

'You don't get lonely?'

'Not at all. I'm too fastidious to tolerate a housemate. You know the sort of thing, hairs in the soap.'

She smiled. There was not one thing in this whole house out of place, not a skerrick of dirt or dust.

He poured the tea into bone china cups. Handing her a cup and saucer, he said, 'What part of England are you from?'

She was instantly aware of the tentative quality of their togetherness, acquaintances courting friendship, uncertain of each other, of how the other feels, what they might reveal or have revealed to each other, just what sort of friendship could possibly exist between them.

'London,' she said. 'I grew up here in Perth though.'

'A ten-pound Pom.'

'I'm too young.'

'Oh, yes. Of course.'

She went on to explain, as concisely as she was able, her oft-told account of her ping-pong Pom life, colouring the narrative with warm descriptions of Heather and Josie.

He listened attentively and as she came to the end of her story he pointed at her cup and said, 'Refill?'

She shook her head and passed him her cup. Their hands brushed together briefly and she was drawn into an unexpected intimacy, that sensuality of human touch, at once soothing and exhilarating, and commonly experienced at the hairdressers.

'Thank you for today,' she said.

'Did you enjoy it?'

'Very much,' she said, with heartfelt gratitude.

'Same time in a fortnight suit?'

'I wouldn't miss it.'

3.16

It was a still evening. The air was fresh. The sunset glowed rich crimson over South Beach. Lazy waves flopped on the shore. A kilometre of golden sand stretched between the breakwaters. Beyond, to the north, the lights in Fremantle Marina and on the cargo ships anchored out at sea twinkled in the deepening dark. Now her shoulder bags were empty of junk mail she felt physically buoyant. Emotionally, she was anything but.

She wondered how much longer she would be able to endure this junk-mail run. Pride vied with the abiding darkness of her predicament, shutting her into a private world, a guarded, self-protective and lonely world of regret and self-recrimination, a world poised to eclipse her enceinte otherworldliness at every turn. She summoned her resolve. She told herself she had to be strong for the sake of the little ones inside who would surely be absorbing her vibes.

She reached into a shoulder bag and extracted with care a white paper bag. The bag was warm. Grease darkened an area of the bag's underside and a small brown stain was showing through the paper in one of the bottom corners. She pulled back the paper to expose the meat pie she'd purchased from a bakery down the road. It was the last pie in the pie warmer—no doubt it had been languishing there all day —a lonely old plain meat pie. The crust had turned rubbery and a dribble of brown slurry had broken through the seam at one end.

Tilting her head back she took a bite, careful not to bear down her jaws too quickly for fear of causing a spurt through the split crust, for she'd become an adept meat pie eater, the result of numerous spillages and the occasional burnt tongue. She chewed, ignoring the rancidity that filtered through the heavy dousing of salt and pepper that the contents of all pies are subjected to, and, after several more bites, the film of grease hardening on the roof of her mouth.

She scrunched the pie wrapper, dropped it back in her shoulder bag and belched. She was, without a doubt, disgusting.

She stared at the ocean and the sky, wishing she could step off this reality into a seascape, painting her own image climbing aboard a boat bound for Africa, a slim-waisted version of herself gripping the arm of a swarthy stranger. Yet she couldn't flee her circumstances. The pie fiends were right here inside her.

Heading back home she crossed Wilson Park, a flat rectangle of lawn edged with towering Norfolk Pines. The park was empty. She tried to imagine scampering about with her progeny, something she often saw parents do, playing chase, or throwing their children in the air, all joyous smiles and squeals of laughter. Did she belong in that cohort of devoted parents, keen to nurture, prepared to sacrifice her own wishes to fulfil the needs of another? Or was Thomas right? She'd never thought of herself as selfish. Perhaps she was. In months she'd be a mother, forced to forego her freedom to attend to the demands of the creatures growing in her belly. From time to time she wondered if she were capable of it.

A burning sensation rose from her stomach and she belched again.

3.17

She was helping Heather clear the table for dinner when Thomas phoned. He sounded chirpy and wasted little time arriving at the purpose of his call.

'Would you like to come to a play?'

'Yeah. What is it?'

'The students from Anton's Academy are performing a show at Subiaco Arts Centre.'

'Are you in anything?'

'Not this year. I'm working on something else.'

They arranged to meet in the foyer Friday night at seven.

The Subiaco Arts Centre was a modular building set in neat gardens. It was almost dark when she walked from the train station down Hamersley Road and entered the car park. As she approached the building she saw Varg in the foyer chatting to a small gathering. Trepidation pulsed through her. Was this the purpose of Thomas's invitation? Surely not. She squashed an impulse to veer off into the gloom, assuring herself that he was probably not that good at maths.

The moment she entered the building, Varg left the foyer through another door. She didn't think he'd seen her. She stood in the foyer, spacious with polished floors, a large canvas taking up the greater part of the far wall, a figurative depiction of a water turtle, the painting rendered in dots, wavy lines and circles. The work was elegant and she appreciated the form and the rich ochres. Indigenous art held a strange appeal, one curiously more compelling than any work she'd seen by white Australians, as if locked into the dots themselves was an appreciation of this land.

She drew her long and baggy cardigan around her middle. Casually attired folk flowed past her and joined the audience inside. She waited, and waited, and at last Thomas appeared, rushing through the doors with Anthony trailing his heels. She struggled to maintain her composure.

They exchanged kisses and polite hellos.

'So pleased you could make it,' Anthony said with contrived sincerity.

'Why?' she said, unable to disguise her hostility.

'Oh, you'll see,' he said with an ironic twist to his mouth. He was dressed flamboyantly in a lurid pink crushed silk blouse and purple cravat beneath an over-sized grey suit, shoulder pads reaching far beyond the flesh beneath.

Thomas stood off to one side, shoulders hunched, adjusting the alignment of his shirtsleeves. He was distinctly out of sorts, which seemed unusual, even for him.

With his usual ersatz, Anthony proffered his arm and steered her into the auditorium. Thomas followed on behind.

The theatre was grand with tiered seating facing a corner stage. The venue seemed rather lavish for an amateur production; little more than a review performed by students. Perhaps there was a mid-week discount on hire fees. Yvette sat between Thomas and Anthony in the second row from the front. She looked around. People continued to stroll in. Before long, all the seats in the four rows behind them were occupied. The front row was empty save for a chair on the far left, where Anton sat, holding a clipboard. Yvette read through the program she'd picked up from her chair before she sat down. Varg's piece, an extract from Harold Pinter's *Betrayal*, was last.

There was a brief moment of hush as the lights in the auditorium dimmed and Anton rushed to the stage. After his lengthy introduction the curtains parted and the show began.

On the stage, a spotlight illumed two neatly moustached men in their twenties, both seated at the wooden table. It was the opening act from John Osborne's *Look Back in Anger*. The men were flicking through newspapers and a young black-haired woman standing stage left was ironing shirts. As one of the men launched into a tirade of antagonisms, Yvette glanced over at Anton, who was grinning, his hands clasped together in salutary fashion.

An excerpt from Noël Coward's *Cavalcade* followed, played competently by a middle-aged couple bedecked in Edwardian costume—both plump, both plain, both pompous.

A slender, dark-haired girl played Eliza Doolittle alongside a bespectacled and lanky boy struggling to come across as the erudite Henry Higgins. But the audience loved them.

And the excerpt from Samuel Beckett's *Waiting for Godot* was performed outstandingly by two teenage boys in dark suits and bowler hats. Between them, they commanded the stage. When their piece came to an end the audience gave them a rapturous applause. The boys left the stage and the curtain closed.

When it opened, a slender woman was seated at the end of a red *chaise longue* set at an angle so the audience could view her in three-quarter profile. The woman was plainly dressed with long fair hair framing a round, nervous face. She was reading a book. Before her stood Varg, his hands in the pockets of his high-waisted pants, his flaming red hair pinned back in a ponytail at the nape of his neck.

He made a gesture.

She looked up at him.

He hesitated.

She mumbled a line.

Their entire performance lacked the repressed ardour and

tension of a Pinter play as if they'd veiled their emotions and motivations so thickly they caused them to vanish.

Yvette wanted to slide from her chair. Thomas remained still but Anthony became fidgety. First he shifted in his seat. Then he leaned his elbow on their shared armrest and slid a hand down his cheek. He winced whenever Varg spoke. Yvette looked over at Anton, now scribbling notes. When Varg and his co-actor bowed to a smattering of light applause, Anton leapt from his seat and made for the stage.

'That was embarrassing,' Anthony whispered loudly.

Yvette was certain those seated nearby had heard him but no one glanced their way. Thomas had his gaze fixed on the row of seats in front of him. In the dim light of the theatre, she couldn't read the expression on his face.

Soon the lights brightened and the actors lined up in order of appearance. They held each other's hands and bowed. The audience came alive with whistles and cheers. Thomas was sitting forward in his seat with hands raised in a steady clap. Even Anthony made an effort to conform, his hands clapping in time with Thomas's.

Anton thanked everyone for coming, the curtain fell and the audience began to filter out.

In the foyer Anthony was acerbic. 'I wouldn't call that acting. Varg mumbled his lines with no conviction whatsoever.'

'Don't be nasty!' Yvette said.

'I'm being honest.' He emitted a supercilious laugh.

'And blunt,' Thomas said, lifting his hand to his mouth to obscure, ineffectively, a titter of his own.

Anthony postured his weight on one leg, hip outthrust, arms folded across his chest, head tilted to the side. 'Where, pray tell, was the emotion?'

'Obviously the part didn't call for any.'

'Oh come on, Yvette! Varg couldn't act his way off the end of a diving board! He's a pretentious loser.'

'What have you got against Varg?' she hissed.

'Oh nothing,' Anthony said with an airy glance at her belly.

She froze. Was there nothing redemptive in Anthony's character? That he would choose to be scathing of the possible father of her children as if to demonstrate to her the depth of her folly was maddening. And, she noted with bewilderment, based on an assumption they both seemed to have made. What could it possibly matter to him anyway? They were barely even friends.

With that last comment Anthony steered Thomas out of the foyer. Thomas looked over his shoulder, pressed his hand to his face in the shape of a phone and mouthed, 'I'll call you.'

She watched them walk across the car park and disappear, the chagrin she felt magnified by her knowledge that they were right. Varg couldn't act. And she hoped neither one of her babies had red hair.

3.18

Another week slid by. Yvette was sitting on the back step overhearing Viktor yelling at his wife and her muted anguished replies. She must have been in the house. Yvette had no idea of the subject of their altercation—the exchange was in Serbian.

A door slammed then all went quiet. Yvette hoped the woman was okay. Viktor appeared an unctuous type capable of brutality across the ironing board.

Any sort of domestic tension reminded her of her father. It was a fast track in her psyche, one the grabbing hand used to whizz her awareness back to her childhood with the alacrity of a bullet. And there she was, standing in the hallway of number fifty-two, facing her father and his two bulging suitcases. He was struggling to open the front door. Tears splashed down his cheeks. She stood firm and urged him on his way. She was sixteen. Her mother was somewhere in the house, probably the garden, and Debbie was hiding in her bedroom. Jimmy was a broken man and they were leaving it to her to bid him goodbye.

Two years later Leah had met and married Joe, and secured permanent residence for the newly rearranged nuclear family to return to Australia, the whole series of events unfolding at a hasty and to this day puzzling pace.

Yvette eased herself to her feet and went inside. She found her phone on her bedside table. She dialled her mother's number and waited.

'Where have you been, Yvette? I've been worried.'

'Didn't you get my texts?'

'I was expecting a phone call.'

'I've been busy.'

'Don't suppose you've heard anything.'

'No.'

Silence.

'How are you?' Yvette said.

'Spent the morning chasing a heifer that had got into the neighbour's paddock. Rolled under the wire. They can be buggers you know.' She went on to deliver a blow-by-blow account of the drama until the heifer was back with the herd, Yvette waiting for a chance to interject.

When Leah's last sentence trailed off, she said, 'Mum, I'm having twins.'

'*Twins?*'

Yvette didn't speak.

'You don't do things by halves. How long have you known?'

'Not long,' she lied.

'And how's the pregnancy?'

'Fine.'

There was another moment of silence.

'Mum?'

'Yes?'

'Why *did* you come back to Australia?'

'He was stalking me.'

'Who?'

'Your father.'

'Stalking?'

'Malicious phone calls at work. Letters to my bosses. His car parked outside the house. There was no end to it.'

'Why didn't you tell me?'

'I did.'

Yvette paused, searching her mind. She only recalled, and dimly at that, her mother's anxiety. Now Leah's swift decision to leave England made sense and Yvette admonished the maverick eraser of her memory. Her mother only wanted what any woman would want, her freedom, a new life far away from the father of her children, turned adversary.

Yvette still despised her father even as she felt for him a sort of sympathy. She wouldn't exist if her mother hadn't married him. It's an odd feeling, wishing you had at least one different parent, when really, you are wishing yourself non-existent. Yvette pictured Leah, sitting on her sofa, her timid face, her white hair thinning around the forehead. He'd beaten the spontaneity out of her. Leah had little choice but to replace it with reserve.

'Why did you marry him?' she said softly.

'To get away from my mother,' she said without hesitation. 'She was too judgemental and interfering.'

For a single ghastly moment Yvette imagined her gran, Leah and her, a trinity sharing unsavoury traits, as if a baton were passed down the generational line. She felt like a cliché tramping through life, oblivious to the ordinariness of her reactions, fighting now against the realisation that, whether by gene or upbringing, there was a part of Leah that lived in her.

She conjured an excuse and hung up her phone.

3.19

An easterly wind fanned hot desert air across the city. Early afternoon and the sea breeze that usually arrived by lunchtime couldn't battle its way across the coast. Yvette knocked on Gordon's front door and immediately heard the shuffle of footsteps. The door opened. 'Come on through.' Gordon hurried her inside before closing the door on the wind.

Inside was cooler, the living room dim with the Venetian blinds closed, but sunshine baked the kitchen window, the curtain that would have shielded the room drawn back to allow in the natural light. Already, sweat prickled on her brow.

She sat before her sketch that Gordon had placed on the table in front of a small easel. On the easel was a canvas. The three still-life objects were gone. Gordon's sketch, lying beside hers, engaged her sharply comparing eye. His was looser in style, more evocative, dramatic. Hers, she had to admit, lacked vigour.

'If you don't mind me saying,' Gordon said, following her gaze, 'your sketch is too literal.'

'I don't mind.'

He took up the chair beside her, squaring his sketch with the edge of the table. Then he picked up a speck of something, standing up again to put it in the kitchen bin and rinsing his hands before returning to his seat.

'Today I thought we might start to paint,' he said, observing her closely.

'So soon?' she said doubtfully.

'Nothing like the deep end.'

'I used to make scores of sketches before I dared approach a canvas.' She emitted an uncertain laugh.

'Let's liberate ourselves. Let the imagination take control.'

Never had a blank canvas appeared more confronting. She was back at school, forced by the curriculum into one tiresome exercise after another, from an upside-down chair to whole lessons devoted to negative space. Looking back she suspected her art teacher drew most of his inspiration from *Drawing on the Right Side of the Brain*. She turned her gaze to her sketch.

'Don't have such high expectations,' Gordon said encouragingly. 'Think of it as playing.'

'Um ... okay.'

She reached for her shoulder bag and pulled out a bundle of brushes and the tubes of acrylic Dan had given her. Before she'd left Heather's house she suspected this would be a painting day although she'd also brought her tin box. Gordon waved back the contents of her bag.

'But ...'

'No buts.'

She breathed a thank you and selected a wide brush from the collection on the table. Gordon squeezed burnt sienna onto a palette, dipped his brush in a jar of water and proceeded to give his canvas a thin undercoat. She did the same.

While they waited for the paint to dry, he said, 'You know what? Kandinsky and Chagall developed as artists through the attention they paid to myth and fairy tale.' He paused. 'Back in a tick.' He placed his hands on his thighs, pushed himself up from his chair and left the room. She was reminded of Josie, the way she would pop her head round the partition wall that separated their studio spaces at Goldsmiths and with an identical 'You know what?' she'd launch into a lengthy explanation of the trouble artists like Séraphine Louis took to find pigments for their paint: the clays, the flowers, the animal blood. It was what drew Josie to Malta, inspired by the rich soils, the honey-coloured stone and the Neolithic heritage. Art, for Josie, was earthy and primal.

Gordon returned with two art books—Kandinsky and Chagall. She wondered then if the source of his interest in the two artists derived from his acquisition of these books, or if he'd chosen the books out of a pre-existing affection for the artists. He handed her the Kandinsky and she leafed through the pages.

'Both used extremes of colour and tone to create tension in their work,' he said, looking on.

He seemed quaint and she admired his naïve yet wholehearted engagement. It had been many years since she'd given either artist more than a cursory glance. Her prejudices seemed to her now as flaky as lime plaster drying in a frost, crumbling from the walls of a false edifice she'd constructed in her mind.

The paint soon dried and they both roughed in the large shapes of the still life. Gordon had become chatty. 'There was a spiritual renewal in art in the early twentieth century,' he said. 'It was an explosion.' He listed scores of artists and movements, all of them famous and none of them Australian. As if he'd swallowed Gombrich like a pill, he supplied a *soupçon* of information for each, bursting forth with enthusiasm as he spoke. She listened politely, watching his gestures, the way he'd jerk a relaxed hand back and forth as if flicking through notes, tilting his head a little, first left, then right, mannerisms she found endearing, what might once have been affectation had become in him natural. She waited for him to finish without interruption.

'Why are you drawn to those particular artists?' she asked, at last keen for clarification.

'Kandinsky and Chagall? Because they both struggled.'

'So many artists do.'

'Maybe all of us.'

'Maybe.'

He lightly touched his canvas. 'The benefits of an easterly.' He began roughing in the darkest areas of his composition. She followed suit. She started to enjoy the uncertainty, the anticipation, knowing she had no idea how this painting would turn out and realising she didn't care.

'Kandinsky had a tough upbringing in Siberia,' he said, returning to his favoured painters. 'And then he was shunned over and again by the conservative art scene in Munich. Chagall was a Jew of course, caught up in both world wars. Here...' He left the room again and returned a short while later with a framed print. '*The Falling Angel*. My favourite.' He gripped the dark wooden frame with both hands, arranging the painting around waist height for her perusal. 'Serves as a memoir of his life. It's all there: war, revolution, persecution, flight, exile.' She stared at the painting, soaking in the drama, the woman painted in the brightest of reds, and there was Gordon himself, and suddenly all of the tribulations expressed in the work were extended beyond the frame.

He took away the painting then returned to sit beside her, dabbing a finger lightly on his canvas. It was dry. Yvette quickly appreciated this simple value of the medium. They both began exploring colours, applying them sparingly, roughly accentuating the features of the bust, the petals, the swirls of the conch.

The afternoon wore on. Gordon gave his work a final flourish of cadmium yellow then jiggled his brush in the water jar and went to make tea. A few more strokes and Yvette plopped her brush alongside his.

Gordon came back and stood behind her.

'See the story emerging?' he said.

'Sort of.'

'You will. This process sidesteps the analytical mind. It's so quick

216

you don't have a chance to pick at what you're doing so the imagination takes over.'

She was impressed. He'd given latitude to expression; he trusted his creativity, whereas she'd spent her artistic life adhering to a bunch of rules. She watched him prepare the teapot with the same fastidious attention she admired last time she was here.

He handed her a slice of orange cake on a small plate replete with silver-plated fork and linen napkin. 'Thank you,' she said, and broke into the cake. It was moist and aromatic, little short of heavenly. 'This is delicious.'

'I made an extra effort,' he said, glancing at her belly, 'for the three of you.'

'We're honoured,' she said. After several more mouthfuls, wondering where next to take the conversation, she said, 'You sound Australian. Were you born here?'

'No. Liverpool. I was sent here in the 1960s. I was five.'

'*Sent?*' I thought the convict era was long gone.'

'I was one of the forgotten children, transported here mostly from orphanages.'

'Transported from orphanages? That's outrageous!' Mrs Thoroughgood never mentioned this part of Australia's migrant history. 'Forgive me,' she added. 'I had no idea that went on.'

'Oh, it did. For decades.'

He poured the tea and passed her a cup and saucer, returning to the kitchen for his own. 'More cake?' he asked, as she finished her last.

'No, no, but thank you.'

He took her plate and set it down in the sink and came back to sit beside her.

Her mind whirled with questions. Who were those orphans? Why were they sent to Australia? What sort of government would dream up such a scheme riven with inhumanity? Where did the children go once they got here? Where were they now? She was in the company of one. It was a sensitive subject but she had to know more.

'What happened to your parents?' she said cautiously.

He placed his cup in its saucer, setting them down on the table. His hands had a slight tremble. 'My mother couldn't cope after my father died, so she gave me up for what she thought would be a better life for me.'

'That must have been so hard, for her and for you.'

'It was. She was French you see. My father was English. They met in Blackpool during the war.' He gazed absently out the window as if beyond the glass the scenes of his past were unfolding. 'And they fell in love. Despite disapproval from both sets of parents, they married and she moved to Liverpool. I came along many years later. A happy accident, you might say.'

'And your father?'

'He was a docker. That day he found himself underneath a falling load. My mother was heartbroken. After she sent me away she went back to France. I had a hard job tracking her down.'

'But you did.'

'Thankfully. Dear Mother. Dear Semille.' He looked wistful. 'She did what she thought was best.'

'And what happened to you?'

'I was sent to Fairbridge Children's Home.'

She stiffened. Fairbridge? It had to be a coincidence, surely not the same place as the festival. Fairbridge, she assured herself, must be a town.

He went to open a drawer in the dresser behind her, lifting out a small photo album. He showed her a photograph of a line of boys of varying ages and sizes standing before an unpainted weatherboard hut. The boys were dressed in shorts and shirts. All of them were smiling.

'Don't be fooled by the smiles. None of us were happy.' He pointed to a scrawny boy at the end of the row. 'Except him.'

'Oh?'

'He came from one hell of a rough background. He was wild when he first came to the home. But he responded well to authority. He liked the discipline.' Gordon froze momentarily. 'He especially liked the hard work. Fairbridge was a farm school you see. We all had to work on the land.'

He closed the album and returned it to the drawer.

3.20

That desolate feeling returned. Setting aside her friendship with Heather and her new bond with Gordon, her friends had become straws, her own heart a grabbing hand. She missed Josie terribly and still no email. She'd often thought of contacting her friend, but her resistance won every time; she must have twenty attempts stored as drafts in her email account. Their friendship demanded resolution like an incomplete artwork waiting for those final brushstrokes to tie the whole thing together. She hadn't heard from Thomas since the play; another friendship requiring resolution, or at the very least an air-clearing conversation.

She was wandering around the back streets of Fremantle's café strip, about to enter a small shop in search of baby toys when, straight ahead of her, walking with a peppy gait, was Thomas. She felt a jolt at the sighting, her world again shrunk by happenstance: from her early encounter with her childhood friend Heather in Pinar's café; the cockroaches in Thomas's old flat driving her to stumble on *Profits of Doom*, opening in her an understanding of asylum seekers she might otherwise never have gained; Thomas introducing her to Dan, who had spontaneously gifted her a trove of art materials; and

Gordon rushing to her assistance in Myer's, with his pre-existing acquaintance with Anthony and the revelation of his sad childhood spent at Fairbridge children's home—the very same town that was hosting a music festival in which she was to sing in a choir. Little synchronicities, or all pure chance, nothing to do with fate, could happen to anyone. Yet part of her shimmied at the notion that her own thoughts carried the power to manifest, like devil talk, and there was no way of knowing where it was all heading, if it was heading anywhere at all.

Dressed in a colourful short-sleeved shirt and jeans, with a black beret tilted to the side, he looked altogether different from the uptight and scuttling Thomas of a few weeks before. She hardly recognised him. He was about to walk past her when she called out his name.

He turned in the direction of her voice, looking puzzled. Then a light of recognition appeared in his face.

'Yvette!'

'Fancy bumping into you.'

They grinned at each other.

'How are you?'

She refrained from telling him the despondency she felt now her bump had become larger than a watermelon. She didn't want to incur a told-you-so reproach.

'You look so different,' she said quickly.

'So do you.' His gaze did a sweep of her torso.

She emitted a short laugh. 'No, really. You've changed.'

'I left my computer programming job. I'm teaching English as a second language and best of all,' he said enthusiastically, 'I've a lead role in a play. We open at the Deck Chair Theatre in April.'

It was an astonishing transformation, like a costume change for the next act. 'You must come along.'

'I'd love to.'

'Here.' He unravelled a poster from a roll under his arm.

'Orpheus Descending,' she read aloud.

'It's a Tennessee Williams play.'

'Is this with Anton?'

'Yes. He auditioned his most promising students,' he said with a measure of pride.

'Congratulations, Thomas. You must be thrilled.'

She wished she could attach to her words more sincerity than she felt. Their lives had cleaved on different trajectories, his filled with creative expression, hers with babies, ultimate creation in the first instance, giving birth to new life, yet filled with obligation and responsibility and hardship and no doubt relentless selflessness. She was jealous of his freedom. And there was something else in his manner. She wondered if he were still with Anthony. It seemed impolite to ask.

'We must stay in touch,' she said.

'Here's my new number. I guess that's why I haven't heard from you these last weeks. I changed my number. I had a heavy breather.'

They both laughed. Yet he hadn't bothered to call her and she never called him.

3.21

Saturday and she woke again low in spirits. She lay on her back, eyes fixed on the ceiling. She heard footsteps in the hall. There was a knock and Heather peered round the door and asked if she fancied a cuppa before disappearing back to the kitchen. Yvette turned on her side then raised herself upright, kicking aside the twin-rearing guidebook she'd been reading last night. She pulled on a thin dressing gown and traipsed across the hall.

'You look tired,' Heather said.

'I'm okay, well, sort of.'

'What's the matter?'

'I'm exhausted.'

'I can imagine.' Her voice was warm. 'I thought you might be feeling weighed down.'

The kettle boiled and Heather poured the water into two large cups. Then she went to the pantry and took out a large round tin. 'Tell me when,' she said, knife poised over a date and walnut cake, arcing slowly until Yvette called out. Heather placed the slice on a plate and passed it along the counter. 'That's for starters,' she said, heading for the fridge.

Yvette watched Heather slice bread for toast, then fry bacon, mushrooms, halves of tomato and eggs in a cast-iron frying pan. Admiring Heather's capable ease she realised her friend had taken the place of her mother. No, more than that, she was the mother Yvette never had. And in Gordon, with his avuncular nature, a father. He was the kindest older man she had ever met. It was as if she'd acquired new parents. She continued to admire her friend, the self-assurance, the ease with which she went about her day.

'How did you become a holistic counsellor?' she asked, baffled as to how anyone whose mother had abandoned them could dedicate their lives to helping others.

'Ah, the march of the wound. I studied psychology at university, found the course too mainstream and branched off into myotherapy then holistic counselling.'

'Do you enjoy it?'

'Immensely.'

All this achievement, and here Yvette was delivering junk mail. She changed the subject, asking if Heather had heard from Angus—she hadn't—before searching for other topics of conversation and realising the limits of their bond, circumscribed by their shared past, a place she had little desire to visit, and choir. She never talked to Heather about Malta. Or London. Or Art.

They were silent for a while.

'Heather?' she said cautiously, hoping the answer to a question that had been nagging her for days would not be the one she anticipated.

'Yes?'

'Can you tell me where in Fairbridge is the Fairbridge Music Festival.'

'Fairbridge isn't a town. It's a children's home.'

Yvette was silent. Her guts did a single somersault. Flashing into her mind was that photograph of Gordon standing in a row of boys with forced smiles before an unpainted weatherboard hut. Who would choose to hold a music festival at a former children's home? It would be like Hogmanay at Bethlem. She didn't mention her misgivings. Heather passed her a plate of the most delicious-looking breakfast she'd ever seen. She picked up her fork.

3.22

The choir were midway through the sweet lullaby, 'Inannay', when they entered the hall. After Heather's sumptuous breakfast they'd spent the morning attending to the laundry and household chores and compiling a list of baby things, which Heather pinned to the fridge. Now Fran, Sue, Beth and Karen were standing at the back of the altos.

Yvette stood beside Fran, catching her eye with a light smile. Fran smiled back. Without hesitation Yvette joined in the chorus, her voice blending with the others, carried along by that swell of voices, rising and falling, the different pitches of the three-part harmony merging and surging forth in sublime dovetail.

The song finished and Fran turned and folded Yvette in her arms.

'How *are* you?' she whispered in Yvette's ear.

Yvette hugged her back, somewhat surprised by the familiarity. When she loosened her arms Yvette said, 'I'm good. And you?'

'Hectic, but I'll live.'

Yvette had no idea what she meant.

She was about to ask when Fiona, who Yvette could barely see past the gathering of altos in front of her, called out. 'That was wonderful. I think we've nailed it. See you all next week and thanks for coming.'

Yvette looked inquiringly at Fran.

'I was late too. Last week she moved the time forward. We start at one now.'

'Ah,' she said, vowing not to miss another rehearsal. She turned to Heather. 'Do you have time for a coffee?'

Heather glanced down at her watch.

'Sure.'

'Gino's?'

'Where else?'

They said their goodbyes to the others and left the hall.

They headed down South Terrace past the shops and cafes housed in the prettily painted neo-colonial buildings, protected by awnings from the sting of the sun, their skin cooled slightly by the sea breeze. They chatted about choir. They were two friends enjoying each other's company. Yvette could have remained in that zone of polite conviviality, but her urge to vent her woes grew with every step.

They crossed the road and entered the café. After a short while in the queue, they ordered at the counter and sat at a table nearby. There was nothing at Gino's that was soft or intimate, nothing to suggest that it might serve as a sort of secular confessional, but the effect of the bustle of customers, their voices blending with the hiss and clatter behind the counter and reverberating round the walls in a dull roar, the cosmopolitan flavour of the room with its high windows and al fresco seating, and Heather herself, buxom, wholesome and kind, and an avalanche of divulgences tumbled out of Yvette: Carlos, the abortion, the palm reader, the triptych of men and her mounting desperation. Blood coloured her cheeks. She felt awkward and uncertain but she couldn't stop the flow.

'I'm worried sick, Heather.'

'I thought you might be. They sure like to keep you waiting.'

'Immigration? I know. Part of me hopes they'll lose my file.' She looked down. She had to be sure she wasn't overstaying her welcome at Heather's as well, although even after the list of baby things pinned to the fridge nothing would convince her that she wasn't. 'I can't stay with you forever,' she said, lifting her gaze.

'Take as long as you need.'

'But you won't want a house full of nappies and crying babies.'

'Might be a challenge, but what are friends for?' She gave Yvette an understanding smile.

'No, Heather. It'll be too much.'

Yvette took a sip of coffee. An ebullient young woman and her ebullient young man walked by with their ebullient young brood. Heather followed Yvette's gaze to where the family had gathered round the counter. 'What about your mother?'

'Mum?'

'Do you think she'll come over to help?'

'She hasn't mentioned it. I'm sure she thinks if she holds out, I'll go back.'

'It won't be long and you'll be unfit for travel.'

They both glanced at Yvette's ballooning belly.

3.23

The house was quiet. Yvette slumped down the hall and slung her junk-mail bags in her room before heading to the kitchen to make tea. She was about to sit on the back step when her phone rang. She pressed the phone to her ear. It was her mother.

'I have some news,' Leah said without preface.

Yvette waited, expecting another account of Debbie's wrangling with Peter's teacher over her son's lackadaisical approach to handwriting.

'Debbie's pregnant.'

'*Again?*'

'Don't. She's having twins.'

'Twins?'

'You better phone her and tell her you're pleased.'

She would, once she'd gotten past feeling trumped. She was uneasy too. Now that Debbie was pregnant, and with twins, her mother would not even consider flying to Perth to help her. How could her sister be so thoughtless? No, that was ludicrous, but she struggled to continue the conversation and quickly broke into her mother's flow with a quick excuse and hung up. She felt like an outcast.

3.24

She'd begun to waddle. Try as she might to maintain a normal gait, her belly was so swollen she had no choice but to lumber behind it. She was growing more tired by the day, prone to spells of breathlessness and endless trips to the toilet. One afternoon she alighted the bus to Gordon's house succumbing to a sudden dizzy rush. The day was warm and bright and she stood in the shade of his veranda and waited for the panting to subside before she knocked.

Gordon opened the door wide and beamed at her. 'Come on in.'

In his presence she felt alive and full of optimism, as if in entering his house she were stepping into an alternate reality, one of benevolence, creativity and joy. She followed him to the kitchen, set up as before, the two easels side-by-side, and tubes of acrylic, brushes and a jar of clean water laid out on the table.

At first glance her painting held a surprising appeal. 'You like what you see?' he said, standing beside her.

'I think I do.'

'Excellent.' He made a wide sweep of his arm. 'Shall we?'

'Yes.'

'Then let the fun begin.'

They took up their chairs like two enthusiasts waiting for the starting gun.

This time she applied paint spontaneously, yet not with reckless abandon, more an intuitive pulse, that led her first here then there, taking in the curves, sweeps, accents, negative space and highlights in turn. The flower began to burst with life, the bust more human with every brush stroke, the shell revealing its hidden depths in the shadows, the form emerging out of deep shade like nature's lamp. With Gordon beside her, his flourishes and steady craftsmanship seeping into her like osmosis, it was a miraculous hour. Too soon Gordon was filling the kettle.

'Gordon?' she said tentatively, at once not wanting to proceed with what she was about to say, yet realising if she didn't it would be a betrayal of their friendship.

'Yes, my dear?'

'I'm going to Fairbridge.'

He hesitated. 'And why would you be going there?'

'For the music festival. I'm in a choir.'

'Oh, my,' he said, bringing a hand flat to his chest.

'I'm sorry. I've upset you.'

'No, no,' he said, although clearly flustered. 'Just taken by surprise.'

'You knew a festival is held there?'

'Yes. It's a space for hire these days. And a museum.'

'I won't go,' she said, suddenly not wanting to trample his past.

'You must. You are an artist,' he said. 'You must go as an artist.'

She doubted her ability to do anything of the sort.

He continued to prepare the tea.

'I can't imagine what it must have been like for you,' she said as he handed her a plate of blackcurrant cheesecake. 'I'd have crumbled under the institutionalisation of it all.'

'I did.' He went back to the kitchen bench. 'I spent two decades of my adult life an alcoholic.' He returned with the tea. 'Then there was the spell in Graylands.'

'The mental hospital?'

'Best place for me at the time. I was a lunatic and it was an asylum.'

'Sounds dreadful.' She was appalled and impressed all at once, by the frankness, the honesty, the willingness to reveal.

He went on. 'It was hell. But it was my own emotional hell. It took me a long time to take responsibility for myself.' He reached for his tea, taking a slow sip before returning the cup to its saucer. 'Anyway, I came good in the end. After I reunited with Semille.'

'That's nice.'

'It was then I learnt about love. You see, the legacy of those homes, above and beyond the abuses, is that you don't know how to love.'

'You seem very loving to me.'

She took a mouthful of the cheesecake and swooned. It was luscious, so smooth and tangy. 'You made this?' she said.

'Of course.'

'It's divine.'

'You are very kind, Yvette.' He looked into her face. 'Something tells me you've been through a lot too.'

'Nothing compared to you.'

'Now why am I finding that hard to believe?'

She reached for her tea wondering how he could see into her past.

3.25

The following Saturday afternoon, Yvette headed down High Street in Fremantle's northeast, carrying with her an ambivalent curiosity; she'd never seen Thomas act. She couldn't imagine him being anyone other than himself, nervous, neurotic, introspective, with an appalling taste in men.

Deckchair Theatre was housed in Victoria Hall. Surrounded by a nonsense of modern building design, the hall was classically symmetrical in style, its stucco façade replete with pilasters and parapet. She rushed through the entrance doors. She was late. Her mother had phoned as she was about to leave the house and before she had a chance to interject, proceeded with a litany of questions and advice concerning her residency application and had she thought about finding a lawyer just in case. She suspected Leah had seen something on television. No word about Terry or Debbie this time. She hung up as soon as she could but missed the bus and had to wait half an hour for another.

There was a woman seated at a small table inside the hall. Yvette rifled through the contents of her shoulder bag then, feigning apology, held the woman's gaze and asked for the concession price of ten dollars. The woman didn't ask for identification.

She walked through to the auditorium, cavernous with rows of temporary seats arranged before the stage. She took a seat in the back row. The seats in front of her were occupied by men and women of all ages, dressed smartly as if their very clothes anticipated a quality performance.

The curtain rose. The stage was set out as a dry-goods store in southern America in the fifties. Lining a back wall were wooden shelves filled with tins, glass jars, earthenware jugs and wicker baskets. Two chairs and a round table were set to one side. And there was Thomas, casually dressed in an open-neck shirt and loose pants, leaning against a high wooden counter, fingering an old-style cash register. A middle-aged and coquettish woman in a calf-length dress and pillbox hat walked on stage. She approached Thomas, curls bobbing, lashes fluttering. And in about half a minute Yvette realised she'd been mistaken: Thomas really could act. In fact, he was superb, all smouldering passion and erotic intensity. He wasn't playing Val, he was Val. The drawl, the mannerisms, every gesture and posture, from the way he leaned across the counter to his movements about the stage.

She was not the only one impressed. As the curtain descended on the second act the audience applauded energetically, and when the curtain rose and Thomas bowed there were whistles and cheers.

Yvette hung back as the audience filtered out the room. The theatre emptied and she wondered if she should leave when Anton approached her inquiringly and, once she'd explained, promptly sent off the ticket woman hovering nearby to search backstage for Thomas.

Before long, Thomas appeared through a side door and walked towards her with a swift glance at her belly. She held out her arms and hugged him fondly. 'You were amazing.'

'Thanks.' He was flushed and slightly breathless.

'Where's Anthony?' she said, glancing around.

'We've split up.'

She searched his face. He didn't appear troubled. 'For good?' she asked.

'For good.'

They chatted briefly about the wonderful opportunities Perth afforded, Thomas with sincere enthusiasm, Yvette struggling to concur. Sensing he was about to walk away, she said, 'Will you go back to England?' not even knowing why she asked the question, noting that she didn't care how he answered.

'What for?'

'I mean, now you're not with Anthony.'

'I have no one there.'

'Your mother?'

'She passed away last month.'

'I'm sorry.'

'Don't be. It took my mother's death to show me how callous Anthony can be.'

She was curious, imagining the airy quips, but refrained from prying. 'I wondered when you'd realise,' she said.

'The power of lust.' He let out a snigger. 'The truth is, I feel liberated.'

'I'm really pleased for you,' she said with genuine warmth. And she realised while she'd been screwing up her life, he'd found himself. He shone, radiant as a summer sun, their lives on two distinct paths, his now a sojourn through a fete in a park, hers more a stony descent through the gloom of a haunted wood.

'I don't suppose you have time for a coffee,' she said.

'Sorry. I have a rehearsal. Never stops.'

'Another play?'

'No. The Romanas. We're playing at the Fairbridge Music Festival.'

'Then I'll see you there.'

'You're going?' He sounded astonished.

'I'll be singing in the Cushtie Chanters,' she said, grinning with sudden pride and amazement, realising it was the first time she'd valued her participation in the choir. She'd never doubted they sounded good, but the Cushtie Chanters had always been to her just a choir.

She gave him another hug and watched him walk back to the stage.

3.26

The day was hot and windy, the pavement had little shade. Following her doctor's advice, she'd enrolled in natural birthing classes at a community centre on South Terrace. She lumbered on down the road, knowing she was late. Ten minutes after the time she needed to leave she'd been caught in a hiatus of doubt about whether or not to ask Heather to join her. She'd decided to go alone, leaving Heather at home and unaware. The intimacy had seemed too much, even as she thought her friend might be waiting to be asked.

The community centre must once have been a family home. She pulled open the gate, then a few paces later the fly screen.

Inside, the original weatherboard cottage was high ceilinged with rooms to either side of a wide hallway. She followed a sign cut in the shape of an arrow, entering a spacious back-room extension with glass sliding doors opening onto a children's play area. Already in the room were eight birthing pairs, each pregnant woman sitting on a yoga mat with her partner beside her. The instructor, a slim woman in her forties, had the ultra-alive demeanour of a gym trainer. She glanced at Yvette and pointed to a vacant mat near the sliding doors.

'My name's Susie,' she said, 'for the benefit of the late arrival.'

There was a murmur of laughter. Yvette eased her body down on a vacant mat, ignoring the inquisitive eyes of the others.

Susie rummaged through a holdall, removing a plastic pelvis and a large wide-eyed doll. She explained the processes of head engagement and cervix dilation from zero to the critical ten centimetres, swiping the doll through the pelvis with a scoop of an arm to simulate the passage of the baby through the birth canal. 'No matter how severe the contractions,' she said with a wagging finger and a cheesy wink, 'you must not push until the cervix is fully dilated.' She looked at all the mothers-to-be with a knowing smile on her face. 'You'll want to push, believe me. Once the cervix has reached seven centimetres the labour goes into what we call transition and the contractions are more frequent and more intense.' She put down the pelvis and the doll. 'Birthing partners, this is where you come in.' She scanned the room, eyeballing each partner. 'It's a breathing exercise. Puff, puff, blow.' She inhaled then puffed out two short blasts of air followed by one long rush. 'Come on everyone, puff, puff, blow.'

The whole room puffed and blowed and puffed and blowed. It was a ludicrous scene, the women and their partners engaging in the exercise with incredible zeal. They seemed almost professional, perhaps into their second or third child. Yvette's debut on the birthing scene was lacklustre. Seated in this room she confronted the full force of a disconnect between replacing a lost foetus and actually wanting to have the babies growing inside her. She felt like a fraud.

Susie moved on to the next phase of the demonstration, calling the group to attention with a raised hand. 'Sometimes mum-to-be experiences back pain,' she said. 'Birthing partners, you can help with gentle massage. Like this.' She squatted down behind the pregnant woman nearest her and massaged her lower back.

The other birthing partners copied her. Yvette glanced around the room. All the partners had a caring look about them and displayed keen interest and dedication. They really wanted to help.

Now she regretted not asking Heather. She'd never felt abandonment like this before. She anticipated her impending parenthood with horror.

Susie came over and kneeled behind her, whispering in her ear not to worry. But she couldn't stop the welling of tears.

3.27

The following evening, she lumbered down to South Terrace like a weighed-down mule. She had to whip her haunches to keep going, giddy herself up to the next letterbox, her will locked in battle with her resistance.

At the corner, she stood and looked down the street at the cars heading her way. The pavements were flat and flanking all the side streets, the old sandstone houses with their small gardens tucked behind stone walls and high fences were comforting and alienating all at once. Inside those homes, families were watching television or eating dinner, having a glass of wine, smiling, laughing, maybe playing board games like Scrabble or reading a book. All this while she plopped junk mail in their letterboxes on her way by.

Her bags were empty when she came to the end of South Terrace. She crossed Wilson Park and went on through the car park and down a sandy track through the sand dunes. The beach was deserted. Eager waves slapped the shore in a rhythmic crash, rush and suck. The sun had set and the sky was clear. There was no moon. The city lights cast a dull pinkish sheen on the sky to the north and east. She made out Orion and the Southern Cross. She tried to find a constellation of the zodiac, Libra maybe, but she had no idea where to look or even what to look for.

The stars winked indifferently. They were mute. Despite what astrologers believe, the stars could tell you nothing. They were useless. Worse than useless, she thought, if you imbue them with portentous power. Patterns in the stars were like lines in a palm. She was astounded by her own stupidity, giving in to a grief-induced wish, standing here now with her bulging belly, the product of one of a triptych of entirely undesirable men. She pictured her mother's tight-lipped ethnocentric chagrin at the very thought of any of them being the father of her grandchildren. Her own view of the contenders cohered with her mother's for entirely different reasons: Varg the Viking seemed a vainglorious man with pretentions not far short of delusional; Lee with his half-Portuguese, half-Chinese heritage, treated his consorts like pieces of furniture; and Dimitri the Russian scarcely knew the difference between seduction and violation.

She took off her sandals. The sand was cold. She went to the waterline and let the shallow wash sweep over her feet and draw back again, enjoying the cool water rippling against her skin, and the fresh, tangy smell of it. Then she walked to the heads.

What should she do? It was too late to fly back to her mother's farm. She hated to admit Leah was right; she should have married Terry, or someone, anyone. Should she get married after all? Yet who would take her now, even as a favour? Her, an English-born chancer? When genuine asylum seekers had a far more compelling justification for such an act, even a woman who was pregnant with another man's child. Unlike them, she'd brought this entire situation upon herself.

She turned and stared back along the beach and the houses beyond. She envied Heather then, her cosseted life in Fremantle, comfortable on a large income, assured a stable life. She envied Debbie, with her hubby and her two boys scampering about on the farm. They had life too easy, for sure. She envied Thomas, who had found himself here in Perth after months of anguish yearning for a life with Anthony. She envied Gordon for coming to terms with his troubled past. She even envied Angus his casual will, the easy way he pursued his goals.

She went back along the beach, then on through the park, where she dusted her feet free of sand and slipped on her sandals. It was a long walk home. With every step she tried to clear the turmoil from her mind. Instead she added to her discomfiture two burning thighs and a couple of blisters on her feet.

3.28

The days and weeks wore on and with each sunrise Yvette withdrew a little more from the world around her. She forced herself out of the house when she had to deliver junk mail or visit the doctor for a pregnancy check-up. Even choir was a drain on her scant energy, and the trip to Gordon's house for painting sessions were now too far. After her last visit, she'd phoned to explain, insisting he keep her painting. Sadness had tightened her throat, not knowing when or even if she'd see him again. She couldn't face calling Thomas. She suffered her mother's occasional phone calls, ignoring her advice and her references to Terry, annoyed each time that she didn't offer to visit. She spent her days waddling about the house, listless and bored. Nothing held her interest. She was floating about on a dead calm sea, waiting.

It was Easter Saturday, and after trying to read another book on rearing twins, she retired early, drifting to sleep to the soft tones of Heather's meditation music spilling through the adjoining wall.

The house was silent when she opened her eyes and lay on her side staring into the dark. Somewhere in the house there was a creak. Then another. Was it the timbers contracting in the cool? Or something else? Dark panic invaded her, an army of tense pulses. There was a presence, she was sure there was a presence in the hallway, right outside her bedroom door. Where was Heather? She huddled down and threw the doona over her head, the dark menace now hovering right above her. She was terrified. Each breath an effort. She couldn't move. She was a child filled with dread, unable to emerge from beneath the covers, unable to stop the loud thump of her heartbeat.

She woke to flashes of memory, sharp as knives, of lying in a bed, alone in a house, petrified. Her mind whirled in feverish desperation. She was five, she was ten, she was all the other ages when the night terrors had consumed her. She thought she'd outgrown them. The terrors hadn't consumed her since she was eighteen. Why now? What the hell was going on?

The terror diffused, leaving her father's footsteps carved in the landscape of her mind. After a decade of resistant determination never to walk that trail, now she felt doomed to follow, her mind trotting back through her past like a dutiful dog. Somewhere inside of her, she was an island. An island so young it never had a chance to know itself before the fissures in him spewed their molten rock; before cascades of his invasive ash crippled every living cell of her.

And in a flash of illumination that made her mind boom with the sheer force of it, she knew that all her adult life she'd been an island lost to itself, lost to the world, trapped beneath this kernel of his alien matter. Now her father filled her with his presence and along with the terror of him she felt a thick treacle of loathing. Not only had his temper been a scourge in her childhood, his very existence was her only obstacle to staying in this country, and she blamed him then, for everything.

That morning Heather left for Rockingham to visit her father. Over breakfast, she pressed Yvette with an invitation, but no, there was something she needed to do. A look of concern had appeared in Heather's face. Yvette reassured her friend with an 'I'll be fine', and waved her goodbye. Then she went straight through the house to the back garden and on to the shed. Angus had left behind all the paraphernalia of his bus renovation, various lengths of battening timber and pine-lining boards, scraps of carpet and old cupboard doors. Stacked against the back wall were sheets of recycled plywood in a range of sizes. Yvette pulled out the sheet second from the front, about a metre by a metre and a half. She carried the sheet to the garden where she propped it on the edge of an old table, the plywood leaning against the back fence. She hesitated and went inside the house, returning with a handful of Dan's brushes and an old newspaper.

She went back to the shed and scanned the tins of acrylic paint that Angus had used on the bus. Among an array of colours there was a large tin of white, a small tin of pillbox red and another of bright blue, and an unopened tin of black. She took a floor brush with her and gave the plywood a thorough sweep before spreading out the newspaper. She returned to the shed and using an old screwdriver levered the lids off the paint tins and took them outside. Her alfresco studio was complete. Normally she sat when she worked on a painting. This time she stood.

She was barely aware of the hebe hedge that ran the full length of the side fence, in full bloom and covered in ecstatic bees. The hills hoist, the border of impatiens edging the wide strip of crazy paving directly outside the house, the row of furrows filled with herbs and leafy greens, the paperbark over by the shed that provided much needed shade, even the day itself, the heat building steadily as the sun arced higher—none of this she took in, yet no image filled her mind.

She dipped the largest of Dan's round brushes into the red and swirled the paint round and round in the centre of the board. Then she took another brush and smeared black around the red. Her brushstrokes were thick and unmeasured. She'd never before painted so fast and without method or design.

The form of a body emerged from the red centre and as she

streaked the paint down the plywood she succumbed to an upsurge of feeling she couldn't make sense of.

She dropped her brush and took a step back. It was an unbearable step. She was compelled forward again. She needed to be closer, needed to merge with the work. She no longer cared what the painting looked like. All that mattered was her intimate proximity, as if an inch of distance were an ache of miles.

Without a moment of hesitation she plunged a hand into the tin of blue and slapped the paint onto the plywood. The paint was slippery and cold. And delicious. She dipped first one hand, then the other, in black and red and white and blue, and smeared on the paint in an eruption of creative impulses, a frenzy of colours she stretched this way and that with her fingers and palms, creating the belly, the breasts, arms akimbo, legs splayed. She was at one with her creation, as if the paint on her fingers were her own blood.

She was molten.

At last, after time that was no time, she stood back again. And there the woman was, in perfect proportion, reclining, her torso receding from the red at the centre, her womanhood. Yvette had no idea how she managed to produce a form satisfying to the eye.

A headless form, for she'd given her woman no head, because her woman had no head.

IV
_____
FOUR

4.1

The hotter than average autumn lingered on. Yvette woke to the comforting sounds of Heather moving about in the kitchen. The fridge door opened and closed. There were chinks of cutlery and plates, the rustle of paper. Before long a soft knock on her door and in walked her friend with a mug of tea.

'Here you go,' she said with a motherly smile.

'Thank you.'

'Breakfast in five,' she said, drawing the curtains on her way out.

Yvette turned on her side. She could scarcely believe she'd woken in this room every morning for months, ensconced by Heather's earthy femininity that was in every colour of paint and texture of fabric, in the vibe her friend created that emanated from even the floorboards that shone honey brown, a room that had replaced her bedroom in Carlos's house in her heart. Looking back, that room was austere, with its white walls, heavy beams bearing down from the great height of the ceiling, the dark timbers of the four-poster, the antique lace that covered the old dressers, the bedside tables and the bed in ivory and white, a room that had matched perfectly the crispness of her mood.

She turned to face the window. The sky was a wash of pale aqua. The sun had yet to crest the low roofs of the suburb. She watched a magpie peck about on the lawn. Then she raised herself up on her pillows and sipped her tea.

Her painting was leaning against the wall over by the door. Once the paint had dried that day, she'd taken the plywood inside. After scrubbing her hands and forearms, she'd searched through the large pile of magazines Angus had left in the living room, a distasteful collection of soft porn and cars. She'd torn photograph after photograph of semi-naked women with over-sized breasts and come-hither gazes and once she had a sizeable pile she hacked off heads and sliced round bikini bottoms, leaving a smaller pile of dismembered limbs and torsos.

She arranged the fragments into a flesh collage, loosely in the shape of a teardrop. Satisfied, she glued the collage to her painting between the woman's splayed legs.

Next, she tackled the head. It seemed wrong to leave her figure headless, yet another collage didn't seem right. She felt like a thief ransacking draws and cupboards in the kitchen, laundry and bathroom; there had to be something in Heather's house that would be just right.

Eventually, in the bottom drawer of the bathroom cabinet, she found a small round unframed mirror.

And the artwork was complete.

Heather returned about an hour later. Yvette had tidied up the house and garden and was in the kitchen taking in her artwork propped against the back door, unsure what to make of it.

'You've been busy,' Heather said, wrapping an arm around her waist.

'Do you like it?'

'It's amazing.'

Yvette looked at her friend and waited for her to say more. Heather observed the work in silent admiration. At last she said, 'Makes quite a statement.'

Yvette was puzzled. To her, the work was cathartic, nothing more.

'The mirror seems to be inviting the viewer to look at herself.' Heather gestured with her hand as she spoke. 'And the body is giving birth to despair.'

'That hadn't occurred to me.'

'It hadn't?'

'Do you really like it?'

'I love it. It's so ... primal.'

Yvette stared again at the woman emerging from the black and the blue, the red in the centre blending with the softer tones of the belly and thighs.

'Where did you find the materials?'

'Um ...' She looked sheepishly at Heather. 'The whole thing is the result of your brother. I found the plywood and old tins of paint in the shed.'

'Glad you found a use for that stuff. And the collage?'

'I raided the *Ralphs*.'

Heather laughed. 'About time they went into the recycling.'

She finished her tea and slipped out of bed, wrapping a sarong around her belly. Before she left the room she caught an image of her profile in the wardrobe mirror, the swollen breasts matching the swell of her belly, the buttocks that had taken on ballast in counterbalance. The base of her spine had developed a sharp curve. She looked full term. Strangely, and despite her eternal preference for the svelte, she felt complacent. The pregnancy had long been a condition that couldn't be changed. And her gravid form was temporary. She would shrink again. What was immutable, carved as if in marble, was a future of motherhood. Yet she couldn't judge her instincts even as she knew they'd betrayed her. Common sense had taken a holiday the moment she set foot on Malta's shores. By the time she'd arrived in Australia little wonder she'd mistaken her fate. She faced the mirror and watched her reflection smile. Foolish woman. Nut.

Awaiting her in the kitchen was a plate of scrambled eggs

topped with grated cheese and chives, garnished with quarters of tomato and surrounded by slices of lightly buttered wholemeal toast.

'Just in time,' Heather said, sitting down to a plate of the same.

Yvette marvelled over her friend's unwavering propensity for home and hearth. 'You are an angel,' she said.

'Tuck in,' Heather flicked open a holistic health magazine and read an article as she ate. When she finished she drew together her knife and fork and said, 'Ready in an hour?'

Heather's question prompted in Yvette a jolt of apprehension. Today they were going to Fairbridge. 'Yep,' she said, and continued to eat.

An hour later, Yvette glanced around the bedroom, checking she had all she needed before grabbing her shoulder bag, packed with clothes for the weekend. Heading outside she noticed the unseasonal autumn heat, the brightness of the sun. Her time in Perth so far had been one long summer.

Heather was waiting in the car. Once Yvette had eased herself into the passenger seat, she backed out of the driveway and drove off down the street. Yvette leaned back in her seat. Heather had packed, loaded the car and now she was chauffeur.

They passed a for-sale sign outside one of the houses near the corner of the next street.

'It must be great to live here,' Yvette said.

'You do live here,' Heather said with a short laugh.

'I mean own something.' She paused, taking in the charming frontages of the houses passing by. 'How long have you lived in your house?'

'Five years.'

'I don't think I've lived anywhere for that long.'

'Time to grow some roots.'

'I'd never afford the deposit.'

'Yeah. These houses are expensive. I guess I was lucky.'

'Did you win the lottery?' Yvette wondered how anyone could

accumulate enough wealth in the first decade of adulthood to afford even a small square of lawn in Fremantle.

Heather turned into Hampton Road. 'No. The house was my mother's. She left it to me in her will.'

'That must have been weird. I mean, considering.'

'It was. I think of it as my mother's way of atoning.'

'Doesn't it feel strange living there?'

'I'm used to it. Although I do think it's ironic that my fate was determined by guilt.'

Even so, Heather's life seemed all bon bons in cellophane tied off with a pretty gold bow.

Yvette wound down her window and watched the humdrum suburb of Hamilton Hill slip by, the suburban houses contrasting poorly with the quaint streets of Fremantle. Heather's driving was reassuring and Yvette felt a wave of contentment, as if she were protected by the soft gauze of Heather's presence.

Heading south they took the Coogee route to Kwinana, and before long they came to an intersection, where the alumina refinery perfumed the air, a distinctly metallic odour that Yvette found instantly nauseating.

'I hate that smell,' she said. 'Reminds me of my father's clothes.'

'It reminds me of my mother.'

'Your mother worked there too?'

'In the office.'

Yvette gave Heather a quick glance. She looked troubled. She said no more as she turned into the next road. Following the signs for Rockingham and Safety Bay, she held a steady speed in the inside lane, indifferent to the four-wheel drives whizzing by on their right. Several minutes passed before she spoke again.

'Yvette,' she said cautiously. 'I have something to tell you. I think you have a right to know.' There was an apprehension in her tone that made Yvette uneasy.

'Go on.'

'You had no idea that my mother knew your father?'

'No.' Although it did seem plausible. She pictured her father as she always did, with a toothy grin and an unrelenting blink, a caricature that made him seem at once ridiculous and harmless, now standing in the refinery office in his overalls.

'They knew each other very well,' Heather said.

'Really?'

'They had an affair.'

'What?!' For a few moments her mind was a dizzy rush. She wondered if there were other vile deeds of which she knew nothing, realising straight away that what she already knew was bad enough. The curious thing was she found it hard to imagine her father a seducer; she assumed her own contempt and Leah's contempt were fragments of a universal contempt and without exception. 'How do you know?' she said.

'My father found out.'

'Shit.'

Little wonder Heather had waited all this time to tell her.

'So he threw your mother out?'

'No. She left. But I didn't find out why until I reunited with her.'

It took Yvette some time to take it all in. She thought Heather's eagerness to catch up with her, her warmth and willingness to let her live in her house, were based on simple goodwill. It had even crossed her mind in one of her more paranoid moments that her friend might have developed an attachment to her that went beyond friendship, musings she quickly dismissed upon the absence of evidence, Heather having made not even a hint of an assignation. Now Yvette felt strangely responsible yet powerless to atone for her father's actions. What he had done was beyond fixing. Even an apology seemed pointless.

'I'm sorry. I'm really sorry,' she said.

'I'm sorry to spin you out.'

She felt bonded to Heather now in a way she could never have imagined. Of all the people she might have met in Perth, Heather had come into her life that day in the café, a woman who looked familiar, and she'd felt an echo of the sad little girl who never got to parade about in a pretty dress.

Heather must have felt something similar. 'Somehow I always knew I'd meet you again one day,' she said.

As they approached the sprawling housing estates of Rockingham, thoughts stampeded through Yvette's mind like a herd of startled gazelles. She blinkered her vision, not wanting to take in a place that was once, for her, hell: a place where her father betrayed her mother, and Heather's father; an affair that caused Heather's mother to abandon her own daughter.

She felt better once they were on the straight stretch of road heading to Mandurah and she could look out at the flat sandy plain of salt bush and grass trees.

'You know, I can't understand why my father didn't go back to Scotland after that,' Heather said casually.

'Maybe he was settled.'

'No. He still isn't. Dyed in the wool Scottish nationalist. You should hear him on Anzac Day. He rants to anyone who'll listen, raving on about Australia's stuck-on American culture. He reckons "Lest We Forget" should be "God, we've forgotten".'

Yvette laughed. 'He's right. I think I like your dad.'

'He doesn't understand that most migrants come here to escape economic insecurity. They want a better life.'

'I guess what he's saying is they might not find one.'

They slipped into silence. The road went on through the unchanging landscape. Yvette adjusted her seatbelt that had started to pinch.

She was wondering what to talk about when Heather said, 'Life is strange.'

'Sure is.'

'It can be a long hard road. And sometimes it's a razorback with a precipice to either side.'

What did she mean?

Heather glanced in her direction but she couldn't read her face. 'I'm so glad you're coming to Fairbridge,' she said.

'Me too.'

Before long they passed through the neat and unremarkable town of Pinjarra, turning left when they reached the town centre, little more than a suburban parade of shops. On the other side of the town they crossed the bridge over the Murray River, where the riverbank trees grew tall, the still water reflecting the canopy and the brilliant blue sky in tinges of violet, sienna and ochre, a landscape worthy of Constable's brush, yet at once distinctly Australian. She knew in that glimpse what it was that drew artists to paint this land.

The road beyond the town was another long stretch of straight and flat highway through yet more of the same sort of bush, now interspersed with paddocks of bleached grass. The trees were less stunted, the whole forest no longer coastal scrub, yet the soil still grey-brown sand.

There should have been a large sign saying 'Children's Home' and 'Farm School', but the only indication of where they were heading was a small street sign that said 'Fairbridge Road', pointing the way down another straight and sealed road largely empty of cars. Heading towards a range of low hills, the road carved a path through large paddocks of stubbled grasses and patches of sand. It was hard to imagine a farm of any sort surviving here. The land didn't seem worth tilling.

The monotony of the landscape ended abruptly when they reached the entrance to Fairbridge, passing between two pergolas supported by columns of red and brown bricks to join a queue of cars inching their way forward. A thicket of trees screened the festival grounds; only the white tops of the marquees could be seen. There were people everywhere engaged in a hubbub of activity.

'Excited?' Heather said.

'Very,' said Yvette, returning her grin.

At last it was their turn and a festival volunteer, dressed in a loose T-shirt and beige dungarees, ticked them off her list and handed

Yvette through her open window two plastic bags. Inside each bag were pamphlets, instruction sheets, a site plan, an orange and a Cherry Ripe.

Heather drove on a few metres and pulled over.

'Let's figure out where the billet is,' she said, rummaging through her bag for a site plan.

Yvette found hers, opening out the pamphlet, noticing straight away the South Dandelup River that snaked around the perimeter of the site, making sense of how this piece of land came to be deemed suitable to farm. Arranged in rows like obedient soldiers were a series of small huts, each one named after some explorer or military commander or other hero of empire, from Raleigh, Nelson, Livingstone and Darwin to Captain Cook himself. There were larger huts, a church and a building now serving as a museum.

Following the route to Scratton Lodge, Heather manoeuvred the car down a narrow track past a scattering of weatherboard buildings set well back among the trees, avoiding festival goers meandering about in all directions. Yvette wondered if Thomas had arrived and where he was staying.

They pulled up in a small parking area before a cream-painted weatherboard cottage with small Georgian-style casement windows and a deep veranda shading the entrance doors. Rising from the iron roof was a square clock tower, also painted cream. The tower had a low square roof, the white faces of the clocks centred in each of the four sides leaving no doubt about the time of day. For all the grandiosity of its clock tower, Scratton was little more than a Nissen hut. It had the same feel of practical, functional purpose, built with no accoutrements of style whatsoever.

'Reckon we're girl guides for the weekend,' Heather said, stepping out of the car.

Yvette unbuckled her seatbelt, opened her door and eased herself free of the seat. Then she stood in the car park, clasping her hands together behind her back before rubbing the base of her spine.

'Are you okay?' Heather said, a look of concern appearing in her face.

'I'll give you a hand.'

'Nope. You stay there.' Heather unlocked the boot and heaved out two canvas bags of groceries. Ignoring her, Yvette grabbed one end of an Esky which, judging by the weight, was packed full. Beside it was a milk crate loaded with saucepans, plates, cups and cutlery.

'When did you pack all this?' Yvette said.

'Last night and early this morning. You were asleep.'

'Blimey.'

'Welcome to the great Australian way of life.'

'Where's the barbecue?'

'There'll be one.' She laughed. 'Can you manage?'

She lifted her end of the Esky. 'I'm still delivering junk mail, remember.'

'Even so. Be careful.'

Double wooden doors led to a large room with unpolished floorboards and a brick fireplace at one end. Dark wooden panelling skirted the lower third of the walls; the fibro sheeting above painted a dull cream. A door at the rear of the room led to a kitchen, equipped with a cooker, two fridges, a freezer, a kettle and a toaster. They dumped the Esky on the floor beneath one of the benches.

After unloading the kitchen supplies Yvette grabbed her shoulder bag from the back seat of the car and headed for their room. The bedrooms were situated in two wings to either side of the main room. She turned the key in door number three.

The bedroom contained two sets of bunk beds and an oak-veneer chest of drawers. Like the rest of the building, the room was gloomy and bare. She crouched on one of the bottom bunks and waited for Heather. She couldn't help feeling like an orphan, every cell of her body in rebellion. When Heather entered the room, Yvette looked at her and said, 'What time are we on?', keen for a reason to escape.

'Five.'

'Five?' That was ages away.

'But Fiona wants to meet at the back of the marquee at two. Fancy a cuppa?' She paused before the door. 'I hope I didn't shock you earlier.'

Yvette was caught by surprise, her current milieu eclipsing her friend's earlier disclosure. 'It was shocking. But not surprising,' she lied. 'My father was ...'

'Your father.' Heather smiled at Yvette with a measure of contrition and left the room.

4.2

Yvette rummaged through the festival bag for the Cherry Ripe before again studying the festival site map. The main marquee had been pitched on the near side of the rows of little huts a short walk from Scratton. The other music venues were located in the larger buildings, along with a green room, organisers' office and festival shop, the festival making full use of the farm school buildings. Beyond the complex were the camping areas.

Next she opened the program of events. Thomas's band, the Romanas, was performing in the clubhouse at the same time as the Cushtie Chanters. But tomorrow she'd see them. The choir had a performance in the chapel and Thomas was on later, at Ruby's.

Yvette drew up closer around her waist her baggy cardigan that she'd taken to wearing all the time now the weather was a little cooler, hoping to obscure the mound of her belly. Lately, when she ventured out on her junk-mail run, she'd noticed other pregnant women in shops, cafes and parks vaunting their taut round bumps beneath tight clothes. Single pregnancies, all of them. Even at six months she'd already looked well into her third trimester. 'When are you due?' she would be asked at random by strangers in bakery queues. Then she would be burdened with explaining she was having twins, forced to endure an onslaught of exclamations, congratulations and vignettes. 'Oh, you'll be huge! My sister ...' She would smile vacantly as she caved, her figure-conscious sensibilities revolting, into another craving for a meat pie.

She left the billet and went to the kitchen, finding Heather sipping tea and chatting to two teenagers, both with dreadlocked hair.

'Oops,' said Heather, passing her a mug.

The teenagers stared at Yvette, letting their gazes fall to her gargantuan midriff. Heather knelt on the floor to open the Esky. She straightened, holding a large round tin.

'She's eating for three,' she said, cutting Yvette a hunk of fruitcake.

'Wow!'

One of the teenagers proceeded with a blow-by-blow account of her mother's twin birth. 'It's great to have a twin,' she said with a sideways glance at her brother.

Yvette nibbled at her cake, unable to contemplate the decades of child rearing before her.

Shortly before two, she strolled with Heather through the grounds. As they neared the marquee, she spied a corral of vendors selling all manner of foodstuffs. There were hamburgers, kebabs, pizzas, hot dogs, bacon and egg rolls, ice-creams, a juice bar and a Hare Krishna stall for the vegetarians. And thankfully no meat pie stall in sight.

The Cushtie Chanters were gathered in a huddle behind the stage. At the sight of Heather and Yvette, Sue and Beth pared away.

'Ah, you made it!' Sue said.

Heather glanced at her watch. 'And not late either.'

'Even so, you had us worried,' said Beth. 'We didn't see you anywhere all morning. Where's your billet?'

'Scratton. And yours?'

'We're camping,' Sue said, wrapping an arm around Beth's waist.

Heather opened her mouth to speak but closed it again as Fiona cornered the marquee looking flustered. 'I'm having trouble finding a place to rehearse,' she said. 'Everywhere is full.'

'Scratton has a deep veranda and a large room,' Heather said, 'and there's no one about.'

'Terrific. Everyone happy?'

There was a smattering of yeahs.

Heading back to Scratton, the choir trooped past the stand of boys' huts. Yvette shot quick glances at the façades. With their white-painted windows set in weatherboard walls of dark brown, the huts were entirely out of keeping with appellations that bestowed the pride of Empire. Gordon's photo might have been taken outside any one of them.

The choir filed up the steps to the veranda and congregated in their three vocal groups in the order they would appear on stage. The tenors stood in a single line closest to the railings. The altos edged slightly apart; Yvette, who was last in her line, finding herself looking into the gloom of Scratton's front room. The sopranos took up their positions in front of the others.

Fiona faced the choir. 'Great to see all our colourful clothes.' Every woman was wearing a vibrant outfit, the sopranos striking in shades of burnt orange, the tenors elegantly attired in frocks ranging from turquoise to apple green, the altos more eclectic with Sue, Beth and Karen decked out in shades of yellow, Heather in her flowing purple frock and Yvette flaunting her bulging belly in a wrap-around of dazzling red. Altogether, the choir were a splendid bouquet.

Fiona, demure in a grey shift, raised her arms, scanned the faces of the choir, gave a small nod and led them through the set. As they launched into the second song, Yvette felt a flutter in her belly followed by a sharp little kick. She smiled inwardly at her babies' movements, picturing them crammed into their watery cavity doing little wriggles and jerks.

The choir sang through the whole set without a glitch. At the end of the last song Fiona clapped her hands together in applause. Fran caught Yvette's eye and winked. 'Nervous?'

'A bit.'

'You'll be fine.'

'We'll all be fine,' Sue said, overhearing.

'Group hug,' said Karen and straight away the altos gathered together into a huddle of pressed bodies and hugging arms, Yvette's belly snuggling against the hips of Sue to one side and Fran the other. It was a curious coming together, the intimacy that the others displayed spontaneously, at once contrived in Yvette, the greater part of her remaining stubbornly set apart until she too gave way to the moment.

The choir wandered back to the food court for a quick bite to eat before their show. Heather and Yvette stayed at Scratton to dine on the Hunza pie and the salad in the Esky.

An hour passed and they were back at the marquee, entering at the rear through a side flap into an area of grass that contained a few plastic chairs and a long table. On the table were a jug of water and a column of plastic cups. Beyond, a flight of temporary steps led to the stage; a raised platform, the speakers stacked to either side great towers of black. The act on stage was a male trio on fiddle, mandolin and guitar, playing frantic reels and jigs. As she listened, her nerves rose, her heartbeat quickening to the vigorous applause at the end of the trio's set.

Before long the trio left the stage.

Her palms were sweating. The MC was introducing the Cushtie Chanters.

'We're on,' whispered Fiona, ushering the tenors.

Yvette followed Karen and took her place at the end of the altos. The sopranos followed.

The marquee was full, not a spare seat in sight, latecomers standing around the sound desk.

She could feel sweat trickling down her armpits. She gazed at the audience, a swathe of expectant faces. She was sure every pair of eyes was settling on her belly.

Fiona took her position in front of the choir and the audience hushed. She bowed then waited for the welcoming applause to subside before turning to face the choir. With a quick glance around, she raised her hands. Yvette wondered if her voice would make a whisper.

The opening bar of the first song and their voices merged and blended, a sonorous gale that soon swept away Yvette's nerves. Two bars into the second song and she'd lost her sense of self. She was at one with the choir, the audience, the whole festival. She gave no thought to how she found herself singing in a choir at a festival. Her nephews and their mother never entered her mind. She felt not one awkward moment, not once questioning her presence here in this marquee at Fairbridge Children's Home. Beside her, though she dare not look, was Heather, and she felt her friend sway, knew well the head held high, the open throat, the lips rounding every syllable.

At the end of the final song Yvette was immersed in a euphoria she'd never before felt; the cocaine she'd rushed up her nose in Malta didn't come close. The performance had come to an end too soon, as if their thirty-minute set had passed in seconds. She wasn't the only person in the marquee to enjoy the experience. The Cushtie Chanters bowed to a rousing applause. Yvette walked off stage jubilant. The others looked like they felt the same.

'We'll need something to come down off a high like that,' Fran said.

'Beer tent?' Beth led the way, pushing through revellers walking in every direction, dodging women and men of all ages, children and even babies in strollers.

Passing a long row of food stalls, Yvette couldn't help noticing that just about everyone was white-skinned. And she suspected that the African men walking off into the crowd were part of a band. To eyes used to the vibrant diversity of cultures in London, cultures expressing themselves with bacchanalian aplomb at carnivals like Notting Hill, this mono-ethnic fact was striking. If folk festivals were all the same, attracting a homogenous audience, then what did that say about the multiculturalism of the nation? At best it was compartmentalised, each diverse group celebrating in its own way, or all together at tokenistic events like that of Burswood Entertainment Centre on Australia Day. At worst the deep traditions of the nation enshrined in folk songs, those of the convicts and early settlers, those therefore by white Australians, of white Australians, for white Australians, supported a sense of identity that excluded others, not least indigenous Australians, and while she surmised that festival goers were likely to have positive views of asylum seekers, this entire folk tradition somehow pushed those corralled on Manus and Nauru further away. Make merry and forget about the dark stain on the nation's psyche. Then Anthony sprang to mind with his shallow attitudes and she decided to desist from such a disturbing line of thinking.

A group of revellers were vacating a cluster of plastic chairs near the entrance to the beer tent. Sue made a quick dash and sat down, looking round at Beth behind her. 'Would you get me a beer?'

Yvette followed the others to the counter, a series of long tables lined up end-to-end behind which several tired-looking yet suitably cheery staff served beer in plastic glasses. Heather caught her eye inquiringly and Yvette nodded as her friend pointed at Fran's glass.

With beers in hand, they joined the others, who were all chatters and laughter. Yvette watched the melee of music lovers stroll about all around until her own spirits settled. Sitting beside Heather, feeling the familiar warmth of her being, the generous spirit, the accommodating all-understanding woman that she was, Yvette felt bonded like kin, as if her father and Heather's mother, in a treacherous act of lust, had made of them blood sisters.

She saw Thomas then, walking along with a group of men in loud shirts and straw hats. They were heading for the beer tent. Yvette fixed her gaze on Thomas and caught his eye. A confused look flashed into his face before he smiled at her and came over.

She stood and he gave her a quick hug, curving his torso forward and nearly losing his balance. 'I wasn't sure you'd be here,' he said, flashing an embarrassed look at her belly.

Yvette had no idea what to say. She felt awkward and painfully self-conscious. She turned to Heather. 'Heather, this is my friend Thomas. He's the reason I came to Perth. He offered me his flat.'

Heather held out her hand and smiled. 'Delighted to meet you.'

Thomas smiled down at her.

'I knew Heather when I lived here as a kid,' Yvette said. 'She was my best friend.'

There was a pause. She'd introduced them to each other through the role they had played in her life. It seemed suddenly self-centred. She couldn't think of anything else to say. Fortunately Thomas did.

'Are you part of the choir too?' he asked Heather.

'The Cushtie Chanters.' She glanced at the violin case he was holding. 'And you're performing?'

'The Romanas.'

'Terrific. I'll have to come and watch you.'

Yvette gazed at her friends. They each represented a part of her past. And here they were, and she saw in the warmth of two pairs of eyes, and in the smiles, the gestures and the words spoken, that Heather and Thomas liked each other. They had no reason not to. And she wanted them to like each other. It was an unexpectedly strong wish. She sat down again sensing that she'd been living out her existence since she arrived in Australia on the other side of normal, where chaos and instability reign. She was reminded of the mad woman chained to a chair in her dream and began to wonder if she'd broken loose.

4.3

Back at Scratton her dark gloom descended, shoving aside her recent joys like so many irrelevant toys. She was sitting on the edge of her bunk watching Heather sort through the contents of her bag. 'There's something creepy about this place,' she said.

'What makes you say that?' Heather said without looking up.

'Echoes. I feel echoes of the children.'

'You make it sound like an asylum.'

'Perhaps it was.'

'Fairbridge has a good reputation. Well, better than most.'

'If Mrs Thoroughgood was able to terrorise her students in a primary school in Rockingham in the nineties, it isn't hard to imagine far worse occurring out here.'

'Mrs Thoroughgood wasn't that bad.'

'Wasn't she?'

'She was strict but not cruel.'

Yvette could scarcely believe Heather meant what she said. Mrs Thoroughgood was a battle axe of a woman who should have retired years before. Her teaching methods were archaic, a staunch chalk and talker whose narrow opinions, stifled by a progressive curriculum, she vented on her pupils at every opportunity. Yvette felt peeved at Heather's rosy view of their teacher and couldn't comprehend the latitude her friend was prepared to give the children's home. 'Heather, I know for a fact the Fairbridge kids were poorly treated,' she said, an image of little-boy Gordon uppermost in her mind.

'Maybe. But there's nothing to suggest they suffered the abuses of Bindoon.'

How can you rank abuse? Put on a continuum from the lesser to the greater the evils that took place? And for the first time a chink appeared in Heather's perfection.

The room was quiet. Heather's breathing light and rhythmic. Yvette lay on her side, wide-eyed. She couldn't sleep. She got out of bed, slipped on a dressing gown and gently opened the door.

The corridor was dark, the whole of Scratton silent. Outside, somewhere nearby, there was a sudden screech then quiet. In the distance the festival partied on to an upbeat-sounding band. Heading for the toilets, she crept along the corridor to the sound of her own heartbeat. Fear prickled her skin. With every step she was overwhelmed by images of forlorn boys, the boys in Gordon's photo, only with unsmiling faces, faces writhen with pain. Cruelty seeped from the pores of the walls, prompting a gush of unbidden scenes of cottage mothers presiding over floggings and beatings, brutal women punishing claims of rape with a belt or a banishment. Yvette was a riot of anguish. She could hear the whimpering, the wailing, the torment. Was she the only festival-goer capable of sensing the vibe?

She forewent the toilets and headed to the main room, sitting on one of the wooden chairs. The room was lit by a single bare globe hanging in the centre of the ceiling. Did Gordon spend his last days at Fairbridge in one of these Scratton rooms? She'd thought he was open and frank with her those occasions he spoke of his past. He confided he'd been an alcoholic and spent time in a mental hospital.

Now she realised he hadn't been that open. He was seven when he was sent here. He didn't reveal what must have happened to him, to so many of the children. Maybe he still succumbed to shame, that oilskin that seals away memories, protecting the little boy inside from a rain of judgements and counter-accusations. Uncomfortable on her hard seat, Yvette stood and walked around.

Above the fireplace was a framed photo of Kingsley Fairbridge, the description beneath stating he was a former Rhodes scholar who established the home in 1912 as an experiment in social reform. By taking deprived children from Britain's orphanages and streets, she thought, including children of single mothers like Gordon, to give them what he decided would be a better life in the colonies, pleasing the government by populating Australia with nice little Anglo-Saxons. Fairbridge, an ironic name. A bridge to fairness? A fair and just passage into adulthood? Neither true. Kingsley Fairbridge may well have had good intentions, but what about the others in charge? Goodness is never born out of a context that is fundamentally evil, and this place had the evils of empire, colonialism and paternalism through to its core.

All remained quiet in Scratton but the music of the festival played on. Only now the style of music had changed. All she could hear was a booming bass that reverberated through her, reinforcing her already hag-ridden state of mind.

She stared into the gloom of the kitchen until she felt so oppressed she went outside and sat on the steps of the veranda. Ahead, a large campervan overshadowed Heather's little red car. The trees beyond the clearing were still. There was a slight chill to the air. And now her thoughts settled on a bizarre irony. Here she was, in a repository for children deported to Australia, children wrenched from their mothers and their homeland, about to suffer a similar fate in reverse, for having the audacity to want to be in the same land as her mother. At least she was free, she told herself, not slowly going mad in a tent in a detention camp in Nauru.

How those detainees must suffer!

It was easier when she hadn't cared, easier when she'd ignored the plight of others. Yet she knew there was no returning to her former indifference. She was stuck with the discomfort of engagement.

She went back to Room Three, slid into bed and willed herself to sleep.

4.4

Her mood didn't rise with dawn. She opened her eyes to the brightening day as Heather got out of her bunk. She kept still and watched her friend slip on a dressing gown and head out of the room with her toiletries bag tucked under an arm. Then she threw off the covers and gathered a sarong around her torso, grabbed her own toiletries and followed Heather to the showers.

She returned to an empty room. Heather's towel was drying on the back of a chair. Yvette dressed and went to the kitchen, finding Heather preparing breakfast.

'Morning, sunshine.' Heather handed her a mug of tea. 'Hungry?'

In minutes they were sitting in the main room with plates of fried eggs, tomatoes and slices of buttered toast. Soon there were footsteps and low voices in the corridors, and bleary-eyed risers shuffling by.

Yvette thanked Heather for breakfast and took her plate back to the kitchen where she rinsed and dried it and placed it back among Heather's things. Then she told Heather she needed to clear her head and left Scratton to wander through the grounds.

The stalls were opening but there were few people about.

Revellers must have been sleeping or going about their morning ablutions, the swathe of plastic seating over by the food stalls empty.

Beyond the stalls was the chapel, a stout and severe red-brick building, with rows of small arched windows peering down beneath a mean hood of roof. Under a girth of skillion roofing was a set of smaller windows in identical locations to the ones above. The bell tower, set to one side, looked not unlike a guard tower at a concentration camp. The chapel stood in uncompromising disapproval of all the area around, once only the various buildings of the farm school, now as well rows of clothing stalls flanking the path that led on to the other venues. Stalls selling an incongruous array of batik sarongs, Indian cotton dresses embroidered with elephants and Taj Mahals, tie-dyed clothes for women, men and kids, stone-washed jeans, screen-printed T-shirts and akubra hats.

In the chapel's façade were two sets of entrance doors.

Inside, the chapel was remarkably plain. Rows of wooden pews faced the altar, now a stage. The concrete floor, the bare brick walls and the dark wooden beams high above oppressed her senses, the chapel imposing a strict will, sanctioning the conditions, the ethos, the abuses that occurred here. Poor Gordon. He would have sat on one of those pews, knees pressed together, mouth tight, eyes fixed straight ahead. This chapel wasn't a haven of love and goodwill; it was a citadel of domination, God himself recruited as an object of fear and unquestioning obedience. She could hardly believe she was about to sing here.

4.5

S he went back to Scratton, following a route that had come alive in the short time she was in the church, wending her way past people strolling about, dodging the jugglers and fire spinners entertaining a raggle taggle of parents and children with painted faces, and an athletic man on a unicycle struggling over the rough terrain.

Heather was sitting out on the veranda. She looked up and said, 'Have a good wander?'

'I've been to the chapel.'

'How was it?'

'Austere.'

Heather's smile left her face.

Yvette went on. 'The festival crowd seem oblivious to this setting.'

'I'm sure they're not.'

'Really?' Yvette felt her anger rise. 'I think the festival masks the history of this place with its gaiety.'

'It might be healing.'

'I doubt it.'

'Yvette, you need to chill.'

Yvette knew she was right. Yet she couldn't transcend her distaste for a festival plonked amidst a former home for child migrants any more than she could condone the Fremantle Prison being used as a cultural and tourist hub. What next? Will we all be trooping off to the Curtin internment centre for a sticky beak? Marvelling over the demountables, the razor wire, the dust? She turned away from her friend, sat on the veranda steps and looked off into the spaces between the trees. A soft wind rustled the leaves of a nearby peppermint gum. She felt restless. She turned back to Heather and said, 'Fancy a walk?'

Heather stood without hesitation. 'Lead the way.'

They went back in the direction of the food court. There were even more people about, and the music had begun in the marquee. They cornered the beer tent and Yvette was about to suggest walking on past the clothing stalls when ahead, facing away from her, was Varg. It had to be Varg, no one else had that stature with that mane of red hair. She grabbed Heather's arm and steered her in the direction of the museum.

'What's up?' Heather said.

'I'll tell you in a minute.'

She was relieved to find the museum doors open and hurried them both inside.

They wandered around the exhibits, reading letters and statements from former residents of happy times and escapades. There were scores of photographs of the children, their overseers and the buildings. Odd bits of machinery were dotted here and there. Yvette walked around without taking much notice. When they found themselves in a back corner, away from the others browsing through, Yvette turned to Heather and whispered, 'That was Varg.'

'Varg?'

'One of the possible fathers.'

'Oops.'

'I don't know how good his maths is, but I don't want him to even suspect he might be the father.'

'Why not? Aren't you curious to find out?'

'Nope. All three contenders have shown themselves to be exactly the sort of men I do not want to share my children with.'

'Haven't you considered the rights of the child?'

'Heather, please. If I'm deported, the twins come with me. But what if the father decides to file for custody? Can you imagine the drama?'

They left the museum and walked back through the food court. Yvette scanned the melee, relieved to find Varg nowhere about.

Then, as they walked round the beer tent there he was, heading straight for them, that drunken woman at the Fremantle Town Hall by his side. Yvette froze. Heather stood close beside her.

'Hey, Yvette,' he said, stopping and leaning down to kiss her cheek. 'Long time no see.'

'Hi Varg. Good to see you.' She acknowledged the woman with a weak smile.

'Wow! I see congratulations are in order,' he said, eyeing her belly.

'Thanks. It all happened so fast.' She laughed. 'I met Robert, that's the father, a few days after I last saw you. Incredible! Never expected to get pregnant so easily.' She laughed again. 'Still, we're getting married next month, just in time.'

'Well, then. Double congratulations,' he said. 'See you around.'

When they were out of earshot, Heather said, 'You should take up acting. You'd be good at it.'

Yvette felt sure she detected a note of disapproval in her voice, and she was glad she'd never broached the subject of asylum seekers with her friend, suspecting a less than sympathetic view despite Heather's kindly nature. When it came to human rights, Heather clearly didn't have things all that well thought through, and Yvette decided there and then that Heather's world was too small.

4.6

After a lazy afternoon chatting and sipping tea on Scratton's veranda, Yvette returned to the chapel with Heather for the Cushtie Chanter's second and last performance. They met the other choir members gathered round the side of the chapel and when the music of a string quartet came to an end and the applause began, they entered quietly through a narrow door. The pews were already full. Low murmurs merged into a hollow-sounding drone. Several rows from the back she saw Thomas. She was pleased to see him, pleased he was about to hear her sing, pleased to have him as a friend, yet saddened by her monstrous belly that she knew would separate them forever: he wasn't the child-centred type. Neither was she, but she'd soon have to be.

Yvette took her position at the end of the altos, waiting, less nervously this time, for Fiona to take the stage. Looking down on the audience from the height of the stage, a view the privilege of the priest, it was easy to imagine how the chapel, with its red bricks, arches and vaulted roof kept the gaze of the audience fixed to the altar in commanded obeisance. And the aspect gave Yvette courage.

When Fiona walked on stage, took her bow to the applause and turned to face the choir, a delicious thrill rippled through her.

The choir sang, their voices in unison forming a single echo rising to the roof, infusing the performance with a spiritual quality at once unexpected and inevitable. They were birds in flight, soaring, gliding, banking, swooping and as the last song came to an end and Fiona turned, the audience were rapt. There was a call for an encore, some standing, and in their intimacy behind the sopranos Heather reached for her hand.

Following the others off stage, Yvette was again euphoric, only this time she held onto a thought, not far short of revelation, held on with a tenacious grasp, unwilling to let it slip by. The chapel that stood staunchly, each brick a memorial of dominance and abuse, was also a sanctum for worship, for reverence, and a chamber, not by accident but by design, capable of producing out of a chorus of voices something sublime. This was obvious, yet to appreciate the beauty was not to deny the horror. It was to hold an outlook on life in colour, not monochrome. Was beauty amoral? Perhaps, but more importantly, should the creation of beauty be a moral pursuit? She conjured Chagall's *The Falling Angel* as the remaining vestiges of her attachment to Precisionist art withered away. The approach, she decided, was morally bereft, containing a profound lack of critique; an absence of judgement that was itself an acceptance of the status quo, one able to glorify the manifestations of industry as the old masters might have done a church. She could no longer countenance painting edifices of power, no matter how accurate the representation.

The others headed off in the direction of the beer tent, leaving Heather and Yvette standing by the side door. Yvette took a final look around the chapel, glimpsing Thomas filing through the front vestibule.

4.7

The Romanas were on in ten minutes. Yvette walked with Heather to Ruby's, entering through a set of double doors into a sports hall. Steel girders supported a high raked ceiling. The walls were cream. Coloured lines painted on the highly polished floor set out a variety of court formations. The air was stale and warm and smelled faintly antiseptic. Yvette and Heather hovered by the sound desk scanning the backs of the large gathering that filled the rows of plastic chairs facing the stage. Seeing a couple vacate two chairs halfway up the aisle, they made a dash before someone else nabbed them.

The Romanas had gathered on stage. Thomas was standing stage right with his violin, to the left of a burly man who was tuning his bass. The guitarist, a thin man with a goatee beard, sat on a chair towards the stage centre. Also present were a flautist, an accordionist and a drummer. Before long the troupe members were poised, eyeing each other, waiting for a cue. The guitarist gave the drummer a quick nod, mouthed a one-two-three-four in the direction of the bassist, and the music began.

They played an energetic set. Yvette's gaze fixed on Thomas, who played his violin beautifully, leaning his body forward and back as he glided his bow across the strings. By the third song he'd even begun to tap his feet and wriggle his hips a little.

At the commencement of the fourth song, several women with dreadlocked hair and garbed in flowing frocks wandered to the front and danced freely. Soon they were joined by a group of children.

At the end of the final tune the audience burst into applause. The Romanas bowed, the MC thanked them and as they made to leave the stage went on to announce the following act. Thomas had disappeared. Yvette felt sad for a moment but let the feeling go. He had his path, she had hers.

'Ready?' Heather said.

'Yep.'

They'd decided to head back that evening. Heather had packed up the car after lunch. As they walked back to Scratton one last time Yvette found herself farewelling all the buildings, the stalls, the tents, that curious mix of festival and children's home.

Before long they were heading back down the road to Pinjarra.

4.8

Back at the house, Yvette collected Friday's post from the letterbox and followed Heather inside. In the kitchen she scanned the envelopes. A telephone bill, a bank statement, and one stamped with the Department of Immigration's official crest. She was caught in an eddy of anticipation and dread. She couldn't open the letter. She clutched it in both hands and worried at the stuck-fast fold, levering and flattening the corners over and again.

She watched Heather trudge back and forth unloading the car.

When Heather had placed the last box on the kitchen table, she grabbed her keys and purse and without looking round she said, 'Popping to the shop for milk. Need anything?'

Yvette mumbled a quiet no.

When she heard the front door close she sat at the kitchen table and pulled out the letter. About halfway through the second sentence and she was breathless. It was the deportation order she'd anticipated. She must leave Australia within six weeks at her own expense. She'd known her application would be refused, known she'd been living in a false haze of hope, but she'd done her best to push the inevitable aside. Easy to do as she'd been free to move about the country, socialise, work and sing in a choir. Bizarre.

She was about seven months pregnant, convinced she was unfit to travel. If she returned to England she wouldn't be in any physical danger, unlike real asylum seekers. But she'd be destitute.

Her mind heaved with the burden of it all. She had no idea what to do. She had no choice. She called her mother.

She had to listen to Leah's blow-by-blow account of the fall-out from last February's agricultural show, how tired she was of committee politics and the long-standing feuds. Yvette waited, without patience, as she informed her that Terry had finished the building of his bush-block house and his art was apparently getting a good price in Melbourne galleries. She said she'd met Tracy, the Buddhist scripture teacher, in the street.

'Such a nice, well-meaning man,' Leah said.

'Yes, Mum.'

'And how are you Yvette?' she said, injecting a maternal tone into her voice.

'I'm okay.'

'Have you heard anything?'

She felt the welling of tears. 'I have a deportation order,' she said in a flat tone, trying to mask her anguish.

There was the inevitable reproach. 'You should have married Terry.'

'I know,' Yvette said heavily. 'Mum, what the hell am I going to do?' She heard the whine of the child filter into her voice.

Silence. Then, 'You can always come back here for the time being.'

'I suppose so,' she said without conviction and searched her mind for an excuse to hang up her phone.

4.9

She waddled into her bedroom succumbing to a widening gloom. She lay on her side on the bed hoping to ease the pain in her back that had been growing with every kilometre on the way back from Fairbridge and had worsened dramatically. She stared blankly at the window, too exhausted to move.

Exhaustion gave way to alarm as a gripping pain coursed through her belly.

The pain eased only to return about five minutes later.

She waited.

Another contraction.

Then another.

She lay in a cycle of pain for what seemed an eternity.

Where the hell was Heather?

At last she heard Heather enter the house. She called out.

Her friend rushed into the room. 'What is it?'

'I'm in labour.'

'Are you sure?'

'I need to pack a bag.'

'Wait there.' Heather rushed from the room, returning with an empty shoulder bag. 'What do you need?'

Yvette heaved herself up and pressed her hands against the base of her spine. It didn't make a difference to the pain but the pressure was comforting.

Then came another contraction.

Breathless, she gripped the doorjamb. 'Toothbrush.' She gasped. 'Slippers.' Another gasp. 'Underwear.'

'On to it.'

By the time Heather pulled up outside the entrance porch of the maternity hospital in East Fremantle, Yvette was not far short of delirium. She took one glance at the hospital's façade, convinced she was about to enter the medieval reality of Gormenghast Castle.

Heather flung open the driver-side door and dashed round the front of the car. She opened the passenger door and scrambled to unbuckle Yvette's seat belt. Yvette took her proffered arm and hauled herself out of the seat.

With Heather at her side, she lumbered into the sparsely furnished and empty reception area. Straight ahead, a prim-looking woman with bouffant grey hair was seated behind a high hatch. A pair of horn-rimmed spectacles hanging from a gold chain rested on her crisp white blouse. Yvette leaned her elbows on the counter for support and without waiting for the woman to look up from the single green ring binder open on her desk, she said, 'I think I'm in labour.'

The receptionist snapped shut the ring binder and gave her an imperious stare. 'How many weeks pregnant are you?'

'Thirty-three, I think.'

'You're huge,' she said doubtfully.

'I'm having twins.'

'Twins? We don't birth many twins here.' The receptionist frowned with confusion and disbelief, as if Yvette had walked into a hardware store and asked for kilo of cheese. 'Why aren't you at King Edward?' she said. 'They have a high tech twins unit.'

'I want a natural birth.'

'Is that right?'

The receptionist handed her a form on a clipboard. Name, address, next of kin. She had never thought of Heather as her next of kin but wrote down her name. When she handed back the clipboard, the receptionist ran an enamelled fingernail down the form, pausing here and there, before shooting her a suspicious look.

'Medicare card,' she said, holding out her hand.

'I don't have one.'

'You don't have one,' she said flatly. 'Private health insurance?'

'No.'

'No?' The woman paused for a moment, nonplussed.

'I'm here on a holiday visa,' Yvette said, wishing she didn't need to explain. It hadn't occurred to her that she'd need to pay a hospital to give birth. She gave the woman a hopeless smile.

'Travel insurance then,' the woman snapped.

Yvette shook her head.

'How do you propose to pay for this birth?'

'I'm sorry.'

'Sorry? You're sorry. I simply can't understand why you didn't return to wherever it is you came from before now?'

Yvette bristled at the intrusive questioning. Her circumstances really were none of this hospital's business. Humiliation gave way to desperation as another contraction coursed through her belly. She gripped the counter, bowed her head and let out a protracted groan. The receptionist observed her with unflinching indifference. The interrogation resumed.

'How far apart are your contractions?'

'I don't know.'

'You don't know?'

'It's hard to tell.'

'Braxton Hicks,' the woman muttered.

'Braxton Hicks?'

'Braxton Hicks can be very painful dear.'

'These are not Braxton Hicks!'

Her shriek reverberated in the capacious reception room, a brilliantly lit space containing a single row of shelving, a lonely laptop on a large desk and a black swivel chair. A room of utmost efficiency, the very presence of a file or piece of notepaper an affront to the scrupulous order no doubt imposed by Ms Horn Rim herself. A speculation confirmed when the receptionist pursed her lips and looked down at her watch, as if Yvette's presence on this Saturday night were an insufferable inconvenience. 'I'll call a nurse,' she said, picking up the telephone receiver and stabbing three buttons in unhurried succession.

There was a long pause.

The receptionist looked over at Heather, now hovering anxiously near a water cooler, and then back at Yvette. 'Sit over there,' she said, pointing to a row of plastic chairs over by the entrance doors.

Yvette did as she was told. Heather sat beside her and gently rubbed her back. 'Try to relax,' she said softly.

Relax? She glared in the direction of the receptionist, overhearing the words that were uttered in an especially loud voice, 'She's an illegal.'

Ten minutes of pain later and a nurse emerged from a set of double doors. She was a plump middle-aged woman with hooded eyes, a beaked nose and a tight down-turned mouth, her bulk squeezed into a nurse's uniform, between an ample bosom and wide hips, her stomach descending in a series of swollen undulations. She looked around before catching sight of Yvette and marched in her direction. Standing squarely before her, hands on hips, the nurse gave Heather, who was stroking a comforting hand across Yvette's shoulders, a hostile stare, before returning her gaze to Yvette.

'You think you're in labour, do you.'

'You can see she's in labour,' Heather said in Yvette's defence.

'I'll be the judge of that, thank you,' the nurse said before beckoning Yvette to follow her with a 'Come on' and an impatient wave of her arm. The nurse had all the matronly command of Hattie Jacques in a Carry On film without the humour or the compassion.

Yvette stood with Heather's assistance.

'You wait here,' the nurse said to Heather, who sat back down at her command. It was a wrench to walk away, Heather her only protection from whatever horrors she was about to step into.

The nurse led Yvette through the double doors and down a wide corridor. The air smelled lifeless. Mottled grey-green flooring curved to meet walls the colour of sunburn on fair skin. A colour that soon darkened beneath the intermittent fluorescent lighting, two out of every three overhead lights switched off, the effect surreal, the walls vascular, herself an intruder in some freakish underworld.

The nurse's footsteps made soft rhythmic clicks. Yvette struggled to keep pace. They passed one heavy white door on the left, another on the right, two sets of double doors facing each other, an intersection of sorts, then more doors, a sharp turn to the left and on still further, the nurse at last pausing to pull the long steel handle of the last door before the fire exit.

The examination chamber was small and windowless and contained a narrow bed, a stack of melamine shelves piled with half-opened white boxes, a small sink and a white swing-top bin.

Without further ado the nurse ordered her to remove her underwear, lie down and open her legs. No smile, no pleasant repartee. Not even a swish of a curtain for privacy. Yvette could do nothing but obey. The nurse plonked her bulk on a stool at the end of the bed, snapped on a pair of surgical gloves and without preface thrust what felt to Yvette like the better part of her whole hand inside her. Yvette clenched her fists and her jaw, shocked by the workman-like indifference, the blatant disregard for her feelings. She was amazed this woman held onto her job; she was inhuman. Did Perth breed these brutal women?

The nurse peeled off her gloves and tossed them in the bin. Without saying a word she reached for a clipboard and extracted a pen from her breast pocket. After a few rapid scribbles she looked at

Yvette, and with the demeanour of a schoolmistress announcing a transgression worthy of corporal punishment, she said, 'Your cervix has dilated five centimetres. You're in active labour.' She paused. 'Just.'

Yvette ignored her sarcasm. She was in active labour. It was validation. It meant for the past few hours the pain she'd experienced really had been labour pain. And she was terrified. Terrified of what lay ahead. There was the ever-increasing intensity of pain. There was the risk of complications. Death. With the rise of another contraction, fear drove a fist through her heart. All she could do was wait for the excruciating spasm to pass.

'Get used to it,' the nurse said. 'You'll be like this for hours.' Then she told Yvette she was sending Heather home. 'I'll let your girlfriend know where you are.'

'What do you mean?'

'We need to move you to King Edward. You're too high risk for here, lovey.'

With the clipboard tucked under one arm, the nurse led Yvette back down the corridor, bumping her hip against a set of double doors leading to a large room of the same flesh-peach tone, containing four beds, each fringed with a leaf-print curtain. The room was dimly lit and, like the reception, the corridor, possibly the whole hospital, empty, the silence of the place broken by occasional distant murmurs and soft, grizzly cries.

She claimed the bed nearest the window.

'Put this on,' the nurse said, handing her a pink hospital gown. 'Ring the buzzer if you need me,' she added abruptly, pointing to a red button beside the bed. Then the nurse stared into her face, her eyes narrowing to slits, lips curling, revealing a markedly protruding front tooth. She was hideous. 'Rest up dearie,' she said, and despite there being no one else in the room, pulled the curtain to the end of Yvette's bed. Then she disappeared.

Yvette disrobed and put on the gown and lay down on the bed, turning on her side and facing the curtain's leafy patterns arranged in sprays. Her vision blurred and soon she was seeing in the spray directly in her line of sight a simian face staring back at her, jeering. The face morphed into another, equally ugly and disturbing, and another and another, a slide show of fantastical overbites and excessively receding chins, grotesque warts and malevolent monobrows. The faces reminded her of the works of Joy Hester, Arthur Boyd and Danila Vassilieff she'd seen in the library the day of her failed cockroach annihilation. But this was little comfort. There was nowhere to look. She turned onto her other side.

She stared through the high, rectangular window at the black emptiness of the night. If she closed her eyes she was imprisoned with the pain. At least with her eyes open her brain could register the existence of another reality, separate from her. With her eyes open she could think in a freeform sort of way. Snatches of memory flashed into her mind, childhood scenes, the beach at Safety Bay, Heather's back yard, the swing set and the paddling pool and the giant, multi-coloured plastic balls. They were nice memories of nice times. But her mind was capricious. It ferreted about, uncovering all manner of dross down memory's dark passages. She saw her mother's face, red with ire, raising the plate of baked beans Debbie was refusing to eat and shoving it into her face. Was that a real memory, or a fabrication based on tales her mother and Debbie told? Her father loomed, a bizarre amalgam of the Joker and Lurch. Another memory seeped into her mind like pus, the night he threw his dinner up the wall because he'd been given an extra potato. She could see, as real as if it were happening now, the rivulets of gravy, the peas on the carpet, a lone chop leaning against the skirting board and three, there should have been two, potato splatters sliding down the wallpaper. Why couldn't she conjure a nice memory of him? There must have been *some* good moments. Her mother told her she used to idolise him but she couldn't remember ever doing that.

She slipped in and out of trance. She recalled her mother relating her birth with enthusiastic pride. Leah went into labour with her on a London bus. She went straight to hospital and two hours later Yvette shot from her loins like a rocket. Debbie birthed each of her boys without much trouble. Both took to motherhood with zeal and, at least in Debbie's case, joy. Mothering was a central part of their identity and purpose as women. Yvette couldn't imagine herself doing the same. Why in God's name had she placed so much faith in that crazy palm-reader's prediction? What had she been thinking? She hadn't been thinking. She'd given way to an irrational urge to procreate.

Hours passed.

When the agonising cramps became so fierce her mind split into fragments that scattered off in all directions, she rang the buzzer.

About ten minutes later the same nurse marched into the room and stood over her bed.

'Well?'

Yvette looked at her imploringly. 'Please,' was all she could manage.

'Get up.'

Yvette struggled off the bed and trailed behind the nurse, hoping to make it to the examination room before the next contraction.

Back on the narrow bed, legs splayed, she closed her eyes against the ghoulish creature about to thrust inside an indecorous hand.

The nurse yanked off her surgical gloves, extracted the biro from her breast pocket and noted down the result before announcing to Yvette that her cervix had dilated to seven centimetres. The birthing instructor had said it had to reach ten before she could deliver the first baby to the world.

'Things will start to speed up from here.'

Another tortuous wave ripped through her belly. Yvette let out a guttural scream, her hands, clutching at nothing, at last finding the sheet beneath her and clenching hard.

'Up you get,' the nurse said with no offer of assistance. The heartless cow.

Once Yvette was standing, she added, 'You could do with pethidine.'

'Can I take a shower?' Yvette said, suddenly recalling Susie telling the birthing class of the wonders of hot showers.

'A shower?' the nurse replied.

'The birthing instructor said it was good for the pain.'

'Hippy nonsense!' She crossed her arms under her bosom.

'*Please.*'

The nurse hesitated. 'Come with me,' she said, adding, 'and you *should* have the pethidine.'

The shower was in the adjoining room. The nurse pushed open the door, forcing Yvette to squeeze past her, before letting the door crash shut. The room was tiled floor to ceiling. A high window stretched along the back wall. Slatted wooden benches were arranged against the side walls beneath a series of coat hooks. Beyond the benches was a row of showers. Yvette slipped off the hospital gown and went into the cubicle at the end.

She ran the tap hot and fast and leaned against the wall, exposing her lower back to the full blast. The relief was beatifying.

She was in no hurry to leave. She could have given birth right here.

About half an hour passed and she heard footsteps clipping across the shower-room floor.

'You can't stay in there all night,' the nurse snapped.

'I'm fine.'

'If you want pethidine, you have to have it now. Or it'll be too late.'

'I want to stay here.'

'Well, you can't.'

She was about to ask why but thought better of it. Defeated, she turned off the taps.

The nurse rammed the needle into her thigh the moment she exited the cubicle, mumbling something about there being no time.

The pain relief was mild. Soon she felt drowsy. Back in the pink room she lay on the bed and waited, hoping that at any moment some kindly paramedics would arrive to whisk her away to King Edward.

No one came.

At midnight the nurse examined her again. The dilation of her cervix had reduced back to five centimetres. She was shattered. If this is what women in childbirth endure, she wondered why the human race had not died out long ago. What sort of choplogic masquerading as reason had she succumbed to all those months before?

She'd lost sense of time. The writhing, sweating, groaning, gasping, the relentless agony, it was all too much. She tried to tell herself she was lucky. She was here, she was safe, she hoped, she was being cared for, sort of, nothing dreadful would happen. She tried to steel her wits, thank her luck she wasn't going through all this in some god-awful hellhole, although she found it hard to imagine anywhere worse than here. She tried to distract herself, tried to recall the news stories she'd read of women in labour in detention centres, how terrifying that would be, how crushing, to have officialdom hovering to lock you back away, lock up your baby, born unfree. But it was pointless. Another surge of pain and she was lost. She reached for the buzzer.

4.10

She opened her eyes and blinked. Daylight brightened the room. She felt a rush of confusion but it soon passed. Moments later she gazed hazily into a kindly female face.

'Congratulations,' the face said.

A nurse was holding a baby wrapped tightly in a pink blanket. Another nurse was holding a second baby also wrapped in pink. Girls! She'd done it. She'd given birth, although she had no idea how she'd managed it.

The nurses leaned over her, tilting the tiny bundles so she could see her babies' faces. They were beautiful. So serene. So delicate. So vulnerable. They were all that mattered. And she was overwhelmed by an enveloping sense of unity, an exquisite oneness, an us like no other. Tears flooded her eyes.

'You did well to get to thirty-seven weeks,' the kindly nurse said.

'Thirty-seven weeks? How can you tell?'

'The weight. Both your babies are three kilos.'

She struggled to take in the news. Thirty-seven weeks. Thirty-seven weeks could mean only one man was the father of her twins—

Terry. She reflected back on her meat pie cravings, resolving to cure their inherited weakness forthwith, through attrition.

She looked around the room, small and bland with pastel pink walls. No sign of the night nurse.

'You've had a caesarean dear,' said the kindly looking nurse. 'We'll help you sit up.' Only now did Yvette recall the progress of her labour. The offer and acceptance of pethidine, the labour collapsing, Saturday merging into Sunday, more pethidine, the panic, someone remonstrating the night nurse for not packing her off to King Edward when there was still time, an ultrasound, straight on an oxytocin drip after the staff agreed they could, they must risk the birth, this gruellingly unnatural birth, the brutal moment when the obstetrician broke her waters, then, nothing.

The nurses placed the bundles into the two small cots situated close to the bed and held Yvette's arms, tilting her forward and stuffing pillows behind her. Then they passed her the bundles.

Yvette gazed at two pretty little faces, eyes wide and blue, noses pert, skin perfect and lips all soft and moist. They didn't look much different from all the baby photos she'd seen in self-help manuals and mothering magazines but to her they were unequivocally unique. She wanted to gaze at them forever but the nurses were fussing to start her breastfeeding, and she entered another sort of hell. They propped the babies on pillows so that their heads were close to her breasts, and she could hold each one under an arm. A nurse loosened her hospital gown. Yvette looked down with dismay. Her breasts were boulders. Would those tiny mouths latch on to those barely protruding nipples?

They managed, miraculously, to suckle until they fell asleep. She admired the domed curve of the first-born's head, the fine down of silky blonde hair. The second born was bald. She wanted to sit like that in a hazy euphoria, enjoying the sense of soft triumph beholding her new work of creation, one trumping with ease her Master's exhibition; a series of exquisitely crafted cityscapes, the luminosity, the grandeur, a renaissance of crisp detail that was quintessentially Precisionist. There'd even been talk of a commission for an oil company in Bahrain. Beholding these babies didn't compare; this was ecstasy, her arms enclosing, possessing, protecting. Then the nurses insisted they put the babies into their cots so she could rest. She knew she couldn't rest if they were not in her arms.

'They'll be just here beside you,' one of the nurses said.

But she couldn't reach them! She couldn't bloody move! The caesarean had rendered her immobile. If one of her babies cried out there was nothing she could do.

'You better let mum rest too,' the kindly nurse said to Heather, who appeared as if from nowhere.

'I'll see you tomorrow,' she said, kissing Yvette's cheek and stroking the babies through their pink blankets in turn.

Yvette didn't sleep. She lifted the sheet and stared with horror at the saggy bag of flesh that was her stomach.

In the days that followed, her breasts engorged and she developed a fever. Something pinged in her guts whenever she heard a soft whimper. She ached inside, an ache of an entirely different kind to any longing she had ever felt before. The two-foot distance between their cots and her bed was an unbreachable no-man's land. It was insufferable.

Every shift change a different team of nurses set her up with a different set of rules. She could have the babies in bed with her. No, that wasn't allowed. They could sleep in a cot by her side. No, they had to go to the nursery with the other babies so mum could sleep. The interference was too much. She wanted to do things her way, not bow to an institution vacillating with the staff roster.

Heather visited every day and listened patiently to her complaints. Together they changed nappies and bathed and dressed the twins. 'You are their aunty,' Yvette would say. And Heather would laugh softly.

On the fifth day Yvette waited for Heather to appear and she discharged herself. She'd had enough of the hospital and its crazy rules. She had no idea how she'd cope at home with breastfeeding, or with all the nappies, all the cleaning, all the cooking. She was so distraught the moment she arrived home she acted on Debbie's advice and phoned Nursing Mothers. A softly spoken woman answered. Yvette told her what had happened. Then, in desperation, she asked if her babies would die of starvation in the night.

'Don't worry dear,' the woman said in a reassuring voice. 'Just relax.'

4.11

The moment she arrived back at Heather's, the wonderment of her creation vanished like the shiny face of the sun eclipsed by a super-sized moon. Nothing had prepared her for motherhood. Nothing could have prepared her. No magazine or self-help book, no friendly advice or suggestion. Nothing. Motherhood had already irrevocably and dramatically changed her life. Childbirth was an initiation into the perdition of nursing, a milky maelstrom, a shitty, pissy nightmare of nappies and sleepless nights. Only Jackson Pollock could have portrayed the chaos, her all garish spatters forced into haphazard positions, constrained by the canvas and the artist who contrived the work. She could only meet with shaky stoicism and bitter resignation the fatigue, her daughters' unquenchable thirst and the barrage of pillows that stockaded her in an armchair for just about the whole of every single day.

She was a cow without the contentment, beached in Heather's living room, forced to stare down at gargantuan breasts and the revolting bulge that was her belly. She couldn't bear to look at it. When she did she was reminded with humiliating intensity of Terry, the father of her children, who'd rejected his previous girlfriend because her post-childbirth belly was no longer flat. Yvette knew not all men thought that way, but his remark had attached itself to her own loathing of her ravaged gut. She'd had a lovely belly, smooth and taut. She wouldn't describe herself as vain, but her self-esteem had always been intricately tied to her body shape. Now she had a belly so ugly, she doubted she'd ever be physically attractive to herself again. And she was not predisposed to informing Terry of his paternity.

There was no respite. When she managed to extricate her sore and cracked nipples from the girls' mouths during their brief sleeps and gently ease their bundled bodies aside so she could move about, she felt as if she no longer had any muscles to support her spine. She shuffled about in Heather's house like an invalid, holding on to furniture as she walked past. In those brief escapes from the shackles of her nursing chair she attended to the tower of domestic chores. There were nappies to soak, wash and dry, along with all the little singlets, bodysuits, sleep suits, all-in-ones and bibs that Heather had kindly purchased last week. There were dishes to wash and meals to cook. Meals she hastily shovelled down her throat anticipating *their* next feed. She had the appetite of a mammoth and the thirst of a hippo. She was disgusting.

She was more aghast at herself than ever for believing that palm-reader's prediction. When that charlatan told her she would meet the father of her children before she reached thirty, she didn't mention it would be entirely at Yvette's own expense. With all that had happened in the last nine months, she couldn't help thinking she'd been conned by the cosmos, even as she knew that was ludicrous. What in heavens had possessed her? She had no idea. No, that wasn't true. She did know what had possessed her. Loss possessed her. Desire possessed her. A single thought imbued with the power of prophecy possessed her. And she'd lost possession of herself.

When her mother phoned she tried to avoid conveying her

discontent. She pretended she was coping very well, all the while wishing her mother would catch the next available flight. She endured the vignettes of Leah's childrearing days, of how easy Yvette had been, how easy she was to forget; of the day she left Yvette's pram outside a shop, got home and wondered what was missing; the day she parked her pram in the back garden and left her there for hours, quite a suntan she had; the day she took Yvette out to the park in the middle of winter, in her slippers. They'd walked halfway down the street before she'd realised. Yvette was not quite two at the time. She'd heard those stories many times—family dramas and little mishaps. Now they took on a different colouring. She'd always known her mother wasn't absentminded but it had never occurred to her before that she'd been neglectful. Why, when she fussed and bothered in other ways, did she overlook her firstborn? Or was she judging her mother against her own dogged devotion to her girls?

Heather seemed to derive genuine satisfaction from the additional housemates. She'd fuss over Yvette, bringing cups of tea and sweet treats on side plates. She would cradle the twins in her arms and even change the occasional nappy, but Yvette knew she wasn't committed, not like a real parent would be. Yvette's new life was a burden, she could see it in Heather's face, the forced patience, the strain. Heather helped whenever she was home, which wasn't often. She spent most of her time at work, visiting her father or running an errand for a friend. Every day there seemed some pretext whereby she would disappear from the house. Yvette suspected it was her way of enduring the situation; she was simply too loyal and considerate to ask Yvette to leave.

One afternoon, as the cool light filtered through the living-room blinds, Yvette tilted her head against the backrest of the sofa, her babies suckling at her breasts. Three weeks old and nameless. Emily and Samantha, Chloe and Sophie, Tasha and Imogen, she mused, but none appealed. She ran through all the names she knew beginning with every letter of the alphabet in turn but nothing grabbed her. The hospital staff had been visibly frustrated and disapproving of the baby

A and baby B nametags on their cots. There were birth registration forms to be filled in, but she had little interest in satisfying Australian bureaucracy. The longer she stalled, the harder it would be for them all to be deported, so she reasoned.

All she knew for certain was she couldn't stay with Heather much longer. Defeated, she reached for her phone.

4.12

Heather pulled up outside the airport departures lounge. The morning was sunny, perky clouds drifted across the sky and a cool wind blew in from the south. Yvette got out of the car and opened the rear-passenger door, unbuckling a baby carrier, grateful yet again to Heather for finding and buying both carriers second-hand.

The twins were asleep. They looked so peaceful. Little did they know the turbulence of these first weeks of their lives. She set the carrier on the pavement and opened the other rear door. Heather had taken her blue travelling bag and canvas holdall from the boot, the stock of Yvette's meagre possessions crammed inside, little more than the amount she'd had when she came to Perth all those months before. She'd forwarded her art materials to her mother's by post.

As they were readying to leave the house Heather had called to Yvette from the kitchen not to forget her painting. Yvette turned back down the hall.

'It's yours.'

Heather paused. 'I couldn't ...'

'I insist. You still like it, don't you?'

'I love it.'

'Consider it a present.'

'Thank you.' Heather reached for her hand. 'Yvette, before you go.' She faltered. 'I want you to know I don't blame your dad.'

'I do,' Yvette said quickly, taken aback by Heather's appeasement. Spontaneous or planned, she couldn't tell.

'I know. I blamed my mother for years. I was gutted when she left. Angus took it really hard too.' Heather stared unblinkingly into Yvette's eyes. 'My mother was a flirt. Even in her later years she had an allure about her, all honey and peaches. She confessed just before she died that she thought Dad was boring. She'd had affairs before. This time Dad found out.'

'How?'

Heather cringed. 'She called out the wrong name.'

'Oh no!'

'When I learned of the affair I felt sorry for you.'

Yvette couldn't speak. Was this the source of her friendship? Pity? Redemption? Atonement for the sins of her mother? They were bound together by the actions of their parents. For the first time since she'd reunited with Heather she felt the depth of her friend's wound, re-opened and weeping in her presence, and how brave Heather had been to face it all.

Heather went on. 'I didn't know if your mum found out. I thought it might have been why you went back to England.'

A bus came to rest a few metres behind them, all hisses and squeals. A couple went by pushing a trolley loaded with suitcases. Yvette picked up the baby carriers and made for the glass-panelled frontage of the departures lounge.

Heather followed with her bags, hurrying ahead to open the door. She gave Yvette a kindly look. 'Will you be okay?'

Sadness dammed in her heart, threatening to burst through her self-restraint.

'I'll stay in touch.'

'I know you will. Come on.'

With loaded arms they went inside and queued at the desk. Her flight to Canberra boarded in twenty minutes. Leah had paid for her ticket without hesitation. Yvette had felt a double defeat when her mother had made the offer, knowing she was following exactly her mother's wishes. She gave her details to the desk attendant, shoved her boarding pass in one hand and tramped through the lounge with the baby carriers, grateful to have Heather walking beside her with her bags, grateful that her babies were still sleeping, dreading the flight and all the awkward manoeuvres of a single mother encumbered with new-born twins. One baby you can carry around while you did other things. Even propped on your hip you had a hand free. You can pick up one baby, supporting its neck, but try picking up the second with the first in one arm. One screaming baby can be comforted with a hug. Not two screaming babies.

'Take care,' Heather said when they'd reached the departure gate.

'I will.'

She set down the carriers and hugged her friend. The weight of finality pressed down on her, separation from the best friend she'd ever had, a sister of sorts. She stood at the gate and watched Heather corner the end of the passageway and disappear.

PART V

5.1

The bedroom felt chilly. There'd been a frost the previous night and the warmth from the wood heater struggled to make it that far. Yvette buttoned her cardigan. Almost a year had passed since she was last here. Then the room was a shrine. Now it was furnished only with a steel-frame single bed and a small chest of drawers to make room for the cots Leah had borrowed from Debbie. Her travelling bag and box of art materials were crammed under the bed. It all seemed so temporary. She shivered and drew the vertical blinds.

The mountains on the western horizon glowed amber in the soft light of the morning sun. Yvette smiled, noticing the old pram Leah had parked under the veranda beside a wheelbarrow of firewood, a gift from someone on the show committee. The garden was as immaculate as ever, her mother no doubt somewhere outside, dressed in track pants and armed with shears.

Yvette turned back to the room. She pulled the doona to the pillow on her bed and did the same with the coverlets in the cots. Then she picked up the postcard propped on the chest of drawers. Debbie had given it to her on their way from the airport. She'd had it in her possession for the last few months, having found its way into her post office box instead of their mother's, and she'd tucked it away in a draw by mistake and forgotten all about it, until Yvette's return. The postcard was from Josie, who, for an inexplicable reason, had chosen the old-fashioned way to correspond. She turned the postcard over to look at the photo: the main chamber of the Hypogeum, an ancient underground temple, with its complex of tunnels and interconnecting chambers. In the photo huge lintels and pillars of cut limestone supported a doorway, the roof a series of bands of stone carved into curves. Josie's way of reminding Yvette of the first weeks she'd spent in Malta, before Carlos had come along and changed her life. Josie and Yvette had explored one ancient site after another, but it was the Hypogeum that mystified them both. Built during the Age of Taurus, the temple was a place of solar worship and shamanic ritual. On one occasion they managed to lose their guided tour party and hid in the catacombs with sketchbooks and a torch. In the absence of other humans, the temple's chambers, with their still air and black spaces became charged with wonder and intrigue. Hours later, they picked up the trail of the final tour of the day, emerging into daylight disoriented and slightly spooked.

Ah, Malta, that rugged land, with all of its temples, forts and churches, emblems of its rich and troubled history. The island had touched her soul. She was at one with the spirit of the place in a way so direct, so immediate, so all-consuming; it was like a spell. Carlos had been part of that spell. She turned over the card. Even with her limited recollection of Maltese—Josie was showing off her new language skills—she recognised in Josie's bunched, untidy handwriting the words 'married' and 'wife' in the sentence that began with 'Carlos'. Yvette was indifferent to the news. So he'd returned to Malta and moved on. He never did waste his time pining for her. And she didn't pine for him.

The holiday in Bali had been a disaster from the start. Carlos had only asked her along to create the appearance of a happy couple on vacation. The truth was he needed to get away for a while to avoid retaliation from a rival gang, who were furious after his latest scam had gone awry. Yvette never knew the details. Carlos had been in a foul frame of mind even at the airport, and by the time they arrived in Kuta his mood was incendiary. She spent two weeks wandering along the beach and the lively streets trying to stay clear of his bullet spitting ire, all the while stricken with the loss of her aborted child. Josie had been right all along: Carlos was no good.

5.2

S he closed the door on the bedroom and walked down the short hallway, catching her reflection in the mirror on her way past the bathroom. Dressed in baggy jeans and a scruffy brown cardigan, she was surprised to find she wasn't troubled by her mother-of-babies frumpiness, the kind of mother that knew she hadn't the time to be bothered with how she looked, adopting the moment she'd arrived in Cobargo a coping-in-spite-of-it-all manner. She was a survivor, having got through the first four weeks of twins.

In the living room, Yvette watched her girls as they slept in their baby carriers on the floor. From the moment they came into embryonic being her life had taken on a surreal quality, as if in flying to Perth she'd entered Salvador Dali's 'Dream Caused by the Flight of a Bee'. Every detail of her life there had been odd in some way and taken together the events formed an intriguing composition as though she, the mother, were an actor in a play she had no script for, a play written and directed by her unborn children.

And now that they were born it was impossible to disengage; they were so much a part of her, extensions like arms. She felt the exquisite embrace of joy. She felt the exhaustion. And she felt the inescapable agony of deportation, a shadow thickening the horizon of the day. She had to grasp the inner steel of her will to cope. Since returning to her mother's farm she felt ensnared by her circumstances. She carried the sort of burden that, little could she have known it then, would remain with her forever.

She wanted to shield her girls with her love, shield them both from the ravages of the world, from all hurt and harm.

Her firstborn stirred. Soon both were fully awake. Awake and crying. She knelt on the floor and managed to lift them both into her arms. And Yvette cried too. They clung to her. She clung to them. As the eastern sun streamed through the window, warming the room, the three of them clung to each other on Leah's carpet and cried.

She had to cope. There was no choice. She breathed deeply.

She changed their nappies and their clothes and fed them both at once. She did it all with an ache in her heart and an ache in her head. What sort of mother was she? She was a mother.

And she'd never leave them behind.

She couldn't fathom how mothers abandoned their children. How could Heather's mother walk out on her six-year-old daughter, never to return? What passion in her overrode her maternal attachment? And Gordon's mother, handing him to an orphanage, perhaps knowing he was destined to set sail for the other side of the world. They must have felt the grief. It was inescapable.

Once the girls had settled back to sleep, she went outside and sat on the veranda, feeling the cool of the concrete on her thighs. The silver birch, with its naked filigree of branches and its crusty white trunk, stood in tender defiance against the backdrop of the Australian bush. Leah was over in the veggie patch, crouching beside rows of peas. Yvette felt no compulsion to join her. Within the confines of the house and garden she avoided her mother as much as she could, now that Leah's 'You should have married Terry' had changed to the imperative. She never missed an opportunity to tell Yvette that she should, she must marry him. Perhaps she should. Yet the entire scenario was fraught with unpalatable implications, sure to result in a situation little better than the uncertain existence she now endured.

Leah stood and made towards the house. Yvette jumped up and went back to her babies in the living room.

A short while later she heard the fly screen slam shut, then her mother opening a cupboard door in the laundry.

'Have you phoned Debbie yet?' Leah called out.

'No. I'll phone later.' Yvette wished her mother wouldn't push. She didn't enjoy Debbie's company and was sure her sister didn't enjoy hers. Throughout the entire three-hour journey from Canberra, Debbie had done nothing but babble on about her boys, and what a joy Alan is now she's pregnant with twins. How he massages her shoulders and makes her breakfast in bed and takes the boys out so she can rest. Yvette didn't want to hear her. But she was trapped inside her car, forced by her willingness to drive up to Canberra, in her condition, to endure her tirade of sentiment. Had the woman no empathy? How did she grow to be so self-centred? Yvette wondered sometimes if they were of the same flesh.

The only respite from her self-indulgent monologue came when a local radio station reported another detention centre riot.

'The government needs to ship the illegals back where they came from,' Debbie said dismissively.

In the past Yvette would have met such a comment with causal indifference, at best vague sympathy for the displaced. Now outrage coiled through her. She was astounded too, by the prevalence of the attitude that had found its way into her sister's heart.

'I suppose that remark includes me,' she said, reminded straight away of that vile hospital receptionist.

'Of course not.'

No two sentences could have been more ill-considered. She, the visa-overstayer, was the 'illegal', although she cringed at the bastardisation of the English language that this usage entailed.

The fly screen slammed shut again. Yvette turned to the girls, who were both woken by the noise.

After an intense hour of feeding and changing nappies, rattling this and that before four tiny grasping hands, the cooing, the chortling and the snuggles, the twins were absorbed, lying on their backs on the floor, quietly entertained by the activity gyms another show-committee member had lent her. She was absorbed too, watching her girls, wondering about her own early childhood, one she could not fully recall. Yet she'd become familiar, as the years of her life went on, with the regimented nature of Leah's mothering, the rules, the strictures, the punishments. It was the old paradigm. Leah was not the sort of mother that subscribed to the liberated ways of the eighties. Now Leah, an immaculate housekeeper, seemed indifferent to the chaos of baby things scattered through the house. This much, she had changed.

Yvette sat on the sofa to enjoy a few moments of stillness, gazing out the window at the dead tree in the neighbour's paddock. A raven landed on one of the upper limbs. If she'd a chance she'd sketch that tree again. In one fleeting moment she wondered what Gordon would have made of the scene in acrylics. Fleeting, because Leah had come in from the garden to make lunch.

5.3

Leaving the girls dozing in their carriers, and Leah transfixed by the melodramatic sagas of *Days of Our Lives*, Yvette went outside. She pulled on the over-sized trainers her mother said she might as well have and walked to the village.

Nothing had changed in the months she'd been in Perth. Even the ruts and potholes on the dirt track to the highway were just as she recalled. There was the smattering of muddy hollows on the other side of the cattle grid. The corrugations on the first bend. The crater beneath a dead red gum. The stretch where the ruts were so deep cars were forced to straddle them, steering one set of wheels along the central raised strip, the other wheels sliding on the soggy grass beside the barbed wire fence.

At the highway she stopped to take in the view of the cemetery where her stepfather rested along with the town's forebears, graves as old as the deaths of the first settlers here, the Tarlintons. A descendant of that family of Catholic dairy farmers was president of the show society. A gentleman, her mother says. A community-minded sort. And that's how isolated towns like Cobargo survive and even thrive—community spirit. Generation upon generation of farming families, shopkeepers and tradesmen all pulling together, running committees, fundraising, supporting each other. Even the feuds bind, like knots in twine.

Heading down the hill, she admired the sweeping views that surrounded the village. She took in the preschool, formerly the golf clubhouse, with its corralled front yard now filled with squealing children making full use of the play equipment and the sand pit.

She passed the bakery with notable ease, pausing nearby to gaze through the Georgian-style windows of the antique-dolls shop. Further on, there was the pottery shop, the curios and collectibles store, the art gallery and two cafes. Altogether Cobargo was a charming village in a charming setting.

As she reached for the key to open her mother's mail box, a buxom woman with short brown hair swung open the post office door and greeted her with a 'G'day, Yvette. How are you?'

'Good thanks.' Yvette smiled at her. She'd forgotten the woman's name but recognised her as the receptionist at the doctor's surgery.

She pulled out a bundle of letters and leafed through the envelopes, all for her mother, except for the last, which Heather had forwarded. It was from the hospital. She opened the envelope and read through the detailed tax invoice, sneering at the exorbitant figure at the bottom. As if she was going to pay even a dollar for that ordeal. She considered suing the hospital instead, before screwing up the invoice and tossing it in a nearby bin.

She crossed the street and entered the newsagency. The large and jolly man behind the counter asked after the twins. 'You beat your sister to it then, eh? Good onya.'

She laughed, handed him a two-dollar coin, and folded the day's local paper under her arm.

Before heading back up the hill she pushed open the door of a newly opened gallery and gift shop, more an exotic emporium in homage to Bali. What was it with Australians and Bali? An island that had seemed to her utterly remote and exotic from the purview of her home in Malta, yet when she'd walked the streets of Kuta, the place was so overrun with Australian tourists, it felt like a colony. Here in this shop, on every wall from ceiling to floor, in every display cabinet and basket, and on every table and chair—Bali. Batik clothing, Buddhist flags, carved elephants, brass bells and chimes, all manner of brightly coloured woven cloth, and packets and packets of incense. She wasn't sure the shop warranted the name 'gallery' until she walked through to the back room.

And there, along with an array of colourful landscapes and intricate paintings of flowers, was Terry's sculpture of Eros. She edged closer. Until now she hadn't wanted to think of Terry. Until this moment she'd had no feelings for him at all. Seeing the delicate, almost invisible layers of leather stretched out finely and pinned to the wooden mount, it was as if Eros himself had pinged an arrow into her heart. And desire welled in her, unbidden, unwanted, a desire for him, a man, any man to sweep her away, transform her life from what it was now into something noble and pure, a life of intoxicating love and endless devoted affection, a trouble-free existence of complete comfort and security. She saw her fate crack open like a walnut and half-anticipated Terry would walk in right then, genuflect before her frumpy frame, and her life would be complete, the drama over and bows taken, curtain falling and the lights of the auditorium gradually lightening as the audience filed out.

No.

That was not real life.

And she'd never be an actor.

She turned her back on Terry's Eros. Turned her back on desire. Terry would never do. Her disfigured stomach would never do for him. People don't change. She wasn't about to fall for a meat-pie loving motoring maniac and go live in a muddy shack in a wilderness. She wasn't about to fall in line with Leah's wishes, or her and Debbie's conniving either. She wasn't a refugee. She was free, despite her new appendages. She could do anything, go anywhere, be anyone. And with the booted foot of her will she stomped on the desire charging about in her, stomped her foot down hard as if it were a cockroach.

She walked through the shop and back outside.

An empty cattle truck jangled its way to the bridge at the bottom of the hill. There were a few tourists about. An elderly couple crossed the highway and a rugged-looking man in a flannelette shirt secured the load on his ute. She was about to turn back up the hill when she noticed a car parked further down the street. It must have just pulled up. Even from this distance she recognised Terry in the driver's seat. Her legs felt weak. What was life trying to do to her?

She turned.

She wouldn't marry Terry to stay in Australia no matter how hard fate pushed. Not because she didn't love him. Not because she had quibbles about the morality or the legality. Not even because her stomach was a crumpled mess. Despite her recent appreciation of the land around this village, she didn't belong or connect to this place. Her mother and her sister were still strangers, so separated by their perspectives they weren't even looking at the same view. She felt stifled here in a land ruled by politicians as cold, hard and indifferent as her mother. She only needed to consider the plight of asylum seekers punished for daring to come here to know that. Back in Malta, that palm reader had said she was better off without her family and she was right. She'd been right all along.

It had been over a year since she'd left Malta. She thought of the enthusiasm written into the last sentences on Josie's postcard, this time in English, the longing for forgiveness, the miss you and the wish you were here. Josie had a new boyfriend, Fonzu, the owner of the bar. The flat upstairs was empty. Yvette knew Fonzu, knew the extended family of sisters, cousins, aunts and especially the grandmothers Sophia and Mari. Two tiny women, as wide as they were tall, with big brown eyes and welcoming smiles. She recalled their rapid talk and exclamations, their joyous laughter, their fussing. They were always busy, those two grandmothers, busy babysitting, cooking family feasts, carrying this here for someone, that there for someone else, popping into the bar with a wicker basket held in a crook of an arm, the contents covered with a square of cotton lace. Sophia and Mari; she thought of them with longing, they were good women. She ran their names through her mind several times and a lesser decision was made. Sophia and Mari—Leah would not be pleased.

Josie, Fonzu, the bar with its upstairs flat, the warm surrogate family who would flock around her, dote on her babies, shower her with all manner of gifts and support. It was too halcyon an image to forego.

She still had her English credit card. All she needed was access to a computer. Would the babies need passports? Probably. And birth certificates. No doubt the application process would be expedited to despatch the undesirables post haste. She'd call Immigration when she got back to Leah's. Explain her circumstances, her willingness, nay her yearning to leave.

She lost her assurance in a burst of panic. What if the Department of Immigration questioned the paternity of her twins? Insisted on tests? She'd have to lie; tell them he was a total stranger who disappeared into the night, someone with a foreign accent, someone of dubious repute, an undesirable, a possible terrorist who'd ravished her against her will. Failing that she'd bolt, take off to the Tanami Desert in search of Angus, who was no doubt still tracking the Leichhardt trail. Anything, no matter how drastic, rather than reveal the paternity of her twins to the authorities, and especially to Leah, who still seemed to have no idea of the father's identity. She was convinced that once Leah knew, the imperative would become an order.

She barely gave a thought to how Leah would feel about her leaving. Leah had Debbie, the boys, twin grandchildren on the way. They all had each other. She'd never be a part of that scene. The separation had gone on too long. It seemed disloyal, almost callous, but she knew she hadn't missed her family in all those years away. She wouldn't miss them this time either. Even if she were to make an effort, it would be fake. She came here because she was running away from heartache, not running towards reunion.

When she reached the preschool she stopped and turned around. She might come back one day. Maybe on holiday. Maybe to live. Maybe.

And with a decisive swing, she faced the direction she was heading.

It was a long walk back up the hill.

Dear reader,

We hope you enjoyed reading *Nine Months Of Summer*. Please take a moment to leave a review in Amazon, even if it's a short one. Your opinion is important to us.

Discover more books by Isobel Blackthorn at https://www. nextchapter.pub/authors/isobel-blackthorn-mystery-thriller-author

Want to know when one of our books is free or discounted for Kindle? Join the newsletter at http://eepurl.com/bqqB3H

Best regards,

Isobel Blackthorn and the Next Chapter Team

You might also like:
Ophelia Adrift by Helen Goltz

To read the first chapter for free, head to:
https://www.nextchapter.pub/books/ophelia-adrift

AUTHOR BIOGRAPHY

Isobel Blackthorn is an award-winning author of unique and engaging fiction. She writes gripping mysteries, dark psychological thrillers, and historical and contemporary fiction. Isobel was shortlisted for the Ada Cambridge Prose Prize 2019 for her biographical short story 'Nothing to Declare', a version of the first chapter of her forthcoming family history novel. Isobel holds a PhD for her research on the works of Theosophist Alice A. Bailey, the 'Mother of the New Age'. She is the author of *The Unlikely Occultist: a biographical novel of Alice A. Bailey*. With a grand passion for the Canary Islands lodged in her heart, Isobel continues to write novels set on Lanzarote and Fuerteventura.

The Drago Tree
Nine Months of Summer
Finding her Father
All Because of You: Eleven stories of refuge and hope
The Cabin Sessions
The Legacy of Old Gran Parks
Twerk
The Unlikely Occultist
A Matter of Latitude
Clarissa's Warning
A Prison in the Sun

CPSIA information can be obtained
at www.ICGtesting.com
Printed in the USA
BVHW030950250121
598677BV00010B/245/J